Catherine Cookson the illegitimate daughter of a poverty-stricken woman, Kate, whom she believed to be her older sister. She began work in service but eventually moved south to Hastings where she met and married a local grammar-school master. At the age of forty she began writing about the lives of the working-class people with whom she had grown up, using the place of her birth as the background to many of her novels.

Although originally acclaimed as a regional writer – her novel *The Round Tower* won the Winifred Holtby award for the best regional novel of 1968 – her readership soon began to spread throughout the world. Her novels have been translated into more than a dozen languages and more than 40,000,000 copies of her books have been sold in Corgi alone. Four of her novels – *The Fifteen Streets, The Black Velvet Gown, The Black Candle*, and *The Man Who Cried* – have been made into successful television dramas, and more are planned.

Catherine Cookson's many bestselling novels have established her as one of the most popular of contemporary women novelists. After receiving an OBE in 1985, Catherine Cookson was created a Dame of the British Empire in 1993. She and her husband Tom now live near Newcastle-upon-Tyne.

OTHER BOOKS BY CATHERINE COOKSON

Kate Hannigan
The Fifteen Streets
Slinky Jane
The Garment
Hannah Massey
The Long Corridor
The Unbaited Trap
The Round Tower
The Nice Bloke
The Glass Virgin
The Invitation
The Dwelling Place
Feathers in the Fire
Pure as the Lily
The Tide of Life
The Slow Awakening
The Iron Façade
The Girl
The Cinder Path
The Man Who Cried

Tilly Trotter
Tilly Trotter Wed
Tilly Trotter Widowed
The Whip
The Black Velvet Gown
A Dinner of Herbs
The Moth
The Parson's Daughter
The Cultured Handmaiden
The Harrogate Secret
The Black Candle
The Wingless Bird
Katie Mulholland
The Gillyvors
My Beloved Son
The Rag Nymph
The House of Women
The Maltese Angel
The Year of the Virgins

Catherine Cookson

FANNY McBRIDE

CORGI BOOKS

FANNY McBRIDE
A CORGI BOOK: 0 552 14067 8

Originally published in Great Britain by
Macdonald & Co. (Publishers) Ltd

PRINTING HISTORY
Macdonald edition published 1959
Corgi edition published 1971
Corgi edition reprinted 1972
Corgi edition reprinted 1973
Corgi edition reprinted 1974 (twice)
Corgi edition reprinted 1975
Corgi edition reissued 1977
Corgi edition reprinted 1977
Corgi edition reprinted 1978
Corgi edition reprinted 1979
Corgi edition reissued 1979
Corgi edition reprinted 1980 (twice)
Corgi edition reprinted 1981
Corgi edition reprinted 1983
Corgi edition reprinted 1984
Corgi edition reprinted 1985
Corgi edition reprinted 1986
Corgi edition reprinted 1988
Corgi edition reissued 1993
Corgi Canada edition published 1996
Copyright © Catherine Cookson 1959

Conditions of sale:

1. This book is sold subject to the condition that it shall not,
by way of trade or otherwise, be lent, re-sold, hired out or
otherwise circulated without the publisher's prior consent in
any form of binding or cover other than that in which it is
published and without a similar condition including this condition
being imposed on the subsequent purchaser.

2. This book is sold subject to the Standard Conditions of Sale
of Net Books and may not be re-sold in the UK below the net
price fixed by the publishers for the book.

Set in 11½/15pt Linotype Sabon by
Phoenix Typesetting, Ilkley, West Yorkshire.

Corgi Books are published by Transworld Publishers Ltd,
61–63 Uxbridge Road, Ealing, London W5 5SA,
in Australia by Transworld Publishers (Aust) Pty Ltd,
15–25 Helles Avenue, Moorebank, NSW 2170,
and in New Zealand by Transworld Publishers (NZ) Ltd,
3 William Pickering Drive, Albany, Auckland.

Printed in Canada
Cover printed in U.S.A.

UNI   10 9 8 7 6 5 4 3 2 1

To Manny and Rita

1

Fanny McBride rolled over on to her back and lay staring at a discoloured patch a foot wide on the ceiling. In a few minutes, she calculated, the sun would light on the side of the window blind and hit the edge of the patch nearest to the door, and that would mean it was a quarter to seven or thereabouts.

For years she had told the time by the light hitting or approaching that patch, for whitewash the ceiling as she would the stain came through. It had been there when she had come into the house as a young bride fifty-two years ago, and she had been scared out of her wits by a ghoulish neighbour across the passage telling her with relish that it was blood that had seeped through after one of the Mulhattans had murdered his wife on the floor above some years before. But the primary cause of this stain had long since faded from Fanny's mind; the stain itself was her sundial and as necessary to the routine of her day as had been the calling of her sons.

Years ago when nine children at one time had swarmed like ants about these two rooms, and their voices yelling their wants had coached her own voice to a pitch that their combined efforts could not drown, she had longed with an intense longing for the time to come when she could lie in bed until seven o'clock in the morning or – miracle of miracles – eight o'clock.

When she was first married she had risen at half-past four, and there was no going back to bed; for after having got McBride off to work she cleaned the rooms, then made him a meal for eight o'clock. For Palmer's shipyard was just up the road and he was never the man to take bait if he could get a hot meal. And when he would leave the house for the second time in the morning she would go with him and away to yon side of Jarrow, near the cemetery, to do the washing for the ladies who lived in their five-roomed houses . . . then back again to make dinner; then out again in the afternoon. And this had been an easy life, a pleasant sort of life. But it lasted for only eight months; for she went down . . . bang . . . literally while standing over a poss-tub in Croft Terrace, and Donald, her first, was born within three hours.

After Donald, they had come thick and fast, an average of one every year for nine years. The tenth had died, and for no reason that she could fathom, except that the Virgin had at last paid a little overdue attention to her, she hadn't seen the sight of another child for seven years. And then Phil came.

It was funny, but right from the start she hadn't known what to do with Phil, and up to this very minute she still didn't know. And then, when Don and the rest were courting strongly and she was nearing the time when all fear of another should have gone, she had to go and have Jack. Oh, the shame of those nine months. And yet, of all her brood, there had been no-one like Jack. Not one of them had teased her, cheeked her, talked to her, and laughed long and loud with her as he had . . . and none of them had broken her heart as he had.

Fanny turned over in the narrow bed, and the coat covering her feet on top of the patchwork quilt sidled to the floor. It was weeks now since Jack had left her. She had only to turn her eyes towards the battered, square, white-topped table taking up the middle of the floor to see him standing there, flinging his things into the suitcase, and shouting as loudly as herself, 'I'd marry her if I hated her guts . . . I'd marry her to spite you.' Yes, he had said that. Any of the others could have said it and it wouldn't have mattered a damn, for they had all gone their own road anyway. But not Jack. Jack was hers, and he had always been a good lad, a God-fearing lad. And that's where the mystery and be-puzzlement of it all came in. He may not have gone to his duties every week, but he had gone to his Mass on a Sunday – at least up to two years ago. She had got at him when he had first stopped going, but then left him alone. Would she though have left him alone had she known the reason for him staying away? No, by God, she wouldn't! And when she had got to know, it had been thrust on her like a bolt from the blue.

All the neighbourhood had been laughing up their sleeves at what was going on, and not one of them daring to tell her. And they were wise, for she would have laid out anyone who dared to come and say that her lad, her Jack, was courting a Hallelujah on the sly; for whoever heard of a Catholic taking up with a Salvation Army piece? No-one . . . until her own flesh had to do it. And there he was, married to her now and living in the far end of the town, so she'd heard. But even so she daren't for the life of her put her nose outside the door after she had come from first Mass on Sunday in case she should see him heading the Salvation Army band down the street and knocking hell out of the big drum. He was capable of anything, she knew, and since he was now in the Salvation family's toils, God alone knew what they'd egg him on to.

Oh! the pains of life, the humiliation!

She lay here now doing what she had always longed to do, lie in. Her body was tired and wanting to rest but her mind was more active than it had been in her life, for now it had time to think and things to think about. It urged her to her feet, and she sat on the side of the bed and scratched the moist flesh under her great wobbling breasts. Her desire for rest had been fulfilled, but now it lay heavy on her heart and filled her with longing for the days when desires were all she'd had and their fulfilment a mirage.

The tin clock on the mantelpiece struck seven. There was another half-hour before she need call Phil. She glanced towards the bedroom door, and it occurred to her yet once again that being alone in the house with Phil was like being with a stranger, or at best a lodger . . . an exact and finnicky lodger, who made you feel that he was staying with you only as long as was absolutely necessary. The thought had the power to frighten her, and she rose from the bed and shambled into the scullery.

Having put the kettle on the gas stove, she came

back into the kitchen and thrust her knickers and petticoat into the old black-leaded oven to warm, then lit the kitchen fire before taking the ashes out. This done, she dressed herself and washed round her face.

She did all this with the blind down; but when finally she had made herself a pot of strong black tea and had drunk three large cups from it, she went to the window and, pulling up the paper blind, looked out into the street.

It was a pleasant morning, she reflected, with a nip of autumn in the air. She'd go out and wash the steps down, for if she left them to the Laveys, the Quigleys, or to Miss Harper, they'd never be done. They were supposed to take their turn, but damn a drop of water they put on them from one year's end to another – the doing of the steps in the tenement had always been left to her and Liz Shaughnessy. But the Shaughnessys were gone. And didn't she know it, for she missed them in more ways than one; the family in the attics now was about as pally as a Jerusalem Jew to an Arab.

She went to the scullery again, returning with a bucket of water; but as she passed the window she halted abruptly and her wrinkled lips pressed themselves together as she squinted between the narrow aperture of her curtains to the far side of the street. Then putting down the bucket none too quietly, she exclaimed aloud, 'Begod! If I went to do 'em at half-past two in the mornin', Lady Flannagan would be there.'

She stood staring at the woman across the road, who with quick, precise movements was washing her buff-painted window sill. She watched her take the cloth and wipe the painted bricks surrounding the door. And as this was finished, Fanny nodded to the window and exclaimed below her breath, 'Now polish your brass knob and stick some furniture polish on your green front door, and make your steps bloody with red ochre. Then go in and titivate your curtains and stand behind 'em and wait for somebody to come by and admire your handiwork so's you can do a bit more bragging . . . And God help anyone so ignorant of the chastity of your front as to put a foot on your step . . . Aw! . . .' With an infuriated movement she turned from the window. There wasn't a woman on God's earth who could get her goat like Nellie Flannagan.

Grabbing up the bucket she returned it to the scullery, then going to the bedroom door she knocked and called, 'Hi! there, it's time you were on your way.'

A clear, decisive voice answered her, saying, 'I'm up.' And as she went back into the scullery she muttered to herself, 'Aye, you would be.'

When the bedroom had held nine of them lying top to toe in two beds, the morning routine had been to wallop them awake with the flat of her hand. Even when, in later years the girls had been relegated to a bed in the corner of the kitchen and the lads were great lumps of fellows, she had still taken pleasure in belabouring them awake. Now, Phil had the whole room to himself like a gentleman. There . . . that was the word that had always raised the barrier between her and Phil. It was a foreign word, at least in this house, for who in his wildest dreams would imagine that anyone who was the product of McBride and herself could fancy himself a gentleman? Not that the word was ever mentioned by either her or Phil, but he was so different from every other member of her brood that to her mind nothing else fitted him.

Philip came into the kitchen, doubling in the neck of an old shirt he always wore while he washed, and he glanced towards the window as he remarked, 'It's a nice morning.'

'Aye, it's all right.'

This daily polite reference to the weather irritated Fanny. None of the others had done it. 'What's to eat, Ma?' they had called. 'For God's sake! Ma, put me more bait up.' Or Jack daring to say, 'Come on, fat old Fan, get a move on!'

But this . . . 'It's a nice morning.' . . . 'It looks

like rain.' . . . 'I think we might have frost.' God in heaven! it got on her nerves. Yet she supposed she should be thankful that that was about all he did say in the mornings, for she got more than her share of talk some nights when he attempted to put her and the entire world to rights.

As Fanny put the frying pan on the gas ring, Philip returned to the bedroom, and ten minutes later when he emerged he was dressed in a blue serge suit and white shirt and collar. His fair hair was watered and for the moment was lying flat, and his face looked as clean, Fanny thought, as a freshly singed chicken. This son's looks never ceased to cause her to wonder. From where did he get his grey eyes and heavy, curved eyebrows? Not from McBride or her. And he had a nose on him, too, bigger and straighter than the stubs that ran in the family. He was better looking than any of them, especially when he laughed, which wasn't often, and was the only one of her brood that touched on six foot. Yet if the truth be spoken, she would swap him this minute for any one of them. God forgive her! What was she thinking? She was ungrateful, that's what she was. He was here, wasn't he, and none of the others would ever come back, for they were married and were scattered about the country far and wide – all except Donald and Florence, and they never put their noses inside the door unless they were after something. She'd get what she deserved if she wasn't careful, for if Phil was to leave her now what would she do? Who would she work for? Who would there be to wait for coming in? She was an ungrateful old slut, that's what she was, and she prayed the Virgin would turn a deaf ear to her ravings. Phil was a good lad . . . he was only a bit too fancy for her, and shouldn't she be proud of that? He wasn't like the others, ignorant or upstarts. Hadn't he gone to night school? Hadn't he come out of the yards and got himself a job in an office, the Borough Treasurer's at that? And wasn't he forever reading his books and learning? The bedroom was like Paddy's market with his books. And hadn't he got himself a lady? Well, anyway, a fancy piece who served in Binns. Not that she had seen her, for it wasn't likely that he'd bring her near the door; but Mary Prout said she had seen her, in fact she knew of her, for the girl had once worked in the same office as her niece, Monica.

Fanny placed the breakfast before her son, and as she did so, another worry born of Mary Prout's gossiping reared its head and attacked her. What if he were to come in some night and tell her he was going to be married? Aw! . . . she went to the hob and lifted up the tea-pot . . . she was always going up the street to look for trouble, and them what looked, the devil saw they found.

She was just about to pour herself out her fourth cup of the morning when a faint tap came on the door, so faint that she wondered if it was a knock at all, until Philip, raising his head, said, 'There's someone there.'

Shambling across the room, she unbolted the door and pulled it open to stare down in some surprise on the child in the hall.

'Hallo,' she said. 'And what are you after?'

The child moved her head with adult politeness. 'I'm Marian Leigh-Petty from upstairs.' She stressed the Leigh.

'Well, I know that. What is it you want?'

Fanny was in no mood to bandy words with a child this morning, and with this one in particular, for the little madam had passed her in the hall numerous times during the last fortnight without as much as a 'Hallo'.

'My mummy says would you be kind enough to let her have a shilling for the gas?'

The words came round and full from the small, pert mouth and were delivered with the suggestion of a demand, and they caused Fanny to think, I'd like to lay me hand across her backside, I would that.

'Wait a minute, I'll see . . . Oh! come in,' she

cried, 'there's a draught. Come in – put a move on now!'

The child did not jump at Fanny's sharp order, but moved slowly into the room, where she stood for a moment looking round her, her face expressing her impression as her eyes went swiftly from the two battered leather armchairs up to the cluttered mantelpiece, then down again to the dresser at one side of the fireplace, over the tattered couch at the other, then on to the rumpled bed in the far corner, finally coming to the table and Philip.

Her eyes lingered on Philip, and he stopped eating and said kindly, 'Hallo.'

'Good morning.'

My God! Fanny opened her purse. He'd met his match in politeness, anyway. 'There.' She held out a shilling, and the child, turning from her fixed contemplation of Philip, took it, saying, 'Thank you'; then without more ado turned towards the door.

'Here!' exclaimed Fanny, 'where you going? What about the coppers or the sixpences or whatever you want change for?'

The child turned again and gazed solemnly at Fanny. 'I didn't want change . . . it was a loan. My mummy will pay you back . . . she will, she promised.'

For once Fanny found no retort ready to roll off her tongue . . . the manner of this creature amazed her. She had met some bairns in her time, but for coolness this one took the cake – she was as sure of herself as a priest. In silence she watched the departure of her early visitor. Then turning towards Phil, her observations on the matter were checked, for there he was having his work cut out to stop himself from laughing. Now if it had been Jack she would likely have let out a roar against herself and they'd have raised the roof, but Phil's idea of humour and hers didn't usually click. So all she said was, 'D'you find it funny?'

He swallowed and looked down at his plate. 'Yes, a bit. She was so cool.'

'Cool! Damn cheek, I'd call it. I've seen the last of that shilling, I bet . . . Fancy' – she turned and stared towards the door – 'sending to borrow a shilling, and her sailing into the house the day they moved in like a delicate-nosed lady on a muck heap, and nobody seen hilt nor hair of her since.'

'Doesn't she go out at all?' asked Philip.

'I haven't seen her, and there's few get past me.'

On this Philip took a long drink from his cup, then wiped his mouth on his handkerchief, clean and white and still in its square.

'I've seen the lass and the lad. The lass goes off to work somewhere, she leaves here at half-past seven, and the lad still goes to school. That 'un' – she nodded towards the door – 'goes to school an' all, but I should imagine there's little they can learn her.'

'Mother.'

'Aye, what is it?' She turned towards the table, where Philip was now standing straightening his tie. That was another of his oddities, this mother business. Never ma.

'What is it?' she repeated.

'I think I should tell you I'm thinking of making a move.'

It came just as quickly and as casually as that. Trust Phil to startle your bowels into action. She'd had the feeling all night and more so since she rose that something was going to happen. She had felt it in the weight of her body, it was achy and tired, depressing her. She could always go by the weight of her body.

She did not make any comment, but her thick, podgy hand moved slowly to her chest, and her fingers, pushing the buttons of her blouse apart, sought the warm, comforting feel of her breast and remained there as she stared at him.

'I stand a good chance of a post in Scarborough. I'm on the short list.' His eyes dropped from hers and for a minute he looked like a shy boy. 'I'm sitting for an exam at the beginning of the year, and if I get this post it could lead to – well, anything. Perhaps one day . . .' He stopped and his colour rose, flushing his fair skin.

Her voice was very quiet as she asked: 'Couldn't you get to the top here?'

'Hardly. And anyway, I feel I should move. And then there's you, you want this place to yourself.'

'Me?' Her voice became high in her head. 'Me want the place to meself? Now don't make that an excuse.' She wiped the air with her hand. 'If you're goin', you're goin'. You'll go sooner or later, anyway, this place isn't fancy enough for you.' She turned from him.

'Now, it isn't that. That isn't fair, you know it isn't.'

He sounded so sincere that she turned her head towards him and asked, 'Well, what am I to think?'

'Not that . . . it isn't that. Although you won't believe me . . . it's only that I want to get away . . . to get on. Anyway, I could have left years ago if it was that.'

Aye, that was true, she thought.

'You gettin' married?' Her eyes narrowed at him.

'No, I'm not!' He said this brusquely and emphatically; then turning swiftly from the table he went into the bedroom.

She continued to watch his movement through the open door, and when he returned to the kitchen carrying a trilby, gloves, and a mackintosh, she asked briefly, 'You goin' soon?'

He placed the coat and gloves on a chair. 'There's nothing settled yet, I've got to go for interview.'

As he adjusted his hat in the half-obliterated mirror above the mantelpiece her eyes spread over him as if she was seeing him for the last time. She watched him pull on the brim, first the back, then the front. Then the look in his eyes surprised her as he turned quickly to her and said, 'You've had enough of us all these years, it's time you had a break.'

She stared at him. Why was he giving her this soft soap? Yet so gentle was his tone that she was forced to believe that he himself believed what he was saying and was acting on that belief. But so separated was she from this son that she could not cry out to him, as she would have done to Jack had he said the same thing, 'Don't go, lad . . . stay. I don't want no breaks such as this. Don't leave me alone, for God's sake.' Yet, if she had cried out now she felt that this one would stay whereas the other one wouldn't have, and it was beyond her power of reasoning to fathom out why she couldn't bring herself to ask him, but she couldn't.

Slowly she went to the table, and under the pretence of clearing away she moved the dishes around. 'You'll do as you want in the long run, like the rest of 'em,' she said.

She did not turn again until she heard the door shut; then almost groping her way she moved to the armchair and sat down. No muscle of her face moved; nor did she allow to reflect in her eyes the pain that was in her heart. The last of them going; not one of them left; all over the country they were spread, and hardly a word she heard from any of them. Molly, Frank, and Peggy in London; Bill and Owen, far away in Devon; Davie and Jane in Scotland; only Don and Florrie lived anywhere near, and Don had an upstart of a wife while Florrie, across the water in Howden, had seven around her and a waster of a man . . . And Jack? The pain in her heart increased, swamping her body, reducing it to the huge shell it was. The pain became almost tangible, a thing to be touched. Her hand pressed against her ribs and she rocked herself.

What was life anyway? Why were you made

to rear them, then have them leave you? All of them, even this one.

All the love she had in her had been lavished on her youngest son, yet after he had left her, in spite of herself, something in her had groped towards Phil. But the feeling was bred of her mind, not her heart, for he was the last defence against loneliness – once he went she would be alone indeed, and what was more, if not actually in want, not far from it.

It had been hard enough to scrape along as it was, with the rent gone up to fourteen and a penny and coals and light, not to mention food. When he was gone there'd still be rent, coals, and light, and out of what? . . . Her bit pension. If she asked for supplementary they'd want to know what her eleven children were doing for her, and if she said, 'Damn all!' they'd likely make them stump up. Well, she'd ask for nothing from one of them, through supplementary or any other way. She'd never begged in her life, although, God knew, she had been near to it many a time to keep the lot of them fed; but she'd never asked for a penny for herself, and she wasn't going to start now. Nor would she when . . . She wouldn't complete her thoughts and say when she was left alone; but she continued to rock herself and press her hand against the pain, which she thought of as wind. And she told herself as she forced her temper to support her, she wasn't finished yet. No, by God! She wasn't. She'd find a job or something. If those pieces from the council houses who hadn't the list to keep their bairns' noses clean could pick up their five pounds in the factories, then surely to God there was a job for her somewhere, part-time or something, that would bring her in a pound or two. There must be . . . there had to be.

2

It was half-past nine exactly when Mary Prout put her pinched blue-ended nose round the door and enquired, 'D'you want anything, Fan, I'm off to the store?'

'Aye,' said Fanny; 'you could get me a bit of bacon.'

'Back?'

'Back, be damned!' Fanny's chin jerked. 'Streaky. Four and odd a pound for back, and the streaky over three bob! Threepence ha'penny it was afore the war, and gammon a shilling. What's things comin' to?' She moved towards the mantelpiece and added, 'How's your leg this mornin'? And come in, don't stand there with the door open, there's a draught.'

'Me leg's killing me, Fan.' Mary came to the centre of the room, her eyes on Fanny as she took her purse from behind an old chipped vase. 'If me job wasn't sit-down I don't know what I'd do. Anyway, I'm goin' to the doctor the night.'

'Aye. Well, it's about time you had it seen to,' said Fanny. Then turning abruptly and looking at the little shrivelled woman, she demanded, 'Do you know anything about our Phil and that lass?'

'What?' Mary blinked her small, permanently startled eyes.

'You heard me.'

'Well, now, it's funny you should ask, Fan, but I did hear something.'

'Well, what is it?' Fanny's fingers sorted out the money in her purse and her eyes concentrated on the operation as though it were of prime importance.

'Well, it wasn't about Phil really,' said Mary, 'it was about her. You see, our John's Monica came in last night cos John wanted to know how I was with me leg bein' so bad, and he told her to call in the lav on her way from . . .'

'Aye, aye; get on with it.' Fanny tossed her head like some mettlesome horse, but still concentrated her attention on the purse.

Mary did not immediately get on with it, but surveyed her neighbour of forty years for a moment before exclaiming, 'You under the weather this mornin', Fan?'

'For God's sake if not mine,' said Fanny slowly, 'forget about me health and tell me what you heard, will you!'

'Aye. Well now, mind, Fan, I don't know how far it's true. Now mind, I don't. It's only hearsay, and I don't want to take nobody's character away, for you know what Father Owen said at second Mass last Sunday about if women kept their mouths shut outside their own homes divorce wouldn't never have been heard of and . . .'

Fanny closed her eyes and Mary stopped, then muttered, 'Oh, all right, Fan. Well, it's just that Monica said that Sylvia, that's Phil's lass, had to leave their office because if she hadn't the boss's wife would have skelped her. She came in one day . . . the wife, and there was a big to-do in the boss's office. And she didn't come back the next day, I mean Sylvia. And then she went to work at Binns.'

'Was she thick with him?'

'Now, Fan!' Mary's eyes blinked rapidly. 'I don't know. Only Monica said she always seemed to have plenty of money and she didn't do a bat of work unless she felt inclined, and they all hated the sight of her. There now, I've gone and told you and I shouldn't . . . cos if Phil's fond of her he'll marry her. But it all came out, and I wasn't asking for it. What started it was that when Monica was setting me back home last night she saw Phil coming in here, and she said what a fine set-up fellow he was, and you'd never think he came

28

from this quarter, and why couldn't you get a council house, and it was a pity he was being taken for a ride by the likes of—'

'All right! all right!' Fanny held out her hand. It always irritated her to have Phil pointed out as a cut above Mulhattan's Hall.

'Them that wants council houses can have 'em. I'm not starving me belly to impress the neighbours. Council houses! Anyway, can you see me in a council house?'

'No, Fan.'

This plain statement of truth slightly non-plussed Fanny. 'I can pass meself when I want to, don't forget that.' She bounced her head to convey the depth her decorum could reach if she was called upon to use it. Then she added, 'Look, get me half-a-pound of streaky and a pound of scrap ends. But mind, don't let 'em pang all the fat bits on you. And you can get me a pound of sausages, and keep threepence for yerself.'

'I'm obliged, Fan. And you don't think none the worse of me for opening me big mouth. And you won't let on to Phil that it was from me you heard, will you, cos I like Phil.'

'You can set your mind at rest there,' said Fanny, 'I'll tell him nothing. It's his business, and let him find out for himself.'

Mary, nodding her head and on the point

of verbal agreement with Fanny, stopped. That the undauntable Fan should allow any of her offspring to mind their own business was a new one on her. Fanny certainly must be feeling poorly.

'If I was you, Fan,' she said, 'I'd lie up for an hour. Yes, I'd do that. And look, when I come back I'll take your ashes out for you.'

'Me ashes are out. Go on, get yerself away,' said Fanny. 'What's up with you? It's you who should be lying up with that leg. Go on, get along.'

'All right, Fan.' Buttoning her coat about her, Mary went out, and Fanny stood looking towards the door, her head moving slightly like that of a golliwog at the end of its wagging . . . So his lady piece was more of a piece than a lady! Well, well. And as for letting him find this knowledge out for himself, had it not been for his curt answer this morning to her question of was he going to be married, she wouldn't have let him through the door the night before she had passed the information on to him, for she wouldn't stand aside and let anybody make a fool of any flesh of hers, not even him.

She turned from her contemplation of the door and moved towards the fire. Yet in the long run it was going to make very little difference to her whether he married or not . . . wasn't he going away?

She now looked at the poker in her hand. Was it the lass who was driving him away, more than his desire to get on? Or, painful thought, herself and Mulhattan's Hall? Could it be, though, that he was wise to the lass? That was something she'd have to make it her business to find out, for, knowing her son, she knew she'd wait a long time before getting anything of a private nature out of him.

The morning passed much as usual, and after Fanny had cooked herself some sausages and mash for her dinner and washed it down with at least a pint of coal-black tea, she brought up a chair to the side of the window and into a position where, without moving her head, she could see the steps that led down from the house to street level, and, taking up a half-finished sock, she began to knit without even casting her eyes in its direction.

The house remained comparatively quiet, with no-one coming or going, until half-past two, when Ted Neilson, who lodged with the Quigleys on the top floor, came in with his hand bandaged up. Her needles stopped clicking for a moment. He'd been hurt; she wondered what had caused it. Well, if he had come home to rest, he had some hope. With old Barry for ever on the natter and fight, it was a poor home for a man. She supposed he stayed with them because he was a relation. Perhaps after Phil had gone she herself would take a lodger. Yes, that would be an idea; for she was doubting very much now whether she would find a job outside, and she was becoming desperate within herself to find something that would take the complete emptiness from the days ahead.

Her needles went on clicking rapidly, then she exclaimed aloud defiantly, 'Aw, sufficient unto the day. . .' Christmas wasn't so far off. And if her Jack didn't show up before then, he would show up at Christmas. Christmas was a great healer.

The needles went on steadily . . . click, click, click, click, until three o'clock, when they were brought to an abrupt halt by the sound across the street of Mrs Flannagan's front door opening. Fanny, with darkening brow, watched the slight lady herself, dressed very neatly and not without taste, step into the street and slowly and methodically lock her door and adjust her blue felt hat and matching coloured gloves before moving jauntily away. The lines on Fanny's face converged to the central point of her mouth, until her face resembled an agitated pumpkin. Lady Golightly. Begod! did you ever see anything like it? But pride always went before a fall. Fanny nodded after the departing figure, and said aloud into the empty room, 'If you're not careful you'll topple off your horse afore it gets you to hell, me lady.' Oh, that one made her want to spit! She brought her lips together but did not perform the function; instead, her needles began a ferocious clicking.

There had been only one other person in her life who'd had the power to arouse her ire as did that lady, and that had been McBride himself – God rest his soul – and if he was getting his deserts she knew where he'd be this minute, and she hoped Nellie Flannagan would one day meet up with him.

McBride had led her a dance, and no mistake. All their married life he'd been at it. If it wasn't beer it was bawds. She wondered at times how she had stood it. But if you had a houseful of bairns around you you had to stand it, or jump in the river on a dark night . . . Aye, and she'd been near that more than once. He had been a waster all his life, had McBride, up to the day he died. And that had been the happiest day of her life. Aye, there wasn't a better dead man than him; nor one so carefully remembered, for didn't she have a Mass said for him as regular as clockwork every year. Father Owen thought it was for the release of his soul from purgatory, and she didn't enlighten him otherwise. But when she paid for and listened to that Mass it wasn't the release of McBride's soul she prayed for, oh! no, but that the good God would prevent her meeting up with him in the long eternity, for when the reckoning came and the coming together was accomplished she didn't want to be saddled with McBride again . . . she'd had her bellyful of McBride. Aye, she'd had that, and in more ways than one.

Her reminiscence had brought her to the conclusion that at least she'd had some sort of a square deal in being allowed to survive the tormentor of her days and nights, when her needles were once again brought to an abrupt stop as her eyes took in a figure moving down the steps of the house. She'd heard no-one come down the stairs or pass her door, and that was very unusual. The woman on the steps was from the attics. She was of slight build and fair, greyey fair . . . dollified, was Fanny's verdict. This was only the second time she had seen the woman, and her attitude now was something different from the day when she had entered the house . . . her head was not high now and her nose in the air, but her whole manner was – Fanny searched for a word to describe furtive, and came upon slinky. Yes, she thought, she had gone slinking off there as if she was dodging the polis. They were a funny lot up in the attics. Would she get her shilling back, she wondered? Well, that remained to be seen.

She watched the woman out of sight, thinking, Aye, she was a slinky piece all right.

Shortly after four she saw the child from the attics come running down the street and dash up the steps, and heard her footsteps pounding up the bare stairs as if she were wearing clogs. There was nothing lady-like about her feet, anyway. Fanny laid down her knitting and went to put the kettle on. And as she did so she wondered if she should make some griddle cakes in case her grandson, Corny, came over from Howden across the water after school. He often looked in on a Friday. She never could decide whether his visits were prompted by a desire to see her or a treat to the pictures, which he usually received.

She liked Corny – he put her in mind of Jack. Jack . . . She screwed up her face again, pushing her wrinkled flesh as a barrier against her thoughts.

Having decided on the griddle cakes, she was reaching for the bag of flour from the pantry shelf when she heard the quick thumping steps on the stairs again almost above her head, and it seemed that at the same moment a double rap came on the door. Putting her head out of the pantry she called, 'Come in! Who is it?'

The door was quickly pushed open, and the

child stood there. But like her mother, her attitude was now changed, for she did not look the same assured child who had come to borrow a shilling only that morning. So different was her expression and manner that Fanny came from the pantry saying, 'What is it? What's the matter? What you crying for?'

'My – my mummy isn't in.'

'Well now' – Fanny stopped dead – 'is that owt to cry about?'

The child turned her head sideways and looked down at the floor, and as Fanny watched the tears trickling down her face she exclaimed kindly, 'Ah now! come on now. You're a big lass . . . how old are you?'

'Seven.' She sniffed. 'Nearly eight.'

'Well, that's an age.'

The child sniffed again and sought for her hankie. And Fanny thought, Ah, God in Heaven, she's only a bairn for all her fancy ways. 'Come here,' she said.

She sat down and waited during the slow approach, and when the child stood at her knee, she asked, 'What brought you down here? Why couldn't you wait till your ma came back, or go out to play?'

'I'm not allowed to play in the streets. Mummy forbids it. And I couldn't wait until she came back because I was afraid. She never goes out, she shouldn't go . . . and . . . and I came to you because – ' She moved nearer to Fanny's knee and with a tentative finger she poked at the none-too-clean apron – 'I wanted to come before – before this morning. Margaret said I could, but Mummy said no.'

'Why did you want to come?' asked Fanny, now slightly curious.

'I liked you.' The voice was small. 'I think you're funny.'

'In the name of God! now would you believe it?' Fanny's smile seemed to spread over her whole body at the questionable compliment. This fancy-tongued piece liking her and thinking her funny! This latter description held no derogatory meaning for her when coupled to the first. She took hold of the small hand and was about to pat it when the fingers gripped hers, and the round blue eyes, staring apprehensively out of the plain little face, looked up at her. 'My mummy will be all right, won't she?'

'Yes, hinny, why not?'

'She shouldn't have gone.'

'But she's only likely gone shopping.'

'No. She doesn't go shopping. Margaret gets everything.'

Fanny recalled the slinking attitude of the

woman. There was something fishy here. Why was the child so concerned?

'Where's your da?' she asked. 'Have you got a da?'

'No, he's dead.'

'Ah, well, now, your mother'll be back in a while. In the meantime would you like a sup tea and a piece bread?'

'Yes, please.'

'Well, let me up and I'll get it.'

The child moved to one side and stood gnawing at her thumbnail while Fanny mashed the tea and cut the bread.

Fanny was spreading the jam on the bread with a gully large enough to carve an ox when the door was unceremoniously pushed open, and a thick-set, black-haired and equally black-browed boy of an age that could have been anything from eight to twelve entered.

'Hallo, Gran.'

'Hallo,' said Fanny casually. 'You're early; you not been to school?'

'Aye.'

Fanny stopped wielding the knife. 'Tell me none of your lies now. You'd have to have flown across the water to get here this quick.'

'I asked out early.' The lad, his head lowered, his eyes stretched upwards under his brows, eyed his grandmother with an open twinkle. Then his gaze flickered to the child who was standing eyeing him, and back again to Fanny as she said, 'You did?'

'Aye.'

'What for?'

'Well, to come across here.'

'And they let you out for that?' Fanny's voice was deep with disbelief.

'No. I said I had to go to a mu-sick lesson.'

Fanny's head now jerked back and her laugh bellowed forth. 'A music lesson! That's rich.'

'It isn't, Gran.' The boy's tone was huffed, and his chin was up and his lips out, and in this action alone there showed the relationship between them.

'I've got a trumpet . . . a cornet. Me da give it me. I'm goner learn.'

'That'll be the day . . . Here.' Fanny handed the staring and seemingly hypnotised Marian a slice of bread, and added with a nod towards the boy, 'This is me grandson . . . Corny.' She did not make the other half of the introduction, but turned to the lad and asked, 'You want a piece?'

'Aye.' Corny was now returning Marian's stare. Yet ignoring her as if she were a street away, he asked of his grannie, 'Who's she?'

Fanny, answering him much in the same vein,

39

said, 'She's from upstairs . . . they call her Marian.'

'From the attics?'

'Aye.'

Corny turned his gaze to the table now and traced his finger round the top of the jam jar. 'I wish Mary Ann Shaughnessy was still there. She was a good sport.'

'Get your fingers off there!' The gully swung out as if it would take off his whole hand.

Corny only grinned, licked his fingers and sat down; and as he did so Marian moved to the opposite corner of the table and concentrated her gaze upon him. Her concern for her mother seemed to be forgotten for the moment, for her face had lost its worried look and was now brightly eager as she asked him, 'Who was she . . . that Mary Ann?'

Corny, eyeing her from under his brows, was slow to answer. He had his method with girls, part of which was to make them ask any question at least twice; and he did not now thank his grannie for interrupting this method when she put in, 'She was a child who lived in your rooms.'

'Was she nice?'

'Oh, aye, she was nice, was Mary Ann.'

'Was she clever?' The question was eager.

'Clever? Well now' – Fanny chuckled – 'if

by clever you mean could she tell the tale, she was clever all right.'

There was a slight pause before Marian spoke again; and when she did her voice wobbled, bringing Fanny's eyes sharply to her. 'I can tell stories, heaps of stories, wonderful stories . . . better than her.'

Fanny looked down at the child, whose face was flushed and lips compressed and who could at any moment begin to cry again. What ailed her anyway?

She was about to say a consoling word when her attention was brought sharply to her grandson on the sound of a baby chant issuing from his unbaby-like mouth.

'This little piggy went to market,
This little piggy stayed at home;
This little piggy had bread and butter
And this little piggy had none.'

With definitely crossed eyes, Corny was gazing at his grubby hand as he plucked each finger, and the child, her face now expressing fury, cried at him across the table, 'You! . . . you! You're a silly, stupid thing . . . a . . . a pig!'

'Now, now!' Fanny cautioned her soothingly.

Then swinging her attention about again she barked, 'I'll skelp the hunger off you, me lad, if you don't stop it.'

'And this little piggy cried, "I can tell stories, I can . . . I'm a clever . . ."'

Fanny's arm swept a wide half-circle, but her grandson, used to her method of attack and the necessary evasive tactics, ducked under the table to come up at the other side and directly behind Marian. Unfortunately this advantageous position held forth a temptation that Corny was unable to resist. His head momentarily on a line with Marian's buttocks, his hand followed his eye and acted according to the dictates of his impish will.

Marian, clapping her hands to her bottom, let out a shrill scream that almost brought Fanny off the floor. 'He – he pinched me!'

'I never did.'

Corny retreated swiftly as Fanny, advancing menacingly on him, yelled, 'If I lay me hands on you it'll be a tombstone you'll be needing, me boy, this night.' Suddenly she made a dive towards him, but Corny, whipping open the door, escaped into the hall. At the sanctuary of the front door he stopped, and holding with outstretched arms to each stanchion, he levelled his puckish grin at her and cried, 'And don't forget to put me full name on it, mind, Gran . . . on me tombstone, Frederick Richard Cornelius Bowen.'

Fanny's face remained grim for another moment, then her wrinkles quivered and she exclaimed, 'One of these days I'll have the hide off you from your scalp to your toes.'

'Excuse me.'

'What?' Corny turned an almost startled face of enquiry to the boy making this polite request, before dropping his arms and standing aside to let him enter. Perhaps it was because the lad was a good head taller than himself and seemingly a good deal older that he checked any mimicry he would otherwise have made.

Fanny looked at the boy making for the stairs, and he looked back at her, but said nothing. And he was already on the stairs when she remarked, 'Your sister's in here along of me . . . your mother's out.'

As if she had hit him with something in the back of the neck, she saw his head jerk forward before he turned.

'What did you say?'

'I said your mother's out, and your sister's in here with me. She was crying because there was nobody in.'

The boy moved down one step, and as he did so Marian pushed past Fanny's bulk and came into the hall. The brother and sister looked at each other, and Fanny looked at them.

What was it at all? Why should two children be so concerned about their ma being out?

'Do you know which way she went, please?' asked the boy.

'Up the street towards the town . . . Now what is there to worry about? Is your ma bad or something? Does she have turns?'

The boy's round, brown eyes blinked, and he pushed his hands through his thick sandy hair as he repeated, 'Turns? . . . Yes, yes, she has turns.' Then he looked at his sister, saying, 'I'll go for Margaret, you stay here. Can she stay with you?'

He appealed to Fanny now, and she said, 'As long as she wants. And would you like a sup tea yourself afore you set off?'

'No . . . no, thank you.'

He went hastily out, and as he passed him Corny asked, with the camaraderie of the young when dealing with a male equal, 'Can I come along of you?'

'No. No, thanks.' The tone, high, polished, different, as much as the abruptness of it, checked Corny's following steps, and his grannie's voice, saying, 'You stay where you are. Come in here now,' brought him back into the hall even as his eyes followed the boy leaping down the steps to the street.

The issue of the pinch was forgotten, and Fanny, a hand on each of their heads, pushed them into the room and closed the door. She looked down on the child, who was standing again with her thumb in her mouth, and her curiosity was very much aroused. She'd like to get to the bottom of this. What was the matter with the woman anyway? To be in the house a fortnight and not show her face; and when she did go out, the bairns to get into this state. Perhaps if she quizzed this one she'd get some inkling of the affair.

'What kind of turns does your ma take,' she asked, 'dizzy ones?'

'No, no, she doesn't take dizzy turns.'

'What kind then?'

Without moving Marian turned her head almost on to her shoulder to look towards the window. 'Your curtains,' she said, 'aren't like ours. Mummy hangs ours like they do in France, crosswise.'

'Is that so?' Fanny nodded her head deeper into her chins. 'Has your mother ever been to France?'

Marian's head came round swiftly now. 'Oh, yes . . . and Germany, and Switzerland, and Austria, and oh . . . all over. My mummy's clever.'

'Is she now?'

'I can speak French, she taught me.'

'Did she now?'

'Yes. She speaks French and German, and she paints. Tony can speak German. And she taught Margaret to paint. Margaret paints beautifully.'

The child was speaking rapidly now. In side-tracking Fanny she had also evaded her own worry for the moment. 'And she reads us wonderful stories. Oh, she reads the *Faerie Queene* beautifully.' Her head moved, emphasising how beautifully. 'Do you know it?'

'No, hinny. What's it all about?'

'Oh, all kinds. About Britomart who wanted to be a boy instead of a girl. And she runs away, and she has a magic spear and magic armour. And she meets Sir Guyon and Prince Arthur and . . .'

'Poloney!'

The rhythm of the story-teller was abruptly cut and she swung round on the disbeliever in fury now. 'You! It isn't paloney . . . you're ignorant. Mummy says you're all ignorant and I haven't got to play with any of you, so there! There!' She thrust out her head at Corny, and Fanny admonished, 'Come! Come now. We won't have any of that highfalutin chatter. Come off your high horse now. And if your ma thinks along those lines why for does she send you to St. Peter's? You

46

go to St. Peter's School, don't you?' And Fanny's indignation caused her to add, 'And why for did she bring you to live here at all, anyway?'

The haughty head drooped. 'Mummy says it won't be for long. We're all going abroad to live. We are, some day.' Her head came up and she glared at Corny as she said again, 'You!'

Corny, a little impressed in spite of himself and his feelings in no way hurt by the stigma of ignorance placed upon him, exclaimed, 'Okay . . . who's arguin' wi' yer?'

They looked at each other, Marian's glance full of childish fury and Corny's amused, cynical. Then, 'I bet you what you like you can't say somethin' in French,' he challenged her.

'Can't I? I can so.' With her eyes hard on him and each word mouthed separately and well apart from its fellow, she delivered, 'Vous êtes un gamin.'

'What's that when you're out?'

'You-are-a-dirty-boy.' Her nose assisted her lips with the translation, and again Fanny admonished, and quickly this time, 'Now! now! there's no need for that, and we'll have none of it.'

'Well' – Marian turned her back on the offender – 'I don't like him.' She looked across at Fanny, and her face suddenly crumpled, and with a sudden rush like a charging goat she made for her. And when her head came to rest in the pit of Fanny's very flexible stomach, Fanny cried with a gasp, 'There, there! Come on, come on.' And at the same time, with her eyes and one hand speaking expressively, she warned the grinning Corny against comment.

'Come on, child. Give over now. Come on, let me sit down.'

Marshalling the temporarily tear-blinded Marian towards the armchair, she sat down with a resounding dull flop, and lifting the child on to her knee she allowed her to bury her head between her breasts. 'Give over now. Stop crying, you'll make yourself bad. Here!' She beckoned her grandson. 'Pour me out a cup of tea. And have you any bullets on you?'

'No, Gran.'

'No, you wouldn't have! Stuffed your kite with them afore you come in.'

'I didn't!' Corny protested. 'I've never had none since last Saturda'; me da only give us sixpence and me ma wouldn't fork out nowt, she said she hadn't it.'

'And that's likely true an' all, with the squad of you she's got to see to. Get the tin down from the top shelf of the pantry. And keep your fingers out of it, mind,' she cautioned, 'I've got them counted.'

In a surprisingly short time, Corny returned from the pantry with the toffee tin seemingly intact, and handed it to Fanny. Then stood with his eyes glued on it, while with her arms still about the child she prised up the lid. Extracting a large humbug, she handed it to him.

'Aw! only one, Gran?'

'Give it back here!' Her arm shot out. Then dipping her fingers again into the tin, she said to the half-buried head, 'Look what I've got. Come on. Do you like humbugs? My! this is a whopper . . . Here, pop it in your mouth.'

The head was turned sideways; the mouth opened, and the humbug disappeared. But the solace of the sweet did not entirely restore Marian to tranquillity, for she continued to lie against Fanny's chest, issuing dry sobs as she automatically sucked at the sweet.

From a safe distance Corny stood surveying her, his humbug traversing the distance between each cheek every few seconds. At one period, failing to make the distance, it was caught and ground noisily between his strong, blunt molars. There was a gulp, a swelling of his throat, then a request, 'Can I have another, Gran?'

'You can if you clear that table and put the kettle on for your Uncle Phil coming in.'

'Aw, nuts!'

'Well, nuts or May, it's up to you. No table, no bullets.'

Fanny smiled inwardly as she watched him stamping back and forth to the scullery. He was another Jack, that one. The same cheeky face, the same nerve, yet more understanding somehow although he was so young. This thought hurt. She would like to have brought him up, but his mother had need of him as she herself had had need of Jack. And God knew her daughter needed comfort against her man as much as she herself had ever done against McBride.

The table set, she said, 'That's a clever lad. Give me the tin here, it's at me feet on the floor.'

As Corny brought the tin from the folds of her skirt a knock came on the door, and she called, 'Come away in.' But when no-one entered, she commanded her grandson, 'Go and see who that is. Are they deaf?'

Corny, running to the door and opening it, paused a moment before calling over his shoulder, 'It's that lad, and – and a lass.'

'Tell them to come in then. Come in!' she shouted. And at the same time, easing herself on to the edge of the chair, she said to Marian, 'Get down a minute, hinny.'

With the comfort of Fanny's flesh and the sweet, Marian had been almost lulled to sleep, but on the sight of the visitors she was wide awake and she ran across the room to where a tall, young woman stood just within the doorway.

'Oh, Margaret, you're back! She went out . . . Mother went out.'

'Sh!' A hand was placed on her head.

'But Margaret . . .'

'Be quiet now. It'll be all right.' It was a command, gently spoken, but not, Fanny noticed, with all the refined accent of the younger brother and sister. Although the voice was sweet-sounding it added to the end of its words the rise of the northern inflection, and Fanny recognised the difference immediately, and was warmed to the girl. She was a bonny-looking lass, she decided, with a pair of fine, dark eyes on her, and a good skin, and hair you didn't see the like of every day, a real nut-brown, a smooth, glossy nut-brown. If there was anything wrong with her, Fanny decided, it was that she was too thin, on the skinny side. Perhaps she'd got that way with worry. She looked worried. For that matter, the bunch of them looked worried.

'Come in. Don't stand there,' she said; 'we're all chained up.' She laughed.

'Thank you, but I won't stay . . . not now. It was very kind of you to have Marian.'

'Now what was kind in that?' Fanny asked the

question, and then put her head on one side as if waiting for an answer.

But the young woman was not to be drawn, not even into a bit of a chat, she only returned Fanny's look. And the worry deepened in her eyes, until her whole face took on a peculiar sadness that sat like a mask on her youth, and caused Fanny to step forward, saying, 'Look, is anything wrong, lass? If I can help you, you've only got to say. I'm used to trouble.' She smiled. 'We're bed fellows . . . Is your mother bad or . . . ?'

'No, no!' It was a double denial, for the boy spoke too, then self-consciously dropped his head. And the girl, after a moment's pause, said, 'She's – my mother's not strong and we worry if she goes out alone. But if it wouldn't be asking too much, would you let Marian stay until we come back? We're going to meet her.'

'Certainly, lass. Would you not like a drop of tea afore you go?'

'No, thanks. But it's very kind of you.'

'Let me come, Margaret.' The child was now clinging to her sister, much as a young baby would have done. And the girl said sternly, 'Behave yourself; you can't come. We won't be long.'

Fanny watched her loosen the child's hands from about her knees. One was too young for her age, she thought, and the other was too old.

She had been made into a woman before she'd been a lass, that one.

'Come here, hinny,' she said to Marian. 'What about another humbug? And what about telling me another story? She tells me she's fine at stories.' Fanny looked at Margaret, who had turned towards the door.

The girl stopped for a moment, and her tone brought a pucker to Fanny's brow as she said flatly, 'Yes, she's good at stories.'

After the door had been closed, Fanny still looked towards it. Now what did she mean by that, for there was more in that remark than hit you in the eye.

'I'll tell . . . I'll tell . . . I will! Mrs McBride, he's stealing the sweets.'

Fanny turned and caught her grandson in the act of depositing a humbug in his trousers pocket, and as she cautioned him with her usual bellow she could not help but wonder at the mercurial change in this other child, who appeared to her quicker than most children at throwing herself from one situation to another. Well, perhaps she'd throw herself into a game.

'Fork out . . . come on.' She held out her hand to Corny as he retreated round the table saying with a lop-sided grin, 'I ain't got none, Gran, honest.'

Fanny liked a game with this grandson. 'Come on!' She advanced steadily on him, ponderously, like an elephant.

'Honest, Gran.'

Dashing to the door, Corny wrenched it open; then stopped and exclaimed, in a high, excited voice, 'Hallo, Uncle Phil.'

'Hallo, Corny. What are you up to now, eh?'

'Havin' Gran on.'

Philip came into the room, and after throwing a glance towards Fanny, which took in the child at the same time, he placed his hat, gloves, and case on a chair, then went to the window, and standing to one side looked up the street.

This was against all usual procedure. The routine was for him to make straight for the bed-room, and on his way there give his verdict on the prevailing weather, to which Fanny would usually reply briefly, 'Aye,' then go to the hob for the teapot.

'What's up?' she asked, her tone expressing both curiosity and perplexity, for this son was above being interested in the happenings of the street; in fact at one time he had dared to censure her for meddling, as he put it, in the business of the neighbours. Should she have a do with Nellie Flannagan his head would be bowed with shame for days. As for looking out of the window, why, the house could be without one for all the notice he took of it. But now he was apparently very interested in something going on outside.

She moved quietly, and taking her stand behind him and peering over his shoulder, she asked, 'What is it? What's up?'

Without turning his head he said under his breath, so that his voice was for her alone, 'There was a woman acting oddly around the top corner, and the girl from upstairs came running up. There was a boy with her. They tried to get the woman to come along. I didn't stop . . . it might have embarrassed her.'

Fanny looked at the neatly trimmed edge of her son's hair where it came to a point on his neck, and at the rim of still clean white collar showing above his coat, and as her mind said, Aye, well, and it should be clean with a fresh one on every day, she set to wondering how he knew the lass was from upstairs; he hadn't let on that he had set eyes on her when she had been on about them this morning.

'Was the woman drunk?' she asked. 'And how do you know they're the ones from upstairs?'

'I saw the girl go out yesterday morning, she must have been late. She got the same bus. She works at one of the factories at East

Jarrow, at least she got off there. . . The woman wasn't drunk, at least I don't think so.'

'No, she couldn't be,' said Fanny; 'they're not open yet and she looked sober enough when she left.'

'Ssh!' Philip, stepping quickly back from the window, almost knocked her off her balance. 'Oh, I'm sorry,' he turned as swiftly to her, his arms out to steady her, but she warded them off saying brusquely, 'It's all right, I'll take some knocking down.'

His colour mounted and for a minute he looked uncomfortable, then turning from her again he stood looking from a safe distance down into the street.

'Are they coming?' asked Fanny.

'Yes.'

She moved in front of him now, and as she did so Marian came across the room saying, 'What is it? Is something happening?'

'No,' said Fanny, now blocking the aperture between the curtains; 'just you go and sit up at the table and I'll give you some tea in a minute.' Fanny did not turn to see whether or not she was being obeyed but kept her gaze fixed on the trio advancing towards her. There was the lass on one side and the lad on the other. They were linking the woman who had slunk out of the house a short while back. But there was no furtiveness about her now for her head was up and she looked as if she was talking away twenty to the dozen. The girl was speaking, too – rapidly and, if her expression was anything to go by, forcefully, but the boy's head hung downwards until you could see nothing but the crown of it from where his hair sprang upwards in tufts.

As they passed beneath the window the woman's incessant and high-pitched voice came clearly to Fanny, saying, 'Nonsense, Margaret, nonsense . . . one must put a face on things . . . one must be gay . . . People live by example. Tomorrow I will . . .'

They mounted the steps now and the woman's voice came to Fanny only as a distant, highfalutin twang. She turned to the door but her movement towards it was checked by Philip. He motioned silently to her, then pointed to Marian.

It was obvious that the child had heard her mother's voice, but it had not made her fly to her, for she was now standing in the corner by the fireplace, her face to the wall and her thumb again in her mouth. And as the sound of the voice came from the hall now, saying, 'Don't . . . don't hurry me, dear, don't hurry me . . . Oh, good evening,' the child moved her head forward until it leant against the wall.

'Hal . . . hallo.' That was Sam Lavey answering. She wouldn't get much conversation out of him, thought Fanny, with his stammer and his tick.

'What is your name?' The demand was imperious and sounded like the lines of an amateur stage duchess.

The front door banged, and that, grinned Fanny, was Sam Lavey's answer.

'Dear, dear! . . . an ignorant man. I . . .'

'Alice!' The name spoken low penetrated the room like a growl, and Fanny knew it was the girl speaking and that she was addressing her mother. But why should she in the first place call her Alice? and why should she speak like that as if the word was being wrenched out of her body? There was no answer to this, only that the cry of Alice had apparently a silencing effect, for there was no longer the sound of the woman's voice only of footsteps going up the stairs and the squeak of Miss Harper's door being gently pulled ajar. Oh, it wouldn't do at all for Miss Harper to miss anything. She was sorry she had missed seeing them herself, but with Philip's eyes on her and the look in them saying, 'Mind your own business,' she had been for the moment deterred. Not that she was afraid of him. No, by God!

'She's bubbling.' Corny's levelling comment brought Fanny's attention to the child again, and as she made her way over to Marian she remarked, 'And she won't be the only one if you don't keep your tongue quiet. Come on,' she said. 'Come on, don't cry. Come and have some tea.'

But Marian would not be coaxed from the wall; she shrugged off Fanny's hand. And Fanny, used to the ways of children, left her to herself and returned to the table.

Philip had now gone into the bedroom, and when he came out again his navy coat had been changed for a tweed one. He went into the scullery and washed his hands before sitting down.

Corny had already started on a piece of boiled ham, a cold sausage and a tomato, and after eyeing his uncle for a time as he applied himself to his food, his gaze slid to Marian's uninteresting back. Then still chewing, he turned his attention to his grandmother.

Fanny was sitting in the armchair, her hand placed under her left breast, gently rubbing her ribs. After gazing at her intently for a moment, he enquired solicitously, 'You got the wind, Gran?'

'Get on with your tea,' said Fanny, without looking at him.

'Why don't you let off, Gran? Me ma does and it eases . . .'

The solicitous advice was cut short. The crash of Philip's knife and fork on to his plate and his outraged cry caused Corny's mouthful of food to make a rapid exit, which in turn caused him to choke and splutter.

'Leave the table!'

'Here, hold your hand a bit.' Fanny was on her feet.

'Hold my hand!' Philip, too, had risen. 'Did you ever allow any of us to say a thing like that to you?'

'No, perhaps not, but . . .'

'There's no but about it. It isn't right that you should allow him to take such liberties . . .'

Oh, my God! he was off again. The last time a thing like this happened was when Peggy's young Joe had said backside. He had gone on for hours trying to make it clear to Joe that bottom would have done. Now if the child had said arse she could have understood it . . . but backside! He could go on for days and hardly open his mouth until his nice, fine sensibilities were shocked, and then he forgot to close it. Now all because the lad had offered his advice on the best way to help nature get rid of a painful indignity which itself had created, he would keep on for days. Corny could be thankful he didn't live here . . . Oh, she supposed it wasn't a proper thing for a bairn to say, but somehow she liked them better that way. Anyway, she understood them better.

'Just imagine if someone had been in,' Philip said. 'And what about . . . ?' He nodded angrily to where Marian was now recovered enough to take an interest in the proceedings.

'She won't hear much in this house that will do her any harm,' said Fanny.

'I don't know so much.' Philip sat down. 'It all depends on what you consider harmful.'

'Uncle Phil.' Corny was coughing into a none too clean piece of rag. 'Uncle Phil, I didn't mean nowt, honest . . . I wasn't trying to be funny or owt.'

The disarmingness of this ugly piece of humanity was too potent. In the face of it Philip could not retain his righteous indignation.

'All right,' he said. 'But try to remember you don't say things like that.'

'OK, Uncle Phil.'

'No matter what you hear in the streets, or what you think—'

'Be quiet, the pair of you,' said Fanny sharply, 'there's somebody coming from up top.'

They all waited now, listening, and when the knock came on the door Fanny said to the child, 'Go and open it, it's your sister.'

As the young woman came into the room Philip rose to his feet, causing Fanny momentarily to close her eyes. That was another daft habit he had

61

acquired which put everybody on tenterhooks.

'Come in, lass,' she said. 'Is everything all right now?'

'Yes. Yes, thank you.' The girl's face was as white as lint and she kept her eyes on Fanny as she spoke. 'You've been very kind. And I understand my mother ran short of change for the meter this morning.' She held out a shilling to Fanny, and as she did so Marian, in a whimpering voice, said, 'She sent me . . . she made me, Margaret.'

'All right, be quiet.' The sister's tone was sharp and had the command in it that Fanny had sensed before, but she drew the child to her, and with her arm about her shoulders, pressed her to her side.

'You caught up with her then,' said Fanny.

'Yes. She had just gone out shopping.'

'Aye well, we all have to do that sometimes.'

'Goodbye. And thank you Mrs . . . McBride, isn't it?'

'Aye, McBride it is, but I answer better to Fan.'

Fanny watched the girl smile, a slow, small smile which softened her face and brought youth to it again.

'Goodbye.'

'So long,' said Fanny.

When the door had closed Fanny turned towards the table again and there was Philip, still standing as if he were glued to the spot. That was an odd thing, wasn't it? The lass hadn't even cast a glance to the side he was on. Give him his due, for all his pernickety ways he was worth looking at. And then about the mother going shopping – she hadn't had a basket with her and not even a quarter of tea in her hand when she came back.

'She looks ill.'

'What?' Fanny looked up at her son.

'The girl, she looks ill and worried. It's odd that type coming here. And the mother's so. . .' He paused, and Fanny, sidetracking anything to do with higher education, purposely misconstrued his meaning.

'Aye, it is odd . . . we may be poor here, but at least there's nothing that you can't put your finger on . . . on anyone of us. Now, will you both finish your tea so's I can clear away, for God's sake.'

3

It was nine o'clock the same evening and the house, after a quiet spell, was starting its last minute bustle of the night. Fanny likened this stir to hens going to roost. 'Cackling themselves on to their barks,' she would say. And tonight, her knitting again in her hand, her eyes directed once more through the narrow aperture of the curtains towards the lamplit street, she thought, 'There they go.'

Even the bustle from the attics reached her. There was a lot up there that even God would find difficult to get to the bottom of. She nodded emphasis to this mental comment. Then as the noise gradually died away she fell to wondering about this and that. She wondered if Philip was with his lady-love; she wondered what Mrs Flannagan was up to behind her fine curtains; she wondered if Mary Prout was having a long wait at the doctor's. Yet she was fully aware that all this wondering was just to keep her mind away for a time from her son and the constant hope that the door would open one of these nights and he would walk in as broad and as cocky, and as casual as life.

Then she stopped wondering, and her mind was being taken up with anxiety that thoughts of this particular son always bred when into her view hobbled Mary Prout, not making her way towards her own house on the other side of the street but to the steps of Mulhattan's Hall. What now? thought Fanny, for by the look of Mary she was in a stew.

Her voice filled the room before Mary's knock had sounded on the door. 'Come away in.'

Mary came in, closing the door hastily behind her and hobbling right to Fanny's side before speaking. Then she brought out tearfully, 'I've got to stay off, Fan.'

Fanny laid down her knitting. 'He's put you off?'

Mary nodded disconsolately. 'For a fortnight at least, he says. What am I going to do, Fan? If I lose me job I'll not get another, not a sittin'-down one. And it's a good 'un.'

'Well, surely they'll keep it open for you?'

'Not unless I can get somebody to stand in, Fan, temperally like. You wouldn't believe there's that many breaking their necks for such a job. Cos

65

it's sit-down, you see, Fan. Most of the time it's sit-down.'

'All right, I know by now it's sit-down. That's about the tenth time you've told me in as many seconds. Well, sit yourself down and stop your agitation. Your life hasn't come to an end yet. What's he say about your leg?'

Mary, easing herself gently on to a chair, exclaimed dolefully, 'I'll be able to carry on if I get a bit of rest now. If I don't me number's up. At least he didn't say that, but I knew what he meant. I can read them.'

'Don't be so daft . . . your number up! Talk sense, lass . . . Well, what d'you 'tend to do?'

Under Fanny's bracing tone Mary recovered herself somewhat. 'I don't know, Fan. If I could only get somebody to stand in for me for a fortnight. Mrs Proctor would keep it open for me – she's the one that gives out the jobs – but it's got to be somebody I know because if she puts a stranger in the devil in hell won't get them out, because you see it's—'

'Aye, aye, I know,' said Fanny, waving her hand. 'It's sitting-down.'

Mary gulped and blinked, then started to clean her thumbnail by the simple process of using a fingernail.

'Is there nobody who'll stand in for you for a couple of weeks?'

'Nobody that I know of, nobody that I could trust not to stand in for me good, once they got set behind that glass plate. Nobody that is, except yourself, Fan.'

This last remark of Mary's seemed to surprise herself as much as it did Fanny, for she looked scared for a moment as she stared at her friend.

The knitting had dropped into Fanny's lap, and her nose was wrinkled and pushing up the bags beneath her eyes, and her lips stretching back over her four remaining teeth made her mouth one large, dark gap, from which she brought the words slowly, 'And what would you be meaning by that, Mary Prout? What's in the back of your mind?'

'Nothing, Fan. I didn't mean nowt. It only came to me as I was comin' out of the surgery, then I would have none of it.

Fan couldn't do it, I said. But she's the only one who could, if she would. If you know what I mean, Fan.'

After this somewhat candid piece of diplomacy Mary looked hard at Fanny, then blinked wildly as Fanny let out a bellow of a laugh.

'Do you know what you're saying, Mary

Prout? Me, in The Ladies. My God! that'll be the day.' Fanny rose to her feet and perhaps there was just the slightest tilt to her chin as she repeated, 'Me in The Ladies!'

She walked to the fireplace and stood looking down into the dull embers. Then addressing them, she remarked, 'And why not? indeed!' Now turning to Mary she asked sharply, 'What's it like? What d'you do?'

'Nothing much, Fan. Maggie's on all day. She takes the tickets and wipes the seats and sees that none of them holds the door open for each other, unless, of course, it's somebody she knows with bairns, or her relations. You just sit in the little glass place and punch the tickets.'

'Is that all?'

'Aye. But mind, Fan, you've got to look respectable.'

The sudden rising of Fanny's bust caused Mary to add hastily and soothingly, 'Not that you can't when you like, Fan. But you know what I mean, Fan. You'd have to put your corsets on.'

'What difference will me corsets make to punching tickets for a lavatory?' Fanny asked this question in a low, aggressive tone, and this caused Mary to move uneasily on her chair, and knock her bad leg as she fought unsuccessfully for words with which to placate her friend.

'Anyway, I'm not goin', so me corsets won't matter.'

'Aw! Fan.'

'Never mind "Aw! Fan". By the sound of it, it's a title you want before you get to work in a lav!'

'I didn't mean that, Fan . . . Oh dear!' Mary was leaning forward towards the window as she gave this exclamation. 'Here's your Philip coming up the steps. By, he's early, isn't he?'

'Phil?' Fanny, too, looked towards the window, then added hastily, 'Say nowt about this if you don't want him to throw a fit at your feet.'

'No, of course not, Fan. Philip wouldn't be for it, I know that. He'd never hear of your doing it.'

This statement caused another rearing of Fanny's bust, and she looked hard at Mary for a moment, wondering if the little woman was fully aware of her incentive remarks or was she just simply being Mary Prout.

'I'll be going, Fan, but will you think it over? I'll pop across first thing in the mornin'. I'd get our Monica to write a note for you to take down if you'd do it.'

'There's time enough in the morning to talk about that.'

'Aye, Fan.'

As Mary opened the door to take her leave, Philip entered, saying, 'Hallo, Mrs Prout.'

'Hallo, Philip. Nice evenin'.'

'Yes, it is.'

'Good night, Philip.'

'Good night, Mrs Prout.'

Fanny moved impatiently towards the table. Oh, the pleasantries. They would choke each other with them in a minute. What had brought him back so early? Had a row with his lady-love, she supposed.

She turned to her son, saying, 'I haven't got your supper ready yet. You're early the night, aren't you?'

'Yes, I've got work to do. I thought I may as well get started on it. I won't want any supper, just a drink.'

'Well, you're easy served. Tea or cocoa?'

'Tea, please.'

As Fanny made the tea Philip called from the bedroom, 'Have you heard any more from those upstairs?'

'You mean in the attic? No, except the young one squealing her head off a few minutes ago.'

'What do you think was wrong with the mother?'

'Your guess is as good as mine.'

'The girl looked ill.'

Fanny lifted her eyes towards the bedroom door. He seemed very interested in the family all at once. Perhaps it was because, like himself, they had a twang.

A few minutes later, as she poured out the tea, a little smile began to lift the corner of her mouth, for she was picturing the effect her words would have on him if she were to shout out this minute, 'What d'you think? I'm off to The Ladies the morrow.' Like as not he would come to the door and say, 'The Ladies? what Ladies?' There passed through her mind a cryptic description of The Ladies, but one that she knew she would never have the face to give him.

But just what would he say if she were to tell him she was going to work in The Ladies? The thought tickled her and teased her as she watched him drink his tea, but when he said, 'Good night, Mother,' she answered off-handedly, 'Good night.'

It was round about three in the morning when she woke up and said to herself, 'I'll do it,' and immediately went to sleep again, to wake at her usual time with a feeling of excitement in her stomach that outdid the pain under her ribs. She lay for some moments savouring what lay before her today, then with a sudden spurt that disturbed her bulk into a protesting waddle, she rose from the bed and going to the cupboard next to the fireplace delved into a cardboard box and retrieved her corsets. After a minute examination as to their pulling power she pushed them into the oven, then set about the business of making a cup of tea and lighting the fire. And this being a special morning she pushed down the top of her vest and washed well down her neck, and she had just finished her unusual toilet when the bedroom door opened and Philip made his appearance.

Fanny turned to him in surprise, saying, 'What's got you up? Something bitten you?'

'I've been awake for some time, I've been working.'

She moved her head in small jerks as if in appreciation. But her mind refused to comprehend, or recognise messing about with figures as work. People who classed figures as working knew nothing about work. She dismissed this controversial subject which was linked up with values and asked herself when she could tell him. When he'd had his breakfast? Aye, she'd better let him get something down him, for he'd need it with the blow she was about to deliver to his dignity.

After cooking his breakfast she sat at the corner of the table sipping her tea and watching him cut the rind from the bacon. She knew he didn't like rind on his bacon, but it was a form of habit or cussedness with her that she had always cooked the bacon with the rind on and she always would. When, as always, he left his plate liberally covered with dip, making no attempt to sop it up with his bread, she could not help an impatient click of her tongue. His fastidiousness irritated her so much that it was with something akin to glee that she thought of the bombshell she was about to drop on his plate.

'I've got a job.' She took a loud gulp of her tea.

Philip looked at her through narrowed eyes, as he repeated, 'A job? You?'

'Aye, me. I'm not dead yet.'

'But why do you want a job?'

'Why does anybody want a job? For money.'

She watched him rise from the table and go to the mantelpiece.

'You needn't have done that . . . I'll send you some each week.'

'I don't want anything off you.' She was on her feet, aggressively gathering the dishes together. 'I want nothin' off nobody as long as I've got a pair of hands on me.'

'Why are you going on like this?' His voice was quiet, and Fanny's hands stopped for a moment. The conversation was taking a wrong turn . . . she had started wrong. She should have thrown the nature of the job straight at his head.

'You're not fit to take a job.'

'What do you know about it? I'm fit to cook and clean, and I'm fit to sit here and end me days in loneliness. Well, I'm not going to do it, d'you see; I'm goin' to sit and get paid for it!'

The expression on his face now was pitying, but she wanted neither his pity nor his sympathy, she wanted nothing from this gentleman son of hers except a big laugh from the look on his face when she sprung on him what she was going to do.

'What kind of a job are you getting sitting down?'

Her chin went up and her hands fell one on top of the other on the layer of her stomach as she emitted through primed lips, 'The Ladies.'

'The Ladies? . . . you mean . . . ?'

'Aye, I mean The Ladies, a penny-in-the-slot.'

That had done it, as she knew it would. His face looked as if strings were pulling it from all angles; there was every kind of expression on it.

The laughter was rumbling audibly in her stomach and in a moment it would have escaped and she would have laughed as she hadn't done for many a long day. But her enjoyment was suddenly whipped away by a wave of anger as she watched her son's face relaxing and crumbling into laughter, laughter which he was struggling hard to hide.

The fact that she had not shocked him, that he had not showered on her any verbal protest, baffled her. He was a mealy-mouthed, sanctimonious, word-knowledgeable upstart, yet he hadn't gone up in the air when she had delivered this bombshell at him.

She began to spurt words at him. 'You find it funny? Let me tell you I can conduct mesel' when I want to . . . And don't you forget it.'

'Oh, Mother, it's – it's not that. Why shouldn't you take such a job if you want to?' He turned from her, his shoulders shaking, and she hated him as he said, 'And as you say, it would be better than sitting here and being lonely.'

She had never seen him like this, with laughter gurgling in him. The truth came at her slowly. He didn't mind what she did because he'd be away and out of the town. Aye, that was it. His reactions would have been different if he had been staying on here, then he would have been his gentlemanly self and put his foot down. He had taken the wind out of her sails but he wasn't going to get away with it altogether.

Her head wagged as she said, 'What will your lady-friend say about your mother being in The Ladies?'

She had been determined to nettle him, and she had succeeded, for his laughter stopped abruptly and he went into his room, saying, 'I haven't any lady-friend, as you call her.'

So that was that, that was finished; he'd likely got wind of her carryings-on. Quite suddenly Fanny sat down again, the thought in her now that she didn't know whether to take the job or not, that's if she got the chance of it.

When sometime later Philip, having come back into the kitchen and going through the usual procedure of brushing his coat and hat, said, 'When do you start?' Fanny kept her eyes directed towards the table and she answered tartly, 'I won't know till I go down and see the woman. Anyway, it's only temporary, Mary Prout's leg's bad.'

He had to pass her as he moved to the door, and in doing so he did a strange thing, for the tips of his fingers touched her shoulder for a moment as he said, 'Enjoy yourself.'

She was staring at the door through which he had gone. Of all the damned unpredictable so-and-so's he was one. Enjoy yourself . . . in The Ladies! What did he mean? Sarcasm, that was it. She could still feel the touch of his fingers, but the emotion they had brought to her she brushed aside. She knew that she was unreasonably angry that he had not flown into a temper when she told him what her job was to be. That he should laugh at it had really been one of the surprises of her life. Now if it had been Jack, they would have roared together, and the captions he would have put on The Ladies would have made her belly roll for days. But this one, he wasn't like that, this one was a gentleman. He should have thrown a fit when confronted with his mother going into The Ladies.

You never knew folks, not even your own. Certainly not your own when they were cuckoos in the nest like him.

'Will I do?'

'Eeh! your corsets do make a difference, Fan. Takes stones off you. Your black coat's hanging like a bag. Don't tell me that's a new hat.'

'No, course it isn't. What would I be getting a new hat for? I changed the ribbon, it had gone a bit green in parts.'

'Aye, it had.' Mary nodded confirmation; then said, 'There's the note. And ask for Mrs Proctor. Tell her it will only be for a fortnight, and I'll be back. It's better that you should go down on your own, because if she feels she's goin' to be stuck she'll take anything.'

'Thanks.'

'Oh, I didn't mean that, Fan. You know what I mean.'

'Aye, I've got a good idea . . . Come on then,' she said brusquely, 'I want to lock me door, and if I don't go now I might change me mind.'

This threat caused Mary to limp hurriedly out into the hall, and just as she reached it her eyes were drawn up the stairs to the woman from the attics.

Fanny turned from the door and placed her key carefully in her black shopping bag, then she, too, looked up at the woman.

'Good morning.' The words were so high and refined that they seemed to chill the muggy air in the hall.

'Good mornin'.' Both Fanny and Mary answered together.

'I was just coming to see you.' The thin woman inclined her head in a condescending bow towards Fanny, and Fanny, on the defensive immediately against both voice and manner, replied, 'That's just too bad, I'm goin' out.'

'I have come with an invitation. I would like you to come to tea.' She inclined her head now towards Mary, as she added, 'And you, too. But I would like to give you some more details about it. May I call again this afternoon?' She was again looking at Fanny, and now Fanny, perplexed in spite of herself at a formal invitation to tea, looked at Mary, then down at her bag, and finally towards the front door as she remarked, 'Aye, me door's always open.'

When they reached the foot of the outside steps Mary whispered, 'What d'you make of that?'

'We're invited to tea,' said Fanny, under her breath.

'Will you go?'

Fanny looked down at her friend for a moment, and a twinkle came into her eye as she said, 'Aye, of course I'll go. And tell her all about The Ladies – that should make her feel at home.' She punched Mary playfully, and Mary let out a giggle that sent Fanny almost gaily down the street towards the bus.

Fanny had joked with the bus conductor, she had joked with the milkman who had nearly bumped her with his electric barrow, she had joked with the young lass who had asked her business in a dingy little room before allowing her into the presence of her superior, Mrs Proctor, but Fanny could not joke with Mrs Proctor, because she saw that Mrs Proctor was summing her up. She did not say to herself that Mrs Proctor was taken aback by the sight of her, but the woman's attitude stiffened Fanny's spine and made her think, Well . . . aye . . . What do you want in such a place? Royalty?

'You understand that the post will only be temporary?'

Fanny nodded briefly.

She also understood that if Mrs Proctor wasn't in a bit of a stew at having to fill Mary Prout's place quickly her own chances of getting in on this job would be very small.

'Have you references?'

'No, I've never had any need of them, I'm well known.'

'Well, I'm afraid you have to have two. Do you think you can get them?'

'Yes, a dozen if you want.' She didn't care now if she got the job or not. References . . . just to serve in the lav! God in Heaven!

'You see you'll be dealing with money, and it's necessary that we have some knowledge of your . . .'

Under Fanny's stare Mrs Proctor became silent, and she added lamely, 'You understand?'

'Aye, I understand, and I've never touched a sixpence that doesn't belong to me in me life and as it's only pennies I'll be dealing with I'm not goin' to start now. If I wanted to go along that line I'd go for bigger game, wouldn't you?'

The question apparently disturbed Mrs Proctor,

80

and she rose to her feet, saying, 'Well now, if you could get me the references you could start tomorrow. And, of course, as I've said, it's only temporary . . .'

'Aye, you told me.' There was deep emphasis in Fanny's reply. One of them was a numbskull . . . and God knew who that was.

'They'll have to be from people in authority.'

'I'm aware of that. One'll be from me priest and the other from me grocer. They've looked after me body and soul for years.' That was a good one, she'd never thought of that afore. A grin at her own humour now split Fanny's face, but found no answering smile on Mrs Proctor's. Instead, the perturbed woman opened the door, saying, 'Good morning. Bring them in tomorrow.'

'Aye, I will.'

There was a codfish if ever there was one. Dealing with all The Ladies in the town had done something to her.

Well, now! Fanny stood in the street and looked up at the sky. It was clear and blue and had a washed look, fresh-like. She had a fresh feeling herself, she had never felt like this for years. Perhaps it was the support of her corsets; perhaps it was getting out a bit, for it was many a long day since she had been further than Braithwaite's or the church, and they were only a stone's throw from each other. She'd go back now and pay a visit to Bob Aiton, who was manager of all Braithwaite's stores and whose backside she had smacked many a time when he was a lad living across the road and playing with her own young 'uns. Of course, he had gone up in the world since then, but she could rely on him to give her a good word.

Fanny felt decidedly better. Perhaps it was because during the last few hours her mind had been taken off her son, Jack, and the longing to see him had not brought its knife-edge between her ribs and made her hands grope for something to do.

But why was it, Fanny thought, that you always had to be interrogated by bits of lasses who wanted to know the ins and outs of your business before you could put a foot over anybody's door.

'You tell Mr Aiton it's Fanny McBride, and if you tell him you've kept me standin' here like Johnny-come-canny he'll skelp the hunger off you, and I'm tellin' you, me girl.' She nodded sharply towards the tallest of the three girls who were staring at her wide-eyed as if, she thought, she was a visitation.

While the tall girl picked up the telephone and became immersed in a somewhat lengthy conversation, Fanny outstared the other two until, their heads drooping, they began to tap their typewriters again. The tall girl looked up from the phone and said, 'Mr Aiton's busy, is it important?'

'Of course it's important, I wouldn't be here else.'

As the girl spoke into the phone she kept her eyes on Fanny, and Fanny held her look. And when the girl, replacing the receiver in its stand, said coldly, 'You'll have to wait a moment, Mr Aiton is busy,' Fanny checked the eloquent ejaculation, 'Well, I'll be damned!' Bob Aiton telling her she'd have to wait a minute! When he was a lad in the greengrocery she had clipped his ear if he didn't push her some pot stuff in extra. And when he was manager of the grocery department he'd make his way to her to have a word with her. But now he had an office and ran the lot she had to wait. Ah well, she supposed that was life. She sat down on a stiff wooden seat and waited for the fleeting glances of the girls as they were lifted to her in curious speculation.

It was some moments before the phone rang. The tall girl answered it, then rose to her feet, saying primly, 'Come this way.'

Fanny went the way indicated, and when her guide knocked on a frosted-glass door and they were bidden to enter and there behind an imposing desk, flanked at one side by a middle-aged woman sitting at a table, she saw Bob Aiton, Fanny gulped openly, for it was not the Bob that she remembered in the grocery department, who still retained a vestige of the lad who had run wild with her own, but a man she thought of, with genuine surprise, as getting on – well on.

He did not rise, but in an over-hearty tone said, 'Come in, Fanny. Come in . . . Well now?'

Fanny looked at him a moment before speaking. It must be all of eight years since she had seen him, but by his changed appearance it could have been twenty. And he was as jerky as a jack-in-the-box, with his hands moving and his nose twitching.

'How's the family? The boys all right, I hope? Years since I saw any of them. Funny what life does . . . throws us here and there. Well, Fanny, what can I do for you?'

'I've come for a reference.'

This, at least, had silenced his jerky flow for he did not even repeat, 'A reference?' but looked at her for some moments in silence, and then said, as if at last getting her statement right, 'Oh yes, who for?'

'For meself.'

'Yourself, Fanny? What do you want a reference for?'

'A job, of course.'

Again her answer had silenced him, until after some moments of staring and blinking, and passing a glance towards the woman at the end of the table, he said, 'Yes. Yes, what kind of job?'

'I'm goin' in The Ladies.'

Fanny hoped that this statement when made last night to her son would shock him into making a protest. To her mind he was the only one that it would shock, yet it had done nothing of the sort. But now she could see she had shocked Bobby Aiton, for his eyebrows were raised and his mouth was forming a puckered 'Oh!' of surprise, and it was only with an effort, she noticed, that he stopped his eyes sliding apprehensively again towards the bent head of the other woman.

As he coughed discreetly in his throat she watched his Adam's-apple bobbing up and down like a cork in a bucket. Now why had he of all people to be agitated? His face was as pink as a smacked backside. My God! Weren't we all very genteel of a sudden. And when she thought how he had been brought up, rougher than any of her own, and that was saying something.

'But – but, Fanny, you are getting on. What – what would you be wanting to do in – in The – The Ladies?'

The unconscious impropriety of this question was not lost on Fanny and she was for answering,

'What would anybody be wanting to do in The Ladies?' but taking it as it was meant, she said, 'It's a sitting job.'

She was about to continue and describe in detail the duties of the position she was after when her eyes were drawn to the startled gaze of the secretary, and the reason for it struck Fanny like a joke from an old-time music-hall, and she was unable to stop the bellow of laughter that sprang from her high, corseted chest. She laughed at the two faces before her, she laughed at what she had just said and the way the woman had taken it, and when the tears sprang into her eyes she dabbed at them, thinking, I've had more fun this mornin' than I've had for years. Then bringing her gaze full on the shocked face of the secretary, she explained pithily, 'We're all grown up, so what does it matter? What I meant was, I'm sitting taking the money.' She turned her look to Bob Aiton again, saying, 'Mary Prout. You remember her, she lived next door to your mother? Well, she's been part-time at the Connolly Street one for years, but now her leg's given out and the doctor's ordered her to be off, so I'm standin' in you might say, or,' her small bright eyes flashed to the woman again, as she ended on a laugh, 'or sittin' in.'

'Yes, yes . . . Yes, yes, and you want a reference? Yes, yes.' Mr Aiton began to write at top speed, and Fanny watched him. Once he paused and looked up at her as if searching for adjectives by which to describe the virtues that would enable her to get into The Ladies, then with a small perturbed shake of his head he went on writing.

Fanny watched him sign his name with a flourish then fold the sheet quickly and stick it into an envelope. And he rose hurriedly to his feet as he handed it to her, saying, 'There, Fanny, that should get you what you want.'

She, too, rose to her feet. And now very quietly she said, 'Thanks, Bob.' No more, no less. She gave him one long look before turning from him, and when he came quickly round his desk to open the door she checked him with a backward wave of her hand and went out, her bust up, her head back, and carrying her bulk as spritely as it would allow her.

In the street Fanny began to walk in the direction of the church. The morning was not so nice now, the sky not so high or so blue. There was a chill in the air that penetrated her fat and made some part of her cold . . . no part in particular, but somewhere inside her she was cold. Bob Aiton hadn't wanted to see her, that was the truth of it. He had forgotten that he ever knew her, or at least was trying hard to dim the memory. Words that her son Don's wife had thrown at her at the christening of their only child came back to her. They seemed in some way connected with Bob Aiton's attitude. 'You take some living down,' she had said.

Well, she'd go to the priest and see what impression she made on him.

Miss Honeysett, the priests' housekeeper, answered her knock. Fanny did not expect Miss Honeysett to smile; she did not expect Miss Honeysett to be civil. Miss Honeysett was Miss Honeysett, an institution in her own right. Protector of the priests from those who had nothing better to do but make their lives a burden, who were forever running after them, like Nellie Flannagan, who took her offerings by hand so's to make sure of the jewels in her heavenly crown. She wouldn't trust her reward to God alone, not her, she wanted a guarantee from Father Owen's own lips. Yes, that was Nellie Flannagan and the likes that pestered the priests. But she wasn't one of them, she hadn't been inside these presbytery doors for over thirty years, and she'd never forget the reason for her visit then either. She had nearly murdered McBride with the frying-pan that day, for she'd had it in her hand at the time he had stumbled in rotten drunk and not a penny of his week's pay in his pocket. Then she had left him flat on the floor and the bairns running hell-for-leather in all directions, and she hadn't known whether to go for the priest or the polis, but God had guided her to this very door, and Father Owen himself had gone back with her and seen to McBride.

'Who d'you want, Father Owen or Father Bailey?'

'Father Owen.'

'Sit down. He's just this minute come in, he's never off his legs. I'll see if he can spare you a minute.'

Fanny nodded understandingly and sat down, and the minute was hardly up before Father Owen appeared in the doorway, his long face longer with astonishment as he surveyed Fanny across the room. And his exclamation was like a warm greeting when he said, 'Well, Fanny, what brings you here? This is a surprise. No, don't get up, keep your seat.' He pulled up a chair close to hers and smiled at her as he asked, 'Are you in trouble, Fanny?'

'Not a bit, Father.'

'Philip all right?'

Fanny's eyes dropped, and then she said, 'He's leaving; he's getting another job. But,' she added, looking at him now straight in the eye, 'it's right that he should. This place is too small for him, he'd never settle here.'

Father Owen said nothing, just bobbed his head.

'He's the last of them, and when he's gone, Father, I'll be lonely, so I thought I'd get meself a job.' It was easy to talk to this man.

If possible the priest's face stretched even to a longer length, his mouth formed an elongated 'oh' as he ejaculated the syllable itself, 'Oh!'

'Yes, Father. I'm after a job. It's just temporary, but when it's finished I'll get another.'

Again the priest nodded his head, and again he exclaimed, 'Oh!' Then: 'What kind of a job are you after, Fanny?' he asked.

'I'm after gettin' into The Ladies, Father, temporary like.'

The priest's mouth closed in order that he should moisten his lips; then they parted slightly and his head bounced once as he repeated in all solemnity, 'The Ladies?'

'Yes, Father, you know . . .'

'Yes, yes,' the priest put in hastily. 'Yes, I know, Fanny.'

Fanny stared at the man who had been her

confessor and friend for as long as she could remember. He wasn't surprised, he wasn't shocked, he didn't think that she was past a job, even The Ladies.

'Do you think your legs will stand it, Fanny?'

Fanny phrased her answer carefully as she replied, 'I'll be only taking the money, Father. I'll be off me legs for most of the time – at least that's what I understand. It all depends on your reference. I have to have two, so I came to you. I've been to Bob Aiton's for the other one.'

'Oh, aye. Oh, you went to Bob? Now there's a fine man. I'm sure he gave you a good one.'

'I don't know,' said Fanny, non-committal about both the reference and him being a fine man. 'Perhaps you'll remember, Father, he was brought up along of my lot.'

'I do, I do, Fanny. They all ran around together. But Bob's done well for himself, and no blame to him, now is there?'

'That all depends,' said Fanny. 'It appeared to me he didn't like to be reminded of his past. And I'm part of his past, for many's the day I've fed him when his belly was empty. And there he was sitting behind his desk as snotty as a new-made bride.'

Father Owen coughed, then he got to his feet and turned his back on Fanny and went to the waiting-room table and picked up a magazine. But before turning to give it to her he coughed again and blew his nose violently. Then coming to her, he handed her the magazine saying, 'There, you'd better take that in case I'm not able to look in on you this week.'

'Thanks, Father. And about the reference?'

The priest stooped over her and patted her shoulder.

'I'll give you a reference that'll get you into the Ministry of Supply, Fanny. I'll say you've had a football team.' The priest threw his head back and laughed down at her, and Fanny, joining her raucous pitch to his, cried, 'And one in reserve, don't forget, Father . . . I've had twelve.'

'And one in reserve, Fanny. And they're all good boys and girls.'

The priest spoke as if her family were still children, and the smile slid from Fanny's face and her eyes dropped to her hands and she tapped her fingers gently together as she said, 'You're forgetting about Jack, Father.'

'No, I'm not forgetting about Jack.' The priest's voice was hearty. 'Jack will see sense one of these days.'

'In the Salvation Army, Father?'

'Oh, that. You worry too much. Jack will never join the Salvation Army.'

'He married one of 'em.'

'Well then, do some praying and get her out of the Salvation Army and into the Church . . . That would cause some rejoicing in Heaven, wouldn't it?' Again the priest's head went back in a laugh.

But Fanny did not join her voice to his this time; instead, she said soberly, 'You don't know my Jack.'

'Oh, I know your Jack very well. Didn't I have the teaching of him? He's going through a bad spell . . . don't we all. No man is worth his salt who isn't tempted.'

'Tempted!' repeated Fanny scornfully. 'He's past being tempted. He jumped in with his eyes open, and he's in it over the eyebrows now and he cannot see his way out. That's why he's ashamed to come near me.'

'What's come over you?' said the priest, sternly now. 'Hope's dead in you and that's a sin. It's as well you're taking something to do, it'll keep your mind from brooding. Well now' – his voice softened – 'let me get my pen and I'll write you a note that'll lead you towards happier times.'

He went out of the room into the hall, and just as he had passed through the door Fanny saw him stop abruptly as if he had been taken aback. And when he spoke the reason was made clear to her and brought her up on to her feet with the suggestion that she had just at that moment been progged with a pin . . . Nellie Flannagan! My God! if she were to go to Hell for a bucket of pitch that Lady would follow her! What could she be wanting here at this time in the morning?

And now Nellie Flannagan's voice told her, for her refined twang floated into the room, saying, 'I've called to see you, Father, with reference to a post.'

Aye, it would be a post with that one, not a job.

'I was wondering if I might ask you for a testimonial?'

Now what job would she be after? Who would take her for anything other than somebody who wanted to learn the art of putting on false airs and graces . . . being an upstart, in short?

She saw the priest's hand move swiftly out and close the door, and she thought to herself, 'Oh, he needn't worry, I know me manners if nobody else does. I wouldn't raise me voice so near to the Holy Church. I'll keep me bawling for me own doorstep.' Then again she thought, 'He needn't have worried,' and she wanted to tell him so when he returned to the room with the pen in his hand and his face bearing an expression that spoke of hurry.

She watched his pen moving swiftly over the

paper for quite some time, and she did comment to herself that he wasn't letting Lady Flannagan cut her reference short, he was giving her her dues. Then when he licked the envelope and pushed in the letter and handed it to her, seemingly all in one movement, she looked at him squarely in the eyes and to the poor man's consternation, she said, calmly, 'Don't agitate yourself, Father. I'd neither hit her nor spit in her eye on your premises. And thanks a lot for this.' She fluttered the envelope. 'And I hope when you're writing out a reference for her you'll give her her deserts as you've given me mine.'

With this telling statement she nodded once, a deferential nod, and turning on her heel she made swiftly for the door into the hall, determined that he wasn't going to lead her out through his private quarters and the main presbytery door.

On entering the hall she did not allow her disappointment to show when there was no sight or sound of Nellie Flannagan. And when the priest, smiling now with a smile that drew up one side of his mouth, bade her goodbye from the door with a 'God bless you, Fanny', she replied, 'And you too, Father'; then sailed down the street in the direction of home with all the lightness she could muster, for her corsets by now were sticking in her at all angles and her feet were bursting out of her good shoes.

'This,' said Mrs Proctor, 'is Miss Toppin.' She waved her hand airily to a tiny, shrunken creature with a face like that of an old bird.

As Fanny acknowledged the introduction she thought, 'God help her, she's got a beak on her that'd pick a winkle.'

'I'm known as Maggie,' piped Miss Toppin in a voice that was as thin and sparse as her body, and she accompanied this information by a smile that did something to her face and made Fanny add to her comment, I'll get on with her all right, she seems a canny sort.

'Maggie is permanent . . . almost an institution in herself.' Mrs Proctor looked down on Maggie with a look of mixed condescension and pity, on which Maggie immediately turned her back and went about her business.

'Mrs Craig comes in in the mornings.' Now Mrs Proctor was addressing Fanny. 'Your time will be from one-thirty till six, with fifteen minutes off for tea.'

'Where do I go to get that?'

'You don't go anywhere, you have it here. There's a ring.'

'That's nice.'

A few minutes later Fanny looked about her at the L-shaped corridor of boxes, at the little glass-fronted office in which she was to sit. She liked the look of that very much, and behind it was the cubby-hole where the stores were kept and where she could go to make her tea; she liked the look of the whole set-up; she liked the smell of the disinfectant; but above all she liked the look of Maggie, and as she had to work with her that was just as well, she felt.

'Now I must go. I will leave you in Maggie's capable hands.' Mrs Proctor was all abustle, which indicated the importance of her position and the many calls upon her services. 'Maggie will show you what is necessary and you'll start tomorrow. Goodbye.'

'Goodbye,' said Fanny.

Maggie did not even nod, but with her thumbnail she made a ripping sound as she tore the outer cover from one toilet roll after another. Then when the door had closed she commented, 'She gets on me tripe!'

'Does she?' said Fanny.

'Aye, she does.' There was another ripping sound and Maggie's long nose jerked up and down and drew Fanny's eyes with it.

'I'm eliterate, that's what she says.' Maggie's head jerked towards the door. 'I heard her say that one day 'bout me, that's why I don't get the job in there permanent.' She nodded towards the glass partition. 'Can't count, she says, but I can take the pennies when we're stuck like now. I can count when I want to. I know how many beans make five . . . You want a cup of tea?'

The ripping sounds were still going on as Fanny said, 'Aye, thanks very much, I could do with one.'

'Come on in then.' Maggie bundled the toilet rolls into a box, then, with a conspiratorial air, went into the little room where she lit the ring and put the kettle on it, saying as she did so, 'Sit down.' Then the relieving smile splitting her face again, she put her head back and looked up at Fanny as she exclaimed, 'That's if you can get in.' This was said in the nature of a compliment and Fanny laughed.

'By! you're big.'

Looking down on the undersized little woman Fanny exclaimed, 'And by, you're little.' Where-upon they both laughed together.

'If we was the same size we would have to play Bad-weather-Jack and find Lady Jane, wouldn't we, one in and one out?' piped Maggie.

'Aye, we would that.'

The more Fanny heard of Maggie's chatter and the more she saw of the wizened little creature the more she liked her. And when Maggie, handing her a brimful cup of tea, exclaimed, apropos of nothing in the immediate conversation, 'Mary Prout's got nothing more up top than me, and she takes the money. Tain't fair, is it?' Fanny, without going into the matter, said, 'No, it isn't.'

'But somehow I don't mind you.' The little woman poked her finger into the region of Fanny's bust. 'I think we'll get on. Not like Mrs Craig . . . you want to see the way she comes dressed up. I says to her one day, "What d'you think this is? You look as if you were dressed for a garden party," and you know what she said?'

Fanny took a drink of tea, looking enquiringly over the rim as she did so into the small, bright eyes below hers.

'She said that she was a cashier in a Ladies' convenience and dressed accordingly.'

As Fanny spluttered into her cup Maggie let out a high squeak that seemed to corkscrew through the top of her head pulling her upwards to the ceiling, for she stretched with her glee. Then she clapped her hands over her mouth, exclaiming, 'Eeh! there's somebody in.'

As Fanny watched her scuttle out of the cubby-hole she thought, 'I'm goin' to enjoy meself here.' Then placing the cup hard down on the shelf opposite as if to emphasise her resolution, she repeated, 'Aye, I am. I'm goin' to think no more, I'm goin' to enjoy meself.'

Fanny had hardly got home when the knock on the door made her turn impatiently, and she cried in her usual way, 'Come away in.' But on seeing the woman from upstairs she was somewhat taken aback. However, she tried not to show it as she exclaimed, 'I've just got in, I haven't got me things off.' Then she added, 'But come in anyway.'

With her hands extracting the pin from her hat Fanny watched her neighbour sail into the room like an eighteenth-century lady on a slumming expedition. And when, without any further invitation, the woman seated herself Fanny sat down opposite her with her hat still on. She'd get her puff, she decided, while weighing up this odd creature.

She was, Fanny commented to herself, sixty-five if she was a day. And how old was the youngest child? Seven or eight, not more. Well now, she granted that every so often there were miracles performed appertaining to creation, although in some cases she believed them only because she must, like the one about John the Baptist's parents. There had been a bit of fiddling there, she'd often thought, but they couldn't get away with that kind of fiddle these days. Taking things as they were this lady would have been close on sixty when she gave birth to her last child, and that was a bit too much to stomach. There was a mystery here.

Because of the mystery and Fanny's natural curiosity to get to the bottom of all mysteries, she now forced a smile to her face as she said, 'You've come about the tea-party?'

'Well, it's not exactly a tea-party, I am merely asking you to tea.' The voice was cool, very cool.

'Oh, aye.' Fanny was determined not to be annoyed. 'Well, I look upon it as the same thing. Is it your birthday or something? By the way, your name's Leigh, isn't it?'

Fanny's tone was at an unusually polite conversational level.

'My name is Mrs Alice Leigh-Petty, and it isn't my birthday, but' – her voice now sounded to Fanny like that of a wireless dame, as she went on in quick jerky tones to explain the reason for the invitation to tea – 'I have always been interested in social work and I have found myself temporarily, I repeat temporarily, sojourning in a quarter that could, I feel, avail itself of my experience.'

Now Mrs Alice Leigh-Petty's voice gathered

speed. It could be true to say that she gabbled at Fanny, but all in a very highfalutin twang.

Fanny sat listening with gathering brows. There was a great deal that she couldn't make of the woman's jabber, but this much she did gather. The poor should be weaned from their grossness by the example of their betters, and that she, Mrs Alice Leigh-Petty, was going to start the crusade in this very house.

Mrs Alice Leigh-Petty proposed, over tea at three o'clock the following afternoon, to guide the steps of the heavy-footed ladies of Mulhattan's Hall on to the first rung of the ladder of culture. They would, she went on to say, talk of books, in a quite simple way, and cover, over other cups of tea on other days, the necessary arts without which women remained, as were her immediate neighbours of necessity, creatures whose lack of intellect placed them in a position akin to animals.

There had been in this discourse wonderful food for Fanny's repartee but she had refrained from using it, for as she'd looked at the thin, lined face of the woman and her pale eyes sunk into large sockets, she had been kept busy putting two and two together. There was something funny here. A blind and deaf mute could tell that.

She next learned that Clara Lavey, Amy

Quigley, and Miss Harper had all accepted the invitation to tea, the former two, Fanny had no doubt, to get a belly laugh – but Miss Harper, Fanny knew, had accepted because she was no doubt, deluding herself that she would be mixing with society. Miss Harper was out for refinement, even if it choked her.

Mrs Leigh-Petty abruptly finishing her discourse rose to her feet, the curl of her lower lip indicating that she'd had as much of the plebeian atmosphere as she could stand at the moment. Then the curl increased and the pale eyes stretched as Fanny explained briefly, 'Thanks all the same, but I won't be able to come.'

'You won't? Why?'

'Well, you see, I'm startin' a job the morrow.'

There was a pause before Mrs Leigh-Petty repeated, 'Starting a job?'

'Aye, that's what I said.'

'May I enquire what position you are taking up?'

'Aye, you may.' Fanny sniffed, a loud, loose sniff. 'I'm goin' in The Ladies. Mary Prout across the way has a bad leg. I'm carrying on for her.'

As if Mary's name had conjured her out of the blue, she now put her head round the door and exclaimed, 'Oh! Fan, I didn't know you had company.'

'Really!' Mrs Leigh-Petty's nose seemed to be actually smelling The Ladies.

'Aye, really.' In spite of her good intentions Fanny's gorge was rising and she shouted now as if Mary was the length of the street away, 'Come away in, Mary.'

Mrs Leigh-Petty turned and looked across the room at Mary Prout hobbling towards them, then she looked back at Fanny and exclaimed with what sounded like genuine regret at the loss of a star pupil, 'Then I won't expect you tomorrow afternoon.'

'You won't,' said Fanny decidedly. 'Good-day to you.'

Without returning the salutation, Mrs Leigh-Petty sailed out of the room, ignoring Mary as if she had no proof of her substance.

'Well' – Fanny moved hastily to close the door on her visitor's back – 'what d'you make of that 'un? If she's all there, then I'm ready for Sedgefield. Out to educate the Tyne she is, and startin' on us.'

'She's been all round the doors,' said Mary, 'asking people to her tea-party . . . But how did you get on, Fan, about the other business?' Mary's face was anxious.

'Oh, fine,' said Fanny airily. 'The job's there when you're fit to go back to it. I'm startin' the morrow.'

'Thank God,' said Mary fervently, and with a little laugh she added, 'And you an' all, Fan.'

'I'm tired.' All at once Fanny sat down in her chair again with a dull-sounding plop. Then looking at Mary, and with a lifting jerk to her head, she added, 'But I must admit I've enjoyed meself the day. Aye, I have. That is, until that 'un came on the scene. Did you say she'd been all round the doors?'

'Aye, Fan. May Brice was in our house and you should have heard what she said to her, pulled her leg no end. Eeh! I did laugh.'

May Brice. Suddenly the knife-like pain returned to Fanny's ribs. May Brice's daughter lived along where their Jack was now living. Anything she had heard of him since he had left home had been through Mary via May Brice.

'Well,' said Fanny, 'and what was she on about?'

'Oh nothing, Fan, she only looked in cos I was under the weather.'

'Out with it,' said Fanny, getting to her feet and pulling off her coat. 'That'll be the day when May Brice has nothing to say.'

'Well, Fan . . . now don't go for me, Fan. Will you, Fan?' Mary started to pick her nails in agitation. 'Well, she says she saw Jack . . . and her, not so long ago. They were arm-in-arm and May says he was well put on . . . dressed to the eyes, that's what she said, in a trilby.'

'A trilby?' Fanny turned slowly and looked down on Mary where she sat perched on the edge of the chair.

'Aye, Fan.'

A trilby. Her Jack who had sneered at and scoffed the lugs off Phil because of his trilby and gloves.

'May says Joyce's folk have moved again, that's twice since they left here – a big six-roomed place they've got now – and . . . Jack and her's with them.'

Fanny swung round and went to the fireplace and screwed the big black kettle into the heart of the dim embers as she cried, 'The halls of Hell are big, they say. Well, I want to hear no more, but mind' – she twisted her head round and glared at Mary – 'if you tell May Brice you told me this, not another farthin' do you get out of me. And mind, I'm telling you.'

'No, Fan, no. Now you know me.'

'Aye, I know, and that's what I'm afraid of.'

'Aw! Fan.' Although Mary sounded hurt she did not appear unduly troubled at the slur on her discretion.

'I'll be goin' now, Fan. I just slipped across

when I saw Nellie Flannagan out of the way, for if she sees me walking about and me on the sick with me leg, I wouldn't put it past her to put a spoke in me wheel.'

'You're right there,' said Fanny. 'Put nothing past that 'un . . . Her and May Brice . . . there's a pair; it's a shame to spoil two houses between 'em.'

'Aye, Fan.' Mary got to her feet. 'Ta-ra, Fan. And thanks again for what you've done. I'll try to come across in the mornin'.'

'So long,' said Fanny abruptly.

As Mary went out Fanny turned to the fire-place again, and putting her hand up to the high mantelpiece she rested it there, staring down on to the kettle. So he was wearing a trilby, was he? It was to be hoped that his head didn't get too big for it. But the news could have been worse, it might have been that he was seen wearing the uniform. My God! that would be the day of shame . . . the Salvation Army uniform. She swung round and tore off her hat, then kicked off her shoes, and in her stockinged feet threw herself into the task of putting the room to rights. And such was her temper that she forgot for the time being that her corsets were killing her.

*　　*　　*

It was some time later, when she had just finished setting the tea for Philip and the energy she had expended in trying to cover the pain under her ribs was beginning to tell on her, that there came another knock on the door. And she called flatly, 'Oh, come away in.'

To say that Fanny was surprised when she saw that her visitor was Mrs Leigh-Petty again was putting it mildly. But it was not the Mrs Leigh-Petty who had left with her nose in the air a short while ago. This Mrs Leigh-Petty came in shiftily, stealthily. She sidled in, softly closing the door behind her.

On the point of speaking, Fanny hesitated. The creature seemed to have as many different guises as a touring act. The fine dame of a while ago, Fanny saw, was gone, and before her stood a pathetic figure, the eyes holding no haughty glint now, but dark and full of pleading. Yet she could do nothing with her voice, for it was still highly refined.

'Am I intruding, Mrs McBride?'

'No, no, not at all. Come away in and sit down. I'm on the point of making a cup of fresh tea.'

'I – I won't have any tea, thank you.'

'What is it? Come and sit down. Are you bad . . . you're shaking?'

'I'm – I'm all right. I wanted to ask you something. I wouldn't go to any of the others.' She motioned her head backwards, indicating the rest of the house. 'I came to you because I feel you understand.'

What Fanny was supposed to understand she didn't rightly know, and she wasn't all that interested, but she said, 'Aye.'

'You won't tell Margaret, will you?'

'Tell her what?'

'Well, anything that passes between us. Margaret's hard, she has very little feeling. I wish Marian was older . . . Marian understands already.'

Fanny nodded, not knowing what was to be understood but appearing to be conversant with it.

'I've run short of money.'

So that was it. Fanny's expression did not change.

'I've told Margaret until I'm tired that I can't manage, but she takes no heed. Would you . . . would you be interested in this?' Mrs Leigh-Petty drew from the bottom of a raffia basket a paper-wrapped object, and uncovering it revealed to Fanny's fixed gaze a silver cake-basket.

Now what in the name of God did the woman think she would do with a silver cake-basket.

'You can have it for a pound.'

A pound! If she had a pound to spare it wouldn't go on a silver cake-basket. On Fanny's silence Mrs Leigh-Petty's voice became urgent. 'Fifteen shillings, then. It's worth four or five pounds.'

'It may be,' said Fanny, 'but I wasn't wanting a cake-basket at the moment.'

'It would make a lovely Christmas present for . . . for one of your family.'

Aye, she was right there, it would . . . but fifteen shillings! Five shillings apiece was her limit for presents, and what with the squad of them and their bairns, she had to take out three money clubs for Christmas each year.

'I'll let you have it for ten shillings.'

It was Thursday and ten shillings was about all she had to see her over till the morrow night, when Phil gave her his pay.

'Please have it . . . please take it.'

So urgent was the plea, so pathetic the creature before her, that Fanny turned to the mantelpiece and taking down her purse handed over the ten shillings. But for a moment she thought that the woman had changed her mind for she clung on to the dish as if loath to part with it; then, almost flinging it from her, she thrust it into Fanny's hands and with only a mumbled word of thanks turned hurriedly away and went out.

The dish in her hands, Fanny looked towards the door. Was there ever such a creature? To her mind that woman needed a doctor . . . and she herself needed her head looking at for being such a damn fool to part with her last ten bob. You couldn't eat a silver dish, now could you, and likely when the lass came in and found the dish gone there'd be hell to pay, but in that case she'd get her ten shillings back. It was a grand dish, though, in fact a fine dish, and worth anybody's ten shillings she would say.

She placed the dish on the dresser among the conglomeration of oddments reposing there, and stood back and surveyed it with not a little pride. Perhaps she wouldn't give it away. She'd keep it and do a bit of bragging on her own within hearing of Lady Flannagan.

The more Fanny looked at the dish the more taken with it she became. Although it looked plain enough it was heavy and had an air about it . . . class-like, she thought. And she found herself eager for someone to come in and admire the acquisition. But no-one did until Philip returned home.

His comments were much as usual. 'Been cold,' he said, 'could be a frost tonight.'

'Aye,' she said. She watched him make for the bedroom, then stop before he entered the door, his head turned sideways, caught by the bright gleam of the silver.

'What's that?' he asked.

'What does it look like?' asked Fanny, pleased that the dish had caught his attention so quickly.

He took a slow step sideward and picked it up, turned it over, then looked towards his mother, and the surprise in his voice gave her a sort of kick as he said, 'It's silver . . . solid silver. Where did you get it?'

'I bought it.'

'Where? Second-hand? Did you clean it up?'

'No.'

'Then where did you get it?' His voice was excited. 'It's a beautiful piece. What did you give for it?'

'Ten bob.'

'What! You're joking. No!'

'Why should I joke? That's what I paid for it.'

He put the dish down and stared at her, his gloves and hat still in his hand. 'This thing's worth pounds, it isn't plate. Where did you get it?'

Nonchalantly, Fanny, raised her eyes to the ceiling. 'The lady . . . from up top, she came in in a stew, nearly went on her knees for me to have it. She wanted a pound, but she dropped quick enough. I didn't want it – what's the good of it to me? – but it's a bargain. I know that, although I've had few in me life.'

'Bargain? What's the girl going to say?'

'I don't know, and it doesn't matter to me what she says, I didn't ask for it.' She could see that he wasn't at all pleased about the deal now that he knew where the dish had come from, and she added, 'Well, it's there, and they can have it . . . that's if I get me money back.'

Philip said no more but went abruptly into his room, leaving her in the air as it were. She went to the oven and pulling out a plate of fish, exclaimed, 'Damn him!' If ever there was a levelling influence in this world it was this son of hers. To witness his attitude you'd think she had pinched the blasted thing.

As Philip ate his tea in silence Fanny sat by the fire, her needles clicking, her mind disturbed and resentful. He hadn't asked a word about her job . . . he didn't care how she got on, whether she sunk or swam. Well, she wouldn't say a blasted word about it. The next minute, giving a whirl to the sock, she remarked in a casual tone, 'I got that job. I'm startin' the morrow.'

He turned surprised eyes towards her, then said, 'Oh, Mary Prout . . . yes. I hope it'll be all right.'

'Why shouldn't it?' She wanted to argue with him, fight, rouse him in some way. She was in a state of mind such that, if Jack had been in the kitchen, she would have gone for him, upbraiding him with her tongue, sure that he would tease her, perhaps put his arms about her and call her 'fat old Fan'. But this one! She gave a loud, derisive huh! inside herself.

An uneasy silence was hanging over the room, and into it drifted the strong smell of kippers. Fanny sniffed. Miss Harper frying again and burning the blasted things to blazes. Then there came the sound of Sam Lavey coughing and spluttering his way up the front steps . . . and then a rap on the door. What could he want? Twisting about, Fanny called, 'Come in, will you!'

The door was not opened, and so, throwing her glance towards Philip, she said sharply, 'See who that is.'

Philip was half-way to the door when it opened slowly and the girl from the attics entered. On seeing him, she appeared disconcerted for a moment and her eyes fell away from him, and looking towards Fanny, she asked, 'Can I speak to you?'

'Aye, lass. Come in.'

The girl moved a step or two, then seemed to hesitate. There was, Fanny thought, a droopiness about her, as if she was very tired. 'Come and sit down,' she said.

'No, thank you, I won't stay. I . . . I want to ask you if. . .' At this point she swallowed as if the words were sticking painfully in her throat, and when her hand went up to her neck and gripped it, Fanny got to her feet.

'Now don't upset yourself. Is it about the dish?' Fanny was speaking with unusual softness.

'The dish?' the girl repeated.

It was at this point that Fanny noticed a curious thing. The girl was on a line with the dresser and the gleaming silver dish was standing out from the objects surrounding it, like a star in a night sky, yet the girl had not appeared to notice it. Or perhaps she was deliberately closing her eyes to it. Aye, that must be it. So she said kindly, 'You can have it back, lass. But you see, if I hadn't taken it somebody else would. Hand it over, Philip.'

Philip picked up the dish from the dresser and going to the girl he stood rather awkwardly before her, and he studied the silver a moment before saying, 'It's a beautiful thing.'

As the girl looked from Philip to the object in his hands, Fanny watched her face. The colour began to drain from it as if a tap had been turned on below her chin; then before, as Fanny said later, you could say knife, it happened . . . the girl went out like a light.

It was a toss up as to who was the most surprised, herself or Philip, but of the two she thought it was him, for the girl could have been red hot so reluctant was he to touch her. She watched him stagger back under her weight, then put his arms tentatively about her as she slumped down him to the floor.

'In the name of God! Lay her here off the lino.' Fanny indicated the mat. 'I'll get some water. That's the quickest passing out I've witnessed in me life.'

When Fanny returned from the scullery Philip had lain the girl on the mat and was on his knees beside her.

'Get me a pillow,' he said.

Fanny dragged a pillow from her bed and passed it to him, then commanded roughly, 'Mind out of me way, till I loosen her things.'

'I've loosened them, there was only her skirt.'

Fanny's eyebrows sprung upwards. Begod! but he had been quick. He wasn't backward in coming forward in some things, she'd give him that.

'Make some tea,' he ordered.

'I've a drop of whisky in the cupboard.'

'No, tea'll be better, make it fresh.'

As she quickly mashed the tea from the ever-boiling kettle on the hob, the girl sighed and Fanny, turning to where she lay, asked anxiously, 'Are you feeling better, lass?'

She watched the girl open her eyes and look up at Philip. She was still in a bit of a daze she could see, for she stared at him for a long while before closing her eyes again, and she did not bother to answer the question.

'Let me have that tea.' Philip thrust one arm out backwards, and Fanny watched him put the other one under the girl's shoulder and raise her up. He had got over his first gliff, for he was handling the situation, Fanny thought, as if it was all part of his day's work . . . all to the manner born. First aid wasn't in it. She watched the girl sit up in a daze, then almost at the same moment as she herself started and turned her head towards the window the girl stiffened into an upright position at the unmistakable sound of her mother's voice coming from the street.

Fanny moved swiftly to the window and there, only a few yards away, under the lamp, was Mrs Leigh-Petty. Her arms wide and her mouth stretched, she was calling out to some bairn playing Tommy-Noddy on the pavement opposite.

'You should be at home learning . . . what about your homework? Go along now, go along.

I won't allow my children on the streets. Get up off the pavement at once.'

Fanny cast a swift glance over her shoulder. The girl, she saw, was attempting to rise, but even with Philip's aid she couldn't make it, and Fanny said, 'Stay still. Stay where you are until you're fit, I'll see to her.' Then turning again to the window and seeing Mrs Flannagan's curtains fluttering, her face tightened and she exclaimed under her breath, 'Aye, and if I don't somebody else will . . . giraffe neb!'

As Fanny reached the hall Mrs Leigh-Petty came up the steps and through the front door, talking all the while, and on the sight of Fanny she did not cease or change her subject matter, and the matter was of such an ungrateful quality, seeing what had passed between them little more than an hour earlier, that Fanny was knocked speechless for the moment.

'Oh, there you are,' cried Mrs Leigh-Petty, with a regal lift to her head. 'I wonder when one could pass through this hall without encountering you. Yet being typical of your surroundings, you are merged in them . . . merged but evident.' Her hand went into action now and waved Fanny aside as she explained, 'There is little hope for a person so encumbered by their circumstances as you, Mrs McBride, for you loll in the broth of squalor, boisterous, bumptious and blousey.' Mrs Leigh-Petty suddenly laughed, a tinkling squeak of a laugh, and exclaimed, 'Beautiful! beautiful! I haven't lost the knack.'

On this note of self-appreciation she turned towards the Laveys' door, adding, 'But this man with his stammer is different. Yes, here we have a plain case of nerves ... inferiority, and complexes ... early environment certainly.'

Fanny had stood enough. Before Mrs Leigh-Petty could raise a hand to knock on the Laveys' door she was seized by the neck and the knickers and propelled without any gentleness towards the stairs.

'You! You! how dare you! Leave go! Leave go of me this instant!'

'Shut up! Shut that word-spewing trap of yours, or I'll shake the innards out of you. Begod! I will. Get up there.' Fanny's technique, learned in the school of marriage, lifted Mrs Leigh-Petty before her as if she was a child.

'Out of me way.' This aside was to Miss Harper, fluttering apprehensively on the first landing, and on the top landing, very very much out of breath and almost blue in the face, she appealed to Amy Quigley, who had preceded them up the stairs, 'Open that door there for me, Amy, afore I push this one right through it.'

The door opened, Fanny gave Mrs Leigh-Petty one last thrust, saying, 'There! and if I hear another word of education and improvement out of you I'll give you the biggest dose of salts you've ever heard of, four ounces, hot, and if that doesn't clear your system, nothing will.' The door banged and Fanny and Amy looked at each other. Then a slow grin spreading over Amy's thin face, she said, 'You've not lost your touch, Fan, it's some years since I seen you do that.'

'She's been asking for it,' Fanny nodded.

'Queer card.' Amy tapped her head. 'Loopy, I should say.'

Fanny was now descending the stairs and she called back, 'And you're not the only one who's come to that way of thinking. If we don't watch out she'll have us all in the same boat. Education! Pshaw!'

On the first landing Miss Harper was nowhere to be seen, having made herself scarce, and it was just as well. Fanny descended more slowly now to the ground floor, and when she stepped into the hall, Philip's voice came to her saying softly, 'Now don't worry, my mother will see to her, she has a way with people.'

This remark brought Fanny to a pause, and putting her head on one side she looked through the slit between the stanchion and the slightly open door and into the room. The girl was sitting on a chair now, and kneeling on the mat on one knee was their Phil. He was patting the girl's hand as if he had known her from birth.

'I – I can't stand it.' Fanny watched the girl's head move rapidly from side to side, as she exclaimed again, 'I can't, I can't!'

Fanny's inner wisdom cautioned her to stay where she was, for at this point she felt she would learn more than if she barged in.

'What is it? What's troubling you?' She watched Philip put his hand under the girl's chin and bring her face to rest. 'Is it your mother?'

The girl's head moved again and Philip said, 'We all have our family troubles, we can't alter our parents.'

No begod! we can't, thought Fanny. It's a pity for your sake we can't.

'Has your mother seen a doctor?'

There was no answer to this, and she watched her son's face take on a tenderness that made him unrecognisable to her for the moment as he said, 'You could tell me about it, it might ease things.'

The girl now put her hands to her face, and above the sound of her crying her mumbled words came to Fanny. 'I wish I was dead . . . I wish we were all dead!'

This statement surprised and troubled Fanny in spite of herself. The other day this girl had given her the impression of being capable of handling any situation that arose within her family. She had seemed a cool young woman who wanted no help, but now Fanny saw she was only a lass, and a very young lass, weighed down with enough worry to make her wish herself dead. Her pity went out to the girl, for how often in her own young days had she wished the same thing.

'It isn't drink in the ordinary sense, is it?' Philip was saying now, and the girl, covering her eyes, choked as she replied, 'I only wish to God it was.'

'Is it drugs of some sort?'

Fanny heard no answer to this, but the silence was admission enough.

'It's a pity, for she's such a highly educated woman.'

Fanny's eyebrows were rising derisively upwards at this remark, when the girl cried, with a sudden startling rush of bitterness, 'Yes, she's an educated woman and you, I suppose, like so many others, admire education. I don't. I hate it! I hate it, I tell you.'

That was one in the eye for him. Go on, lass, go on. Fanny nodded encouragement.

Philip's voice, sheepishly now, admitted, 'I admire education, and you must do, too, everybody does. I've been trying to educate myself for years, and it's been a difficult struggle.' Here he gave a little laugh before going on to say, 'My mother hasn't much use for education either.'

'That's why she's so nice . . . so human. Education makes people think they are gods. They think they can rule because they have it. They think it covers all the sins on the earth. And some people cow-tow to them because of it. But I don't. Do you know what?' The girl's voice was loud now. 'I pray that I'll come in one night and find her dead, for her own sake.'

Following this outburst there was silence in the room, and Fanny tried to still her heavy breathing in case it should give her away, and as she did so her head moved in small pitying jerks.

'I've got to go. I – I've said too much.'

'No, you haven't.'

'I have. I know I have.' Her voice was quivering again.

'You haven't, believe me. And if you had I don't talk to anyone about here. The least said the soonest mended about this quarter.'

Something in this remark annoyed Fanny and told her it was time she put in an appearance, so coughing deep in her throat, she waited a moment before entering the room, and when she did she found them both on their feet.

'How do you feel, lass?' she asked lightly.

The girl's eyes dropped towards the table. 'I'm a lot better.'

'That's good. And you'll feel better still if you remember you're among friends.'

Fanny was standing at the other side of the table, and the girl still keeping her head lowered, murmured, 'I'm so grateful to you and – and I'm glad we live here.' Now she raised her eyes to Fanny and confessed below her breath, 'It's been unbearable in other places.'

Fanny knew that she was supposed to be in the dark as to what made it unbearable in other places, and to keep up the deception she should now start asking questions. But she couldn't bring herself to do it.

They were all quiet, when the girl said, 'It's Tony that I'm worried about. He gets so upset. It doesn't touch Marian so much, but the shame has eaten into Tony and made him old.'

'When things get too much for you up top, lass, you come down here or tell her I'll come up and deal with her. That should settle her hash.' Fanny patted the girl's shoulder. 'What's your name, lass?'

'Margaret.'

'Aye, well then, Margaret it'll be from now on.'

'I'll go up now.' She did not look at Philip, or make any remark about the dish, nor did Fanny allude to it, and when she walked somewhat unsteadily across the room Philip went hastily to the door and opened it for her, then followed her into the hall.

In a minute or so he was back in the kitchen and Fanny was standing by the table waiting for him. She wondered if he would repeat his own conclusion as to what ailed the woman. But as she stood looking at him and he made to speak, the sound of the front door opening, and Mrs Flannagan's voice filling the hall, brought both their heads round in that direction.

With swelling chest and compressed lips Fanny watched Philip make a bee-line for the kitchen and close the door quickly behind him.

As Fanny reached her front door she saw Sam Lavey going into his flat. It was Sam Mrs Flannagan had been speaking to, but Fanny knew it was not he whom she had come to see, it was them up top. With surprising swiftness for her bulk she made for the stairs and took up her position on the second step, and she carried out this manoeuvre under the eyes of the woman who was the antithesis of herself, thin, compact, and neatly clad, with a face branded with the tightness of moral righteousness.

Battling tendencies, like froth from a newly opened bottle of beer, rose in Fanny and brought out the one word, 'Well!'

Mrs Flannagan, with her lips looking as if they were about to eject a whistle, emitted the same word, but her 'Well?' was born in the refined chambers of the nostrils and floated on to the air via the roof of her mouth, and it did not mean the same thing at all as the well that had been dragged from the coarse belly of Fanny McBride. It was not a challenge, but the complete ignoring of an obstacle.

Fanny gulped and champed her mouth before she brought out, in a mock refined tone, 'And who would you be wanting, Mrs Flannagan?'

Mrs Flannagan's body gave a slight wriggle, which gave to her hips a suggestion of a hula-hula dance, and to her neck and pointed face the alerted action of a disturbed snake. 'That is entirely my business. And will you kindly get out of me way, Mrs McBride?'

'I'll see you to hell first, Mrs Flannagan.'

Fanny watched her adversary's lips pull inwards, preparatory to drenching her with words, but before Mrs Flannagan could begin Fanny cut in with, 'I asked you who you'd be wanting. I know it won't be me, God himself would bear witness to that, nor Miss Harper, for she's fed up with the sound of your tongue through her window, and if you were to go near the Quigleys', Barry'd hit you with the first thing that came to his hand, so who up above would you be wanting to see, Mrs Flannagan?'

Mrs Flannagan stepped back, and her head began to wag as if on wires. And now she spluttered as she spoke. 'I'm not the one for complaining . . . I mind my own business, but this is—'

'Oh!' cried Fanny who was now in her element. 'Don't choke, St. Michael.' She cast her eyes ceilingwards. 'Mind her own business. Did you hear her? That's the best yet. And you'll hear more if you hang on a minute. She'll be saying she's just going up top to see if she can be of any help.' Fanny now brought her fiery eyes down to Mrs Flannagan, and bouncing her head to each word, she ended, 'And push her long neb in to find out all she can, then go and spin it round the doors. Don't I know you! Now get out of this house.'

'I'll have the police on you, you see if I don't. And Father Owen. Yes, and Father Owen.' Mrs Flannagan's voice had risen to a croak as she now retreated towards the door under the pressure of Fanny's advancing bulk and outstretched arm.

'Out!'

'I'll bring Mr Flannagan over to you.'

'Oh! my God, the poor little man. Get out, will you!'

The disparaging note in Fanny's voice when she spoke of Mr Flannagan refuelled Mrs Flannagan's staying power, for she paused and her nostrils widened as she stared back at the bane of her refined life. And her next words indeed spoke of the depth of her courage, for her tone now deadly quiet, she said, 'It's no wonder your sons won't live with you, or even own you. Your Jack's never looked back since he left your door. And now your last one's getting out and no blame to him. His efforts to rise above you have got him down at last, and he's going. Good luck to—'

Fanny, with head down and fists up, made a rush like a charging bull, but fortunately Mrs Flannagan was very nimble on her feet, and although her retreat was slightly undignified she escaped unharmed.

Fanny did not follow her usual procedure and bawl after her neighbour from the top of the steps, but she crashed the door shut, then stood leaning against it. She had been enjoying the rumpus, for there wasn't a thing she liked better in life, if the truth were told, than a shindy with Nellie Flannagan. But this was one time Nellie had got the better of her . . . Her last one was getting out an' all. They'd all be saying that in the street. He was trying to rise above her. Nellie had struck where it hurt most.

After taking a deep gulp of air she went slowly across the hall and into the room where Philip was now standing waiting for her. And she thought, God in heaven, don't let him lead off now, for if he does I'll say more than I should to him. She pressed her hand against her ribs, thinking, pushing that 'un up those stairs was too much. I'm past that kind of thing. I should have more sense. She did not count the past scene as detrimental to her health.

As she sat down under Philip's level gaze, she muttered in a form of prayer now, 'Dear God, don't let him start. Keep him off me, for I'm in no shape to tackle him, I'm feeling done up.'

But all Philip said was, 'Take it easy for a minute, you're getting past that kind of thing.'

Something inside her shrank away from the deep kindness in his voice, but pressing her hand tighter to her side, she thought, 'He's right, as usual.' Then casting her eyes sidewards to the dresser where the silver dish was once more reposing she said, tersely, 'Shove that dish into a drawer. It's my belief it's been pinched and we'll hear more of it.'

He looked at her steadily for a moment before obeying her command.

The pain under her ribs seemed to be gathering force and she talked against it, saying, 'There's something very fishy with that 'un up top.'

'She takes drugs of some sort.' Philip had turned towards her again, and Fanny, simulating surprise as best she could, said, 'Drugs? Aye, well now that explains a lot. But it doesn't explain everything. That young bairn, Marian, isn't hers.'

'No?' Philip's tone was enquiring.

'No, she's too old in the loin to have worked herself up to that trick.' As she saw the furrow between her son's brows grow deeper, Fanny did ask herself what it was in her own composition that always made her come out with something raw in his presence.

She rubbed at her pain again, bending forward as she did so, then belched loudly and exclaimed in a tone that robbed the statement of all importance, 'The child likely belongs to the lass.'

'Don't be silly.'

'What!'

She was sitting upright now looking at him. He had used many tones to her before but never one like this, but the look on his face was a familiar one, like the expression he wore when he went for Corny, or was angry about something.

'If you've worked out that the mother's too old

to have the child, can't you see that the girl's too young?'

Fanny did not answer this question, she just stared at him.

'The child must be seven, perhaps eight, and . . . and she . . . she can't be more than twenty.'

She saw that her remark had made him hopping mad, but of a sudden she was too tired to take any pleasure in this achievement. But she did manage to defend her theory by saying, 'She's young all right, but she's over twenty . . . twenty-three or four I should say, and bairns have been born to lasses of fourteen afore the day. It's no unusual thing. And how else would you account for the child and her authority over it? For she has much more say over the young 'un than the supposed mother.'

They were staring at each other, and she did not allow her gaze to falter from his in spite of her tiredness. It was his eyes that dropped away first. Then, turning on his heel, he went into his room, closing the door none too quietly after him.

Begod! that's how it was, was it? And all in a couple of nights. Well, these things happened. Her gentlemanly son had fallen, but before he'd had time to taste the joys of love, the outcome of somebody else's fling had presented him with a problem in the form of a seven-year-old bairn. Here would be something interesting to watch, and she wondered cynically within herself how he would stand up to it. Would his self-education be of any use to him in a case like this? Aye now, would it? Him and his education!

4

Fanny had now been seven days in The Ladies, and so used had she become to the click of the ticket puncher, the faces passing her window, the sound of doors banging and the surging rush of emptying cisterns that she felt she had been here for at least half her life. And during that seven days she had reached the conclusion that nature, and nature alone, is the one and overall social leveller.

She had already got to know the rushing regulars, as Maggie termed the busy shoppers, and the passers through, those who never came again, and the time-killers, of whom there were a number. And it was the sight of any one of these that always brought her mind back to the thought of her Jack. For they would stand titivating their hair in the glass, or talking the hind leg off a donkey, or just sit if the place wasn't busy, and all to get away from their loneliness . . . or to try and forget something that they were forever remembering.

Fanny had thought that here in The Ladies there would be nothing to remind her of her heartache, for Maggie's chatter, unlike Mary Prout's, would have no personal touch about it. But she had not counted on the lonely women, each of whom was a reflection of the great lonely gap within herself.

This particular afternoon had promised from the start to be more than usually busy. Perhaps it was the weather. The few days of sunshine had gone, seemingly forever, and the past three days had been deep November, cold as only a northern November cold can be. A child had been sick in one of the cubicles, somebody had pinched a roll of toilet paper – the Corporation stamp never deterred them – two women had tried to get in for the price of one, one of them saying that she didn't want to go, then changing her mind at the last minute and slipping in as the other one came out. You wouldn't believe the fiddles they would get up to for the sake of a penny. And the dud coppers that were put across the counter had to be seen to be believed. Oh, you had to have your eyes skinned in this place.

It was nearing closing time now, and Maggie had just slipped in to the cubby-hole to make a cup of cocoa to send them warmly on their way, when the door opened and in came a rush of scent that outdid the strong smell of disinfectant and put Fanny's nostrils into a deep sniff. Her finger on the puncher, and the ticket roll in her hand, she looked upwards through the glass and she couldn't prevent her mouth from dropping into a gape at the sight of a highly-painted face before her. It was a good-looking face, but there was something about it that did things to the hairs on her neck.

'Hallo, me dear.'

'Hallo,' said Fanny quietly.

'You new here?'

'Aye, you could say that.'

Now the painted head came down to the opening and the great mascaraed eyes looked into Fanny's, and an unusual, deep voice issued from the feminine lips, whispering, 'Is Maggie about?'

Fanny, in a sort of hypnotised stare, muttered, 'Aye, she's back there.' She motioned with her head slightly. 'Do you want her?'

The eyes widened, the deeply waved blonde head swung from side to side, and the lips formed themselves into a silent 'No'.

Fanny's eyes followed the woman as she moved cautiously into the corridor. There was something about the dress and gait that puzzled her. She looked . . . she looked . . .

How Fanny would have described to herself how the woman looked was cut short by a high-pitched squeak from the cubby-hole behind her, and as she slid from her stool and made for the door she saw Maggie simply leap on the tall, flashily-dressed woman, crying as she did so, 'Get out. Get out of here!'

'Ah, now, Maggie dee-ar.' The tall figure was backing towards the wall with a slack flapping of her hands as if she was thrusting off a moth, but Maggie was no moth. Under Fanny's astonished eyes she saw the little undersized woman actually punch out at the retreating figure as she continued to yell. 'I warned you last time, mind. I'll get the polis.'

'Aw! you wouldn't do that to me, Mag-gie.'

'I'd do it and more. You dirty big looney you! Fan! Fan!'

As Maggie called, Fanny moved hastily forward, and on the sight of her the subject of the oration gave a little giggle. 'Fanny likes me, don't you, Fan? She's a nice girl is Fan.'

It was a situation Fanny found herself unable to cope with. What it was all about she didn't rightly know, but there was Maggie, clawing the woman as if she would tear the clothes off her back, and the weird creature had called her a nice girl. Name of God!

'Open the door, Fan.'

As Fanny went hastily to obey Maggie's order, she cried, 'What's up, anyway? What's the matter with her?'

'It isn't a her, it's a him. He's just dressed up.'

'My God!' Fanny's nose pricked. Of course that was it . . . she was learning something. She had heard about them, but this was the first one she had ever clapped eyes on in all her long days. At least, dressed up like this. There had been a fellow on the trams in her young days who should never have been put into trousers.

When the painted face leered at her and the man with disarming simplicity said, 'Don't you believe her, Fan, I'm more one than the other,' Fanny felt her gorge rise, and she heard herself saying, 'Mother of God!'

The door open, Maggie with one last push thrust the man into the street and into the arms of a passer-by.

'What's the matter? Can I help?'

It was Maggie answering the voice and saying, 'It will take you and more than all your Army to help this one,' that screwed Fanny's eyes up to peer into the darkness at the newcomer.

As quick as she was in turning away Fanny knew that she had been recognised. Joyce Scallen, or Joyce McBride as she was now, had seen her all right! She hurried round into the office and sat down. It was odd, but up to this very minute she hadn't minded him knowing she was working in The Ladies, but now something within her cried out in protest. No! no! I don't want him to find out I'm in here. She did not ask herself why. She did not admit that his derisive laughter about the job might now hurt her. Philip's scorn would have given her a kick, but Jack's would have done something to her last shreds of pride. He would, she knew, have found nothing lowering to her status in going out to do a day's cleaning, or washing, but working in the ladies' lav . . . ! She could hear his laughter now.

Maggie came bustling into the office, her sharp, wizened face red with her indignation. 'Would you believe it! I warned him last time. It's nearly a year since he was on this spree.'

'Who is he?'

'One of the funnies.'

'The funnies?'

'Aye, that's what we call 'em. He works in the shipyard, like a big navvy, he is, but goes on these sprees every now and again. He's been locked up once. Eeh! I feel sorry for him.'

Fanny looked down on her in amazement. 'You feel sorry for him? Then you took a funny way of showing it, that's all I can say.'

'Well, I've got to go for him, woman. Why, if I didn't he'd never be out of here and the polis'd get him. Eeh! I'll never forget the first time I saw him.' Maggie stared at the floor and shook her head. 'Mrs Craig let him through, and when he came out of the lav, he spoke to a woman from another cubicle and she took one look at him and passed out. Flat on the floor she was. That's the time we got the polis. Eeh! it wasn't half a night.' Maggie started to laugh; her hard little body began to shake, and soon she was leaning on the shelf, her head on her arms.

Fanny wanted to laugh with her over 'the funny'. It would have been grand to have a good laugh, to sup at the hot cocoa and laugh, but she couldn't somehow, for her eyes were still seeing the Salvation Army bonnet and Joyce Scallen's eyes looking at her.

Maggie straightened herself, and seeing Fanny's face, her own sobered and she said, 'You see nowt to laugh at in him? – Well, perhaps you're right.'

Fanny could not explain – it would take too long. Moreover, how could a woman who had never had a child understand a woman who had had twelve and only had feelings for one. She couldn't, when she thought of it, understand it herself.

*   *   *

It was the following afternoon when Fanny's daughter-in-law appeared in The Ladies. Somehow Fanny had been expecting her, she had been keeping an eye open for the bonnet. But Joyce was not in uniform, she was neatly dressed, and bonny to all eyes but Fanny's.

All the bitterness of which she was capable rose in Fanny and formed her mouth into a hard line and narrowed her eyes and caused the girl on the other side of the glass to gulp and swallow. It was evident that she was trying to get something out, but Fanny was determined to give her no chance to speak, and she cried, 'Well, do you want a ticket or not? Make up your mind; only you can tell.'

With heightened colour and downcast eyes, the girl groped in her bag and pushed a penny over the little counter, and in return she had a ticket flung at her.

As she watched the girl slowly make her way to a cubicle a feeling of rage engulfed Fanny. She wanted to bang and clash and throw things, but there was nothing to hand to bang and clash, only the ticket puncher, and whatever she threw in here she'd likely be called upon to pay for. But this situation needed some reaction or else it would kill her. In the form of an outlet there sprang to her mind a parody on a Salvation Army hymn

140

the soldiers had sung in the First World War. Although long forgotten, the words and tune now sprang to her lips and her voice startled Maggie, almost causing her to slip on the wet tiled floor she was mopping, when it exploded into song, raucous and loud, near earsplitting, singing the words:

'Whiter than the snow,
Whiter than the snow,
If you wash me in the water
That you've washed your dirty daughter,
Then I shall be whiter
Than the whitewash on the wall.
Oh, whi-i-ter than the snow . . . ow,
Whi-i-ter than the sno . . . ow,
Oh, wash me in the water
That you've washed your dirty daughter,
Then, I shall be whiter
Than the whitewash on the wall.'

Maggie stood leaning helplessly on the mop. Her laugh was of the muted, side-aching sort, and when Mrs McBride junior came out of the cubicle she looked down on the little warped creature, but there was no sign of resentment in her eyes. And when she passed the glass partition and paused for a moment to look at Fanny, silent and breathless now, there was nothing in her expression that gave Fanny any satisfaction. If Fanny could have put a name to it she would have labelled the look pitying, but she wouldn't put such a name to it.

'Oh, Fan, I've never heard nowt so funny.' Maggie was leaning against the doorpost. 'What made you go off like that?'

'Oh, I just felt like it.'

'Eeh! it was funny. It was like a Salvation Army tune,' said Maggie. 'I thought the roof was coming off. Eeh! you should be on the stage.'

On this compliment Fanny turned to the ticket puncher and a customer. She should be on the stage . . . She should be in her box, and she wished she was. She wished the Lord had taken her before her son had married a Hallelujah.

She did not make any jokes while drinking her tea, and this puzzled Maggie, having witnessed her 'funny turn' a few minutes earlier. She kept glancing at her, yet refrained from probing the 'closed look'. But later and just before Fanny said goodbye, she made a generous gesture at the expense of the Corporation and slipped into her bag two toilet rolls, saying, 'God helps those who help themselves, Fanny!' And Fanny, looking down at her, smiled now and added, 'Aye, and

God help those who are caught helping themselves, Maggie . . . Six months, stand down!'

Maggie let out her high, squeaking gurgle. This was the Fanny she had come to know. She slapped her on the back and pushed her out of the door . . .

Although Fanny had capped Maggie's saying with her usual pithy comment, her mind returned to it now in serious vein. God helps those who help themselves. Aye, if that saying was taken to bits it would prove that them who looked after themselves from the start never wanted, whereas damn fools like herself who had given her life for her bairns were left with damn all. With a squad of 'em like she had reared she was left alone or as near to it as made no odds . . . Any minute now. Oh, blast Phil! What did he matter, anyway? When he was gone that would be one irritation less. Her mind began a tirade against Philip, and she let it have its way, for she knew that once it stopped she would be picturing the scene again in The Ladies, with herself yelling that song out, and somewhere in her there was a spark of shame for having acted in such a way. And the spark she knew had been given birth by the look in the lass's eyes as she had gone out . . .

When she reached home the house was in darkness. That meant that Phil wasn't in yet, or perhaps he had been in and gone. This thought made her angry, as it had done the other night, for when she'd reached home at half-past six he'd already had his tea and gone out, and the night had seemed as long as a week, and she hadn't clapped eyes on anybody until he came in again near on eleven. It wasn't that she wanted his company, but when she had somebody to do something for, or even get at, it took her mind off other things.

But she found the table set just as she had left it before she'd gone out, with the bacon and eggs ready to go in the pan. Sitting slowly down in the old armchair she eased her shoes off her swelling ankles and moved her toes about, gazing at them as she did so.

They'd be sitting down to tea now, and she'd be telling him all that happened, telling him what a mother he'd got . . . and her working in The Ladies. Staring at her distorted feet she pictured him rising from the table yelling as she would have done herself, 'I'll put a stop to that. Ladies! Just wait till I see her.' She even turned her head, half expecting him to come bouncing in, yelling at her, 'What the hell do you mean taking a job in a place like that? What'll you do next?' So vivid was the picture that her head reared and she turned her body round towards the door with a retort on her lips, and her heart almost stopped beating when the door was thrust open.

Her hand was pressed tightly against her ribs when Corny backed into the room, saying, 'Come on. Come on.'

'What is it? Why have you come over in the dark?' Fanny lumbered to her feet, then exclaimed, 'What have you there? What is it?' Then her voice rising in amazement she exclaimed, 'Where did you get that thing?'

Corny, pulling on a piece of leather as wide as a horse's rein, cried, 'It's a dog, Gran.'

Fanny moved closer. 'A dog?' she repeated.

'Aye, Gran, can't you see? Come on,' he coaxed the animal. 'Come on.'

'Where did you get it?'

'Me da bought it. He swapped it for wor two rabbits.'

'In the name of God!' said Fanny slowly, looking down on the beast, 'What sort is he? Do you know?'

'No, Gran.'

'No, I should think you don't. And why put a collar like that on the animal; it would fit a horse.'

'Me da says he'll grow. Don't you like him, Gran?'

'Oh, aye . . . Aye.'

Corny appeared slightly hurt at her evident lack of appreciation.

Fanny continued to look down on the dog, and now the dog looked back at her, and of the two he appeared the more bewildered.

He looked an impossible dog, and the expression in his eye as he returned Fanny's scrutiny seemed to say he was well aware of just how impossible he was. His eyes were his best feature, but even they weren't big enough, soft enough, or brown enough to redeem the rest of his body. His head was a bullet shape and his chest had the broad expanse of a bull terrier. But here the similarity ended, for his hind quarters had the appearance of a whippet, and over all he was brindle colour in black, white, and rust, while his long, thin tail defied any label – terrier, whippet, or otherwise.

Fanny, sensing that something was expected of her, asked quietly, 'What do you call him?'

'Joe,' said Corny.

'Joe? In the name of God, why Joe?'

Corny looked at his gran and he felt grieved at her attitude. He liked his gran, on the quiet he even admitted to himself that he loved her. She knew and understood everything, so why couldn't she see the wonder of Joe.

'I call him Joe cos I like Joe.'

'Well, that's as good a reason as any,' said Fanny. 'But what are we standing here for lookin'' at him as if he was goin' to depart this life? Would you like something to eat?'

'Aye, Gran.'

'Well wait till I get me things off . . . Fried bacon or broth?'

'Broth, Gran,' Corny had brightened visibly. This was more like how things should be. 'You know what, Gran?'

'No. What?'

'A man on the ferry laughed at him. He said I should enter him for the Manchester November Handicap, and another man said he was handicapped enough. They did laugh, Gran . . . and Joe barked. He's got a funny bark, Gran.'

Fanny put the heavy pan of broth on to the fire, saying, 'Aye, he would have.'

'I brought him over to show Tony.'

'Tony?' said Fanny. 'The lad that's upstairs?'

Corny nodded.

'But how do you know him?'

'I got talkin' to him last week outside. He said he'd like a dog and one day he'd have one . . . Gran.'

'Aye?'

'Do you like your new job, Gran?' Corny's eyes were well up under his lids.

'It's all right.'

'What do you do, Gran?'

Fanny's lips twisted and she looked down her nose before she answered, 'I take the money.'

'The pennies?'

'Aye, the pennies.'

'What for? Do women have to pay a penny to go to the lav, Gran?'

Fanny moved some plates with slow deliberation. She had many answers she could have given to this, but she had to remind herself of her grandson's age while disclaiming his knowledge or the fact that he was 'having her on', so she said, 'It's a custom.'

There was a deep glow in the back of Corny's eyes. 'Me da says it's cos they take longer.'

'Your da would think up something like that.'

'I'm glad that lads don't have to pay a penny. I'd never have no pocket money. I'm always goin' when it's cold.'

Fanny ignored this confidence, and was about to change the subject to food when Corny put in, 'Me ma nearly laughed herself daft at what me da said. He started to sing a song about the waters of Minnie Tonka, and he called you Fanny Tonka and said he'd send you a record for the grama—'

'Be quiet! And you can tell your da if he sends anything here I'll come across the water and break it over his head . . . before God I will.'

'He was only funning, Gran.' Corny's head was down now and his eyes were no longer merry. His gran was mad. From beneath lowered lids he watched her go to the hearth, and he searched about in his mind for something that might please her . . . And then he had it.

He started to play with Joe before he said, 'I saw me Uncle Jack the day, Gran. He was waiting to get on the ferry as I was coming off.'

Fanny turned slowly from the fire and looked down at the mat where Corny was now wrestling with the dog.

'Stop him a minute,' she said sharply.

'What, Gran?'

'Stop still a minute.'

Corny bent over the squirming dog.

'What did your uncle say?'

'He said, "Hallo".'

'And what else?'

Corny fell on his back and the dog bounded on to his chest, 'Aw! give over. . . . He give me a tanner, Gran, and said watch out I didn't end up in jail, for . . . aw! give over you.' Then sitting up on his hunkers he ended, 'He said watch out I didn't end up in jail for passing off a dog for a horse . . . he was laughing at the collar, Gran.'

'Aye, and what else?'

Corny stopped the dog's antics by taking a firm grip on his head and tail, and he looked up at his gran. 'That's all, Gran.'

Fanny's hand was at her side again, and the boy twisting agilely to his feet said, 'You got the wind . . .' He paused as if expecting to be pounced on, then finished, 'again, Gran?'

'No . . . Are you sure? Are you sure that's all he said?'

'Aye.'

She turned away and Corny looked at her back, then pushed the dog's forepaws from his shoulders. That strange, disturbing feeling which he sometimes got when he looked at his granny and to which he could give no name was attacking him again and caused him to say, 'He did say something else, Gran, I've just remembered.'

'What was it?' Fanny was facing him.

'Well, he just said, "How's . . . how's me mother?"'

'He said that?'

Corny rubbed his nose along the length of his hand. 'Well, not that . . . he . . . he said, "How's yer grannie?"'

'And what did you say?'

'I said she's all right.'

'And then?'

Corny remained silent, his eyes held by the round, dark ones looking at him. He couldn't think of another lie, not right on the minute he couldn't. Given a bit breathing space he could have gone on for hours. Yet not with his grannie, and her looking at him like that he couldn't.

'Come on, lad, think.' It was a demand.

'That's all . . . Gran . . . Joe's . . . Joe's hungry.'

'He would be.' Fanny glared at the dog. 'Was he with anybody?'

'No.'

Slowly Fanny turned away and went into the scullery. But from there she shouted, 'How long ago was this?'

'Just as I was coming here, Gran.'

Perhaps the girl hadn't told him how she had gone on, perhaps she had kept it to herself, for he couldn't have been up in arms against her if he had asked after her like that.

'Gran?'

'Aye?' she called back.

'Me ma thinks she's got the chance of a house. It's fine and big.'

'Well that's a God's blessing. Where is it?'

'Up on the new estate; it'll have a bath.'

'A bath?' said Fanny, coming back into the kitchen. 'That's nothing to recommend it.'

'But it'll be fine to have a bath,' said Corny.

'Aw, what can you do in a bath that you can't do in a tub?'

'Lie down, Gran.'

'You're right there.' Fanny paused as she put the soup plate on the table, then she laughed and looked with fondness at this grandson and added, 'And drown yersel'.'

Now they both laughed, and Fanny said, 'Your ma'll be like the rest and make a showpiece of it. Like your Aunt Lily in Scotland. Do you know, when your Uncle Jack went up there he wasn't allowed to wash his hands in the bathroom, much less take a bath, in case he splashed the paint. Tour of inspection, he said your Aunt Lily had, around that bathroom when anybody fresh came. And there's your Aunt Peggy in London. Years ago they put them in a house with a bath, and what you think they did with it?'

'Put the coal in it,' said Corny with relish.

'They didn't then,' said Fanny. 'They used it as a cold storage like a fridge and kept the fats in it and the bacon, even the bread. It was a few years ago when we were having a hot day or two and your cousin Peter . . . you remember your cousin Peter? Well he turned the taps on and they were so stiff he couldn't get them off again. And he took fright and dashed out in case his mother caught him, and the next thing they knew was that the water was pouring like Niagara Falls down the stairs, and all the food soaked and ruined. The place was like hell let loose. That's baths for you.' Fanny suddenly burst out laughing. She laughed and laughed, but it was forced laughter, and when she stopped as quickly as she had begun she lifted up the corner of her apron and blew her nose on it.

Corny, once again on the mat and fondling Joe, looked up at his grannie. Oh, his grannie was funny. His ma said when they were little they had all been scared of her and daren't answer her back, not a word. He couldn't imagine anybody being scared of his grannie. She was always ready for a bit carry on.

Now he got on all fours and barked at Joe, and Joe, taking a firm stand on his rickety legs, barked back. And the sound made Fanny screw up her face and cry, 'For God's sake stop him making that noise, he sounds like a tormented soul in purgatory! And you stop it an' all. Stop it, the pair of you!'

When Joe's unearthly bark was silenced Fanny held up her hand and said, 'Listen . . . that's the lad comin' in. That's his step. Go and fetch him in if you want to.' And Corny, bounding up, dashed to the door with the dog at his heels, and Fanny was forced to smile to herself as she heard the virtues of the odd animal being extolled on the one hand and appreciated on the other. But the continued draught from the hall swirled into the kitchen and made her cry, 'Come away in, the lot of you,' and when they trooped back into the room, Corny leading the dog and the boy from upstairs patting it, she addressed Tony saying, 'What d'you think of him now? Isn't he a sketch?'

'I think he's fine.'

The boy was unsmiling, his face pale and sadlooking. The sadness lay deep in his eyes, and Fanny felt there was a great deal too much of it to be healthy. What this lad wanted was a month or so spent with Corny.

'Well,' she said jokingly, 'I'm afraid I differ from you. To me he looks a mongrel of the first water.'

'He'll be better when he's grown and filled out,' said the boy solemnly.

'Aye, I suppose he will.'

The lad was so serious there wasn't a laugh within a mile of him. He had a dampening effect.

'Will you stay and have some tea?' she was asking him, when out of the corner of her eye she saw Joe, and with a loud bellow she turned on him crying, 'No, you don't begod! you don't. Not in here. I've had enough,' and grabbing up the big multi-coloured tea-cosy she levelled it at him.

Joe had been in the act of relieving himself against the chair leg, for to him at that moment the old armchair with its varying smells was the most comforting thing in the room, but Fanny's yell, entirely new to him, and the soft woolly thing that hit him were too much for his untrained nervous system. With a loud yelp he sprang across the room with a dribble of water in his train, and as Corny made a grab at him he blindly collided with the corner of the dresser, overbalancing a small work-box standing on the edge.

The bobbins, pins, and oddments from the box, seeming to come at him from all directions, sent Joe's remaining wits out of him and he leapt three times his height, then bounded between Fanny and the boy.

Within seconds the room had become a place of pandemonium. Corny's voice, nearly as loud as Fanny's, was yelling, 'Joe! Joe! give over, Joe. Come here!' Then missing Joe's tail by a matter of hairs, he cried, 'Open the door, Tony, and let him out.'

'Do no such thing!' yelled Fanny on top of this. 'Do no such thing till we catch hold of him, or he'll run so fast you'll never see him again.'

Joe was now partly under the back of the couch. Like an ostrich, his head was well covered, but he could not bring his hindquarters in. Corny, moving cautiously now, grabbed hold of his hind legs, and so causing a series of frantic wriggles from Joe, which almost lifted the couch but still did not afford him adequate cover. The wriggling did succeed, however, in releasing him from Corny's grasp, and with another twist he made his escape from the side of the couch and bounded away.

It was a matter of bad timing that Fanny should be directly in his path, and Joe, not having breath or sense to make a detour, went straight between her legs.

If Fanny had followed the fashions in only one way and had possessed a shortish skirt all would have been well, but her long skirt brought Joe to an abrupt halt, and almost immediately Fanny's legs went up and she was on the floor, and partly on Joe, who proclaimed this in blood-curdling howls. Unfortunately, in her descent, she also clutched the cloth on the table and brought down the broth, the bread, and the dishes, all of them.

As quickly as the pandemonium had begun it ceased. Corny, kneeling on the floor, was clutching the quivering Joe to him, while he stared pop-eyed at his granny sitting in the middle of the mess, and listened to Tony as he enquired, almost tearfully, over and over again, 'Are you hurt, Mrs McBride? Are you hurt, Mrs McBride?'

Fanny made no answer, but from where she sat she turned her head slowly and surveyed her room. It had all been so nice and tidy, she had spent the whole morning doing it, and now look at it. As if it had been hit by the devil in a gale of wind. She looked from the concerned face of the lad to the even more concerned face of her grandson, and then from them to the quivering beast who had made an unholy mess of her room. Then, eye to eye with the dog, a bubble of laughter rose in her, and her fat slowly began to wobble. She had thought she was in for a night of the miseries, and here she was laughing. Thanks be to God and the animal here she was laughing. What matter about the mess, she was laughing . . . really laughing, no make-game.

To join her laughter now came Corny's high-pitched, relieved giggle, but what was more satisfying to her was the sight of the lad. His was a quiet laughter she could see, an aching laughter, and outside of her own laughing she was thinking, 'It'll do him good, the best medicine in the world for him.'

The tears were pouring down her face, her cloth was ruined and her floor was an unholy mess, and she'd have to buy new plates. What of it?

'Here.' She stretched up her arms to the boys. 'Give me a help up so I can lay me hands on that animal. Begod! I'll teach him to pay a penny on me chair.'

'Oh! Gran. Eeh! Gran.' Corny's laughter became hysterical, and Tony's was not far removed. They were pulling at her with more show than strength when the door opened and into the strange scene walked Philip and Margaret.

After one startled glance which took in the shambles of the room and the exclamation of 'Good God!' Philip moved swiftly forward towards Fanny and with his hands under her armpits from behind, and with Margaret's and the lads' help from the fore, he gently eased her to her feet.

Standing leaning for support on the table and trying to still quivering flesh, Fanny looked at the strained, concerned face of her son, and while she listened to his wordy demand to know how all this had come about, she could not help but think, 'Ah, if it had only been the other one, he would have sat on the floor and laughed with us.' But her mind was taken from Jack again by the fact that Philip had not come in alone. The lass was with him. Well, well. What had she said earlier on? He had fallen all right. And for that matter, be damned, so had she, for her hip-bones felt as if they had come through her shoulders.

Corny was singularly quiet. He was proffering no explanation that would bring his uncle's tongue on him, so pointing off-handedly to the dog, she replied to Philip's earnest enquiry as to how all this had happened, saying, 'It was Holy Joe there.'

This light remark of Fanny's caused Corny to splutter, and the spluttering released Tony's dry laughter again, and Philip, now leading his mother towards her chair, said sharply, 'Be quiet now.'

'Oh, leave them be.' Fanny glanced towards the girl with words of welcome on her lips, but the girl was looking at her brother and her face was full of surprise, pleased sur prise. And Fanny watched it slowly crumple, and in a second she, too, was laughing.

Now Joe, suddenly realising that there wasn't anything more at present to be afraid of, yawned, then barked, and the sound, so odd as to appear like an inarticulate voice, set Fanny herself off again. They were all laughing now, all, that is, except Philip. His face was dead straight and full of concern as he looked in perplexity about the room, and when his gaze became fixed on Joe, and Joe, from his temporary haven under the table, stopped his barking and looked back at him with equal solemnity, Fanny's laughter burst forth on a top key. God was good after all . . . He provided distractions from heart-break in the form of Holy Joes.

Later that night when they were getting ready for bed Philip, moving towards his door and without any lead up, remarked, 'By the way, she's just turned twenty. Good night.'

Fanny did not return the salutation. Her apron rolled up in her hand, she stood looking at the closed door. Well, so he had found out that much. He was in earnest an' all, begod he was. She unloosed her clothes and one by one put them across the foot of her bed. Whose was the child then, if not the lass's? There was a mystery here all right . . . there was a mystery about the whole bang lot of 'em up there. She turned slitted eyes towards her son's room. His lordship would sleep better the night now that he had sorted that out. Yes, he must have got it bad.

She was climbing into bed when a thought brought her to a pause on her hands and knees. If he got thick with the lass, would it prevent him from leaving?

Slowly she slid round on to her back and, pulling the clothes about her shoulders, she lay staring into the darkness until she exclaimed to herself, 'But what difference will it make to me? If he gets that job, he goes . . . if he marries her, he goes. He goes in any case.'

Slowly she slid round to go. Her back and pulling the clothes about her shoulders, she lay sinking into the darkness until she exclaimed to herself, 'But what difference will it make so that I go to that job, he says. 'I'll be punished both he goes. She goes in a moment.

5

Mary Prout was installed in bed and she looked at Fanny tearfully as she said, 'It'll be another week or more, Fan. I haven't got to hobble about, he says to keep it up. Do you mind, Fan?'

'That's all right.' These few words succeeded in conveying to Mary that it was a bit of a nuisance having to keep on the job, but for such a friend as herself she would do it.

But Fanny did honestly try to stop herself from hoping that Mary's leg would keep her tied to the bed for a good many weeks yet, for the job suited her down to the ground. That's when she was inside The Ladies. The travelling back and forth wasn't too good, and took toll of her own legs and her puff. Sometimes, when she came back at night, she could hardly get her breath to stagger up the steps into the house.

Now she said kindly, 'I'll tell Mrs Proctor. And don't you worry . . . take it easy, your job's there for you when you want it, and I'll carry on for you till then.'

'Thanks, Fan. I'll never be able to repay you. And I told that to Nellie Flannagan herself this mornin' when she was in. I did, Fan. I said, "I'll never be able to repay Fanny for standing in for me like that."'

Fanny folded her arms across her chest before asking, 'And what did she want?'

'Well, she said she came to see me, to see how I was, but she really came to spill the beans about them in your attics.'

'What about them?'

'Well, she told me a tale, Fan, about the woman stoppin' her and asking her to get some laudanum for her, she said it was for cleaning.'

There was a pause before Fanny said, 'Well, it could have been couldn't it?'

Mary leant forward over the clothes towards Fanny, her voice low. 'No, Fan, it wouldn't be for cleaning, not in her case. You remember Tilly Concert and her methylated spirits. As mad as a hatter Tilly could get on sixpence, and as mad as a hatter she finally went with it. That one over there puts me very much in mind of Tilly, Fan.'

'Well, what of it?'

This disconcerting remark from her friend

nonplussed Mary, and she lay back on her pillows saying, 'Well, it explains the way she goes on, acting educated-like, doesn't it?'

'There's no need for her to act that,' said Fanny, 'she is educated. But that's no credit to her.'

'No, Fan.'

There followed an uneasy pause before Mary continued, 'And there was something else Nellie Flannagan was on about, Fan. She said that the child couldn't be the woman's, she was likely its grandmother. And you know what, Fan?' Again Mary was sitting forward to draw Fanny's interest. 'She says it's the young lass's.'

'It's no such thing. You can tell that big-gobbed, mischief-making madam that the girl is only turned nineteen.'

Philip's defence of Margaret's purity was nothing now compared to Fanny's. Even if she had been convinced that Margaret was Marian's mother she would have still fought for her against the accusations of Nellie Flannagan.

'You tell her that if she's not careful she'll be had up for libel.'

'Yes, Fan.'

Now Fanny leant towards Mary and asked, 'And where did the lad come from? Has she worked that one out? Perhaps the lass had him when she was eight. You tell Nellie Flannagan to work that one out.'

Something had got into Fan. It was usual, Mary knew, for her to go off the deep end when Nellie Flannagan's name was mentioned, but not to take such an aggressive attitude when Nellie's verbiage wasn't directed against herself. 'I never open me mouth to her, Fan. I play dumb. I do, Fan.'

'Well, I'd continue to play dumb,' said Fanny stiffly.

There followed a prolonged silence during which Mary plucked at the threads on the patchwork quilt and Fanny several times adjusted her apron. Then Mary asked what she thought would be a placating question. 'Did Philip have any luck with his job?' she said.

'He had luck all right.' Fanny's voice was flat.

'Oh, I'm glad. Did he get it then?'

'Yes, he got it.' There was no change of tone as Fanny said this.

'When will he be goin' ?' asked Mary quietly.

'Not till the New Year.'

Mary now pulled herself up into a very straight sitting position and, rubbing the top part of her sore leg and with her eyes directed on the business, she said diffidently, 'Fan, there's something I think you should know.'

'Aye?' Fanny's eyes were hard and bright as she looked at Mary's bent head.

'You know the lass, the lass Phil used to go with in Binns . . . Sylvia?'

'Aye? what of her?'

'She's goin' to have a bairn.'

There was no change of expression on Fanny's face. 'You sure?'

'Aye, Fan. Monica told me . . . And, Fan . . . well, Fan, I think you should know this. Well, she's for ever on the lookout for your Phil.'

Now Fanny reared. 'What you suggestin'?'

'Nowt, Fan, why nowt, not a thing. I was just sayin' I thought you should know.'

'You were saying she's for ever on the look-out for our Phil, you're sayin' it's his.'

'No, no, Fan. Why no, I'm not. I wouldn't . . . I wouldn't.'

Mary was in a sweat, and Fanny continued to stare at her, but she was looking beyond her and asking, Was this why he had gone after the job? No. No, it wouldn't be, he wasn't the type to take a lass down. Aw, why didn't she stop kidding herself, he was a man, wasn't he? And these quiet ones were usually furnaces underneath. So that was it . . . or was it? From what she'd heard of the piece she seemed too smart to be dropped in her sleep.

'What about the other fellow she worked for?' asked Fanny. 'She was thick with him by all your accounts.'

'Aye. Aye, Fan, but he's married, Phil isn't. It makes a difference.'

Aye, it did make a difference. She'd seen innocent blokes tied up for life before the day. She had a sudden urge to get across the street and see him before he went out. She had left him at his tea.

She rose, saying, 'I'll be goin'. Keep what you've told me to yourself. And mind—' She raised her finger, and with her eye hard on Mary, she added, 'I'm tellin' you.'

'Aye, Fan.'

'If I hear a cackle of it, you'll get somebody else to do your job. And then you won't have one to go back to.'

'Aye, Fan, I know. I'll keep me mouth shut.'

Fanny went quickly out, across the lamplit road and up the steps into Mulhattan's Hall.

When she opened the kitchen door Philip was putting a woollen scarf inside his coat. The scarf, she noticed, was new and matched the grey coat he had bought last month. This was another thing that always kept them divided. He had, since he was a lad, insisted on choosing and buying his own clothes. Right from when she was married she had bought McBride's clothes and for all the others, too, until they left to be married. Sometimes she had drawn as many as six five-pound clubs together, especially at Easter, to get them rigged out. But my lord Philip would have none of them, and he would madden her further in this direction by always making his clothes last twice as long as the rest of them. Looking at him now, she wondered yet again how he could have any connection with herself. He was dressed like a bandbox, and if you were judging on looks alone, was as removed from her as was royalty.

The scarf discreetly hidden, the coat buttoned up, Philip stood under the light, his head bent as if he were contemplating his shoes.

'It's cold enough for snow,' he said.

She looked at him covertly. The weather topic was out of order, he dealt with it coming in, not going out. For the first time in their long association, Fanny recognised it as a symptom of nervousness, for she saw now that he was definitely uneasy. Her agitation ebbed somewhat and to her surprise she heard herself saying, calmly, 'Aye we'll be gettin' it.' And she added by way of conversation, 'I'll have to see about gettin' some coal by me, before there's a run on it.'

'I'll get you a ton before I go.'

She looked up at him. 'You're really going then?'

He blinked in surprise. 'Why, yes. I told you, didn't I?' But when she made no remark to this he went on, 'Yet it's odd, for I don't know whether I want to take the job or not now . . . Mother.'

Fanny waited a moment, then said, 'Aye? Well, what is it?'

He was looking down at his shoes again as he said, 'I'm in a bit of a quandary.'

Whatever quandary might mean he was saying he was in a fix. So it was right then what Mary had suggested. Her lips tightened.

'It's about Margaret. I suppose it won't come as an entire surprise to you, but I'm fond of her.' He now picked up his hat from the chair and examined it.

This was beating about the bush. There was nothing Fanny disliked more than beating about the bush, but she said as calmly as she could, 'There's no law against that. How does she feel?'

'I don't really know. I thought that . . . well, that she wouldn't be averse, and then she started avoiding me. When I was away at the interview the other day I knew how it was with me and I had to get back. I went to meet her and she seemed pleased, but when I asked her if she would come out with me, she said "No" . . . I don't know what to make of it.'

'Perhaps it's the mother . . . You'd be takin' on

something if she did have you. Have you thought of that?'

'Yes, I've weighed everything up.'

'You've been damned smart, then,' said Fanny tersely. 'And there's those two bairns to be looked after for years yet.'

'I've thought of that, too.'

'The lass has told you nothing about herself?'

'No, she's close there. I thought she might have confided in me after the night she fainted down here. There's something I can't get to the bottom of.' His eyes lifted from his hat. 'There's nothing very much that escapes you, what d'you think?'

Now this kind of directness was up her street. This was how she liked it, but for the life of her she couldn't give him an immediate answer.

He stared at her, then moved towards her, saying, 'I feel you know something . . . tell me.'

'Look, lad.' She felt more kindly disposed towards him at this moment than she had done in her life before. 'All I know is hearsay, gossip.'

'Well, tell me.'

Fanny pushed up her breasts.

'It's not about them upstairs.'

'No?'

'No, it's about the other one.'

'The other one?'

'That one, Sylvia.'

'What about her?'

'Have you finished with her?'

'Yes, yes, of course. It couldn't be otherwise.'

'But she still waits for you, at the top of the street.'

His colour mounted as he said, 'I can't help that. I've told her.'

'What have you told her?'

'It's finished.'

'Do you know she's goin' to have a bairn?'

She watched his eyes become almost lost behind his screwed-up lids, and she saw his lips leave his teeth bare. It was as if he had suddenly been confronted by something terrifying. She did not need to be told that this was news to him, and of a frightening kind.

'Who told you this?' he asked quietly.

'I got it from Mary Prout. Her brother's lass knows the other one . . . When did you see her last?'

He seemed to be raking in his bemused mind to pinpoint the time, then he muttered, 'Nearly a fortnight ago.'

'Well, she's been round here since then. Mary Prout said she was at the top of the street the other night.'

'Yes, yes, I know, but I evaded her.' He wetted

his lips, and his eyes slipped back and forth across the room.

Then Fanny, speaking quietly but abruptly, said, 'Is it yours?'

'No. Good God, no!'

'Then you've got nothing to worry about.' Even as she said it, she knew how far it was from the truth. If that piece wanted a father for her bairn he had everything to worry about.

With a helpless gesture that robbed him of his poise, he sat down opposite to her and said words that drew out of her the first feelings of protectiveness towards him. 'I'm scared,' he said; 'I don't mind telling you, I'm scared. She's . . . Sylvia's an odd girl . . . determined. I never really found it out until recently.'

And Fanny saw he was scared. This gentleman son of hers was scared. If it had been one of the others, they'd have cried, 'Aye, well, let her try to hang anything on to me . . . just let her try.' But not this one. His reading, his copying fine ways, like standing up when even Mary Prout came into the room, his fussiness about his clothes and his eating had left him, she considered, a bit soft inside. Certainly it hadn't equipped him to deal with a situation like this.

'Has she hinted at anything?' she asked.

'No. No, of course not, there was no reason.

I've never. . .' His colour rose and he moved on the chair. 'No!'

'Look, I'm your mother and there's no need to get delicate-minded with me. If your conscience is clear in that direction, what are you worrying about?'

He became still and looked at her. 'She's been saying odd things. I thought . . . I thought she was going a little funny, but now I see where it was leading.'

'Have you ever promised to marry her?'

'We did talk of it. Then I had my suspicions there was somebody else – she let me down once or twice – we had words and I broke it off, that's all.'

Fanny wondered for the moment if she should say anything to him about the girl's previous boss, but she thought better of it. This wasn't the time. 'Look,' she said, 'go out and about your business, and should she waylay you, you put a flea in her ear. But if you can, I'd keep out of her way.'

He sat for a while longer before rising and as he gathered up his hat and gloves in silence a tap came on the door, and Fanny called impatiently, 'Who is it? . . . come in.'

When Margaret appeared in the doorway Fanny exclaimed in a lighter tone, 'Oh, come away in, lass.'

The girl came slowly to the centre of the room, looking at Philip as she did so. 'Hallo.'

'Hallo,' he replied, without returning her glance. Then with a flustered gesture he pulled his hat on to his head and turning went abruptly out.

Fanny could see that the girl was completely taken off her guard by his manner and sudden departure, and she watched her turn and look at the closed door, and saw her composure slip from her like a silk vest.

'Come and sit down, lass,' she said kindly.

'I . . . I can't stay.' A tremor passed over her face, and she bit at her lip before going on. 'I just came to see if you'd do me a favour, Mrs McBride.' She now forced to her face a little smile as she added, 'I'm always asking you for favours.'

'I will if I can, lass. What is it?'

'Tony's gone to choir practice, and my mother isn't too well, she's in bed, and I've put Marian to bed, too, for she has a touch of cold, but she won't stay in the room by herself, and . . . and I don't want her to . . . to disturb my mother. Would it be asking too much of you to stay with her, I mean Marian, till I come back?' Now the words came tumbling out in rapid succession. 'I've got to go to the doctor's, he gives me some special tablets for my mother's head. She has dreadful headaches . . . dreadful.'

After a pause in which Fanny thought, I'm not goin' to relish this, she said, 'Not at all, lass. I might as well be sittin' up there as down here. I can knit anywhere.'

'It was the stairs I was thinking about.'

'Oh, when I can't manage them stairs that'll be the day, they'll carry me out then.'

'You're very kind.'

Now Margaret's voice was trembling and her eyes were cast down and her fingers picking at each other in a distraught fashion.

'Kind? There's not much kind about that. Look, lass . . . aw, come on, what is it? Don't cry. Now . . . now.' She went to where Margaret stood, her face covered with her hands, her body shaking, and putting her arms about her she pulled her to her ample breast, saying softly, 'Come on, lass, come on . . . what is it?'

For a moment Margaret leaned against Fanny's comforting flesh, then groping for a handkerchief, she dried her eyes quickly, exclaiming, 'It's nothing, I just felt like that for a moment.'

'Now look, lass.' Fanny nodded her head. 'I've seen a bit in me time, and I know you're carrying more than your share. You can tell me and it'll go no further, and it'll ease you. Tellin' always eases you. Every time I go to Father Owen I say thank God to him who invented confession. Anyway, lass, I've drawn me own conclusions already.'

Now Margaret looked up at her, her eyes steady, and she asked, 'Have you?'

'Aye.'

'They won't be right, Mrs McBride.'

'You seem sure of that, lass.'

'Yes . . . yes, I am sure, and I wish I wasn't, but if I could tell anyone in the world I would tell you . . . do you believe that?' She put out her hand to Fanny, and Fanny took it between her two bloated ones, saying, 'Well, I'm always here, bear that in mind, lass. But there's one thing I'm goin' to ask you outright.' She brought her chin into the rolls of fat in her neck as she said, 'Do you like my lad?'

On this question Margaret withdrew her hand, and her colour slowly mounted and her eyes moved away from Fanny as she answered with a semblance of Marian's primness, 'Yes . . . he's very nice.'

Fanny sighed impatiently. 'That's not the answer. And you must forget how he went off just now . . . we . . . we'd been having a few words.'

Turning quickly towards the door and with her back now to Fanny, Margaret said, 'I can't give you any other answer.'

'No?' Fanny gave a small laugh. 'Well, that'll do to go on with. I'll just bank me fire down and then I'll be up. Go on and get yourself ready.'

Five minutes later when Fanny mounted the stairs Miss Harper's door opened just a fraction, and then, on the sight of Fanny, just a little wider, and the tall, thin, and ever-curious lady, putting her head out, asked, 'Is it trouble, Mrs McBride?'

'Trouble?' said Fanny without pausing, as she turned round the landing and on to the attic stairs. 'There wouldn't be any trouble without yourself knowing it, Miss Harper . . . No, there's no trouble.'

'Oh, I just thought . . .' Miss Harper's voice faded away, and Fanny commented privately, 'Aye, you're like a lot of other folks, troubles are your amusement.'

Margaret was ready when Fanny unceremoniously entered the attic. She was placing a drink on the table by the side of a single bed which stood in the corner of the room, and when Marian on the sight of Fanny began to toss about excitedly, Margaret said, somewhat sternly, 'Now, mind, I've told you to behave. And don't attempt to get up.'

'She'll be all right,' Fanny said. 'Get yourself away, and don't rush.' And when Margaret moved towards the door she followed her, saying quietly, 'I'd ask him for a tonic for yourself while you're there. You need something. Not that I meself hold with tonics.'

Margaret smiled but said nothing, and when the door had closed on her Fanny walked slowly to a chair by the fire, and without looking again towards the bed, said, 'You read your book, hinny, I'm goin' to knit.'

Marian, after eyeing Fanny's set profile for a few minutes, reluctantly drew a book over the coverlet towards her and began to read.

When Fanny had had a glimpse of this room before, such had been her annoyance at the time that she hadn't carried away with her any impression of it whatever. Now covertly she began to take in her surroundings. She knew these two rooms as well as she did her own, and during the occupation of their various tenants she had visited them, but she had never seen them looking as they did now. In Lizzie Shaughnessy's time the place had been neat and clean, but it hadn't looked like this. There was a different air about the room now. What was it exactly? Fanny looked slowly about her. Perhaps it was the effect of the curtains hung cross-wise, as the child had said, French-style, or the entire absence of even one picture on the wall. But the place nevertheless wasn't without comfort, for there was a carpet covering the floor, and that must be a strange feeling indeed for the attic floorboards. And the round table in the centre was of shining mahogany with feet like claws jutting from a pillar in the middle. The couch, which was a match for the chair she was now sitting on, was well covered in good leather, and against the far wall was a glass-fronted cabinet, full, not of china, but of books. But nowhere, Fanny noted, not even on the mantelpiece, was there a knick-knack or an ornament. Except for a heavy marble clock, the mantelpiece was as bare as a moulting hen's backside.

'Mrs McBride?' The voice was a whisper.

'Aye, hinny?'

'I've got a cold.'

'That'll soon be better.' Fanny's needles clicked . . . click-clack, click-clack.

'Mrs McBride?'

'Aye, hinny?'

'You know that girl you told me of who lived here?'

'Yes.'

'Where does she live now?'

'In the country on a farm.'

'I wish I lived in the country. I don't like living here. I hate this house.'

The statement was delivered with such bitterness that Fanny immediately turned her attention to the child, who was now leaning back against the bed rails, staring straight in front of her.

'You don't like Mulhattan's Hall?'

'No, I don't.'

'Oh well, I meself think it's a grand house, towering above the rest of the street with their potty two storeys.'

'It isn't a proper house, not like we had.'

'Had you such a grand house, then?'

Marian picked up the book, then threw it down again saying, 'It was better than this. And we had a garden, a real garden, and window boxes . . . and we grew mustard and cress.'

'Well, you don't tell me. Mustard and cress?' Something in Fanny's chest softened. She hadn't really much time for this little madam, but after all, what was she but a bairn, so she added conversationally, 'And did you have it for your tea?'

'No, it died,' said Marian flatly.

'The mustard and cress died?' Fanny screwed her face up in simulated interest.

'Yes, the whole window-box full.' Marian brought her eyes to Fanny's. 'The cats did it, they used it.'

'Did they an' all, the varmints. But there's one thing, the cats won't get up as far as this. What's to stop you having a bit window-box up here? Oh, it would be a grand sight, so it would.'

'You couldn't grow a window-box here.'

'And why ever not?'

'They're only attics and the windows are too small.' The child's voice was full of scorn now. 'I don't want to do anything here, nothing, nothing.' Two small fists thumped into the bed, and Fanny cautioned quietly, 'Now, now, we'll have none of that,' and returning to her knitting she added, 'If Mary Ann Shaughnessy had gone on like that nothing special would have ever happened to her. Mary Ann swore these attics were enchanted.'

'Enchanted?' The word held Marian's attention.

'Aye, enchanted. That's what she used to say. She used to say, "You know, Mrs McBride, there's something special about the attics, they're enchanted."'

Begod, she was becoming nearly as good a hand as Mary Ann herself at telling a tale. But it was funny, when she came to think of it, the things that had happened to the folks who had lived up here during the years. They came here when they considered they had reached rock bottom and in each case they had bounded up again. Look at the Ironsides, they'd had the attics before the Shaughnessys, and look what happened to them.

Thomas Henry Ironside would neither work nor want, and every day of her life poor Peggy had to go out and earn the bread because he was ailing with one thing or another. It was his feet that had kept Thomas Henry Ironside down, so to speak, and then when they wouldn't pay him any more dole or sick-pay, he had to take a light job. And what should happen on the second morning on his way to his light job? What indeed? A crane loading a ship with crates in the docks slipped a chain and a crate fell right on top of him, and he had no more trouble with his feet from that day on for the crate cut them off at the hips. But they gave him a grand lump sum for his legs, and now Peggy was living in a nice house up near The Robin Hood and having the time of her life.

'How are they enchanted?' Marian was waiting.

'Oh, well now.' Fanny came back to herself. How to explain it? 'Well now.' As she groped in her mind for some story to satisfy the child, the gleam from the fire, making deep rose patterns in the shiny steel of the fender, caught her eye. The fender had become a permanent fixture in the attic, for no-one could remember who had first brought it there, and no tenant would take upon themselves the bother of risking it fitting into their new home, so there it had remained. And now it gave Fanny a basis, so to speak, for her romancing.

'It's to do with the fender here.' She nodded down to the great ugly piece of steel and iron. 'Mary Ann Shaughnessy swore that the attics were enchanted because of the fender. She only had to sit on it and wish and whatever she wished for she got . . . There now, what d'you think of that?'

Marian looked from Fanny to the fender and back again. 'I don't believe it,' she said flatly. 'That fender couldn't do anything. Anyway, you can't tell a story like Mammy.'

Fanny, with lips compressed, turned her attention to her knitting, and Marian, after waiting for some retort, wriggled down into the bed and made a great fuss of straightening the bedclothes under her chin. Then she exclaimed, 'Mammy hates it here, too. She hates all the people in this house, and she'd go away, abroad . . . to France, and take us all, but Margaret won't let her. Margaret's hard and cruel.'

'That's enough.' Fanny's voice was quick and sharp. 'Who works for you, for you and your mother and your brother? Eh?'

Marian, her two large eyes just visible over the top of the sheet, looked at Fanny as she said slyly, 'She won't work for us if she gets married, will she? Mammy's forbidden her to see your . . . Mr McBride. If she does she'll—'

The clicking of Fanny's needles stopped. 'Go on,' she said quietly.

But Marian didn't go on, and Fanny, looking at her under lowered brows, thought, 'This is a house divided all right, and although this one can't be the old woman's she's a true disciple, if ever there was one.'

'Go on,' she said again; 'tell me what she'll do.'

Slowly the child's lids drooped, and she whispered, 'Nothing.'

'That's not the truth.' Fanny stood up, and going to the bed, she asked, 'Tell me what your mother'll do if Margaret doesn't stop seeing our . . . Mr McBride.'

Marian now brought her knees up, then pushed her feet down hard, and then with the evasive tactics that Fanny had come to recognise, she said, 'My mother's ill.' Then not being fully capable of completing the evasion, she added, 'It's Margaret who makes her ill.'

'Now look you here, me girl,' said Fanny, under her breath, 'I want to talk to you. Move over there a bit so's I can sit down.'

Reluctantly Marian moved over, and Fanny was just about to seat herself on the bed when a low tap on the door checked her, and moving across the room she opened the door to stand for a moment and gape at Philip.

Philip in his turn gazed back, and it was evident to her that he was as surprised as herself. After a quick glance back towards the bed Fanny moved out on to the landing and, pulling the door closed, demanded, 'What do you want, sneakin' back up here?'

'Sneaking?' The colour swept over his face making even his eyes look red. 'Who's sneaking?'

Watching his neck stretching out of his collar Fanny said more quietly now, 'That wasn't what I meant at all. But why had you to come up here when the old 'un's in?'

'I want to see Margaret. Isn't it evident?'

'Ssh!' Fanny cautioned, her eyes flicking back to the door, 'keep your tongue down, you don't want to tell the house, do you? She's not in, she's gone to the doctor's and the child's got a cold. And anyway,' she whispered, now almost fiercely, 'what talkin' do you expect to do up here, with the ears of the house on you?'

'I have to see her.'

'All right then, catch her comin' in, and take her in home and have it out there. And don't go acting like a seventeen-year-old sprig.'

Philip's colour deepened still further, and she

saw his jaw tighten as he turned on his heels and ran down the stairs.

After a moment, during which she sighed, Fanny went back into the room and was just in time to see Marian skip into bed. She paused and looked towards the bedroom door. It had been closed, but was now open, and from the room now came Mrs Leigh-Petty's voice, high, peevish, and demanding, 'Mrs McBride!'

Fanny walked slowly towards the bedroom, and standing in the open doorway she looked through the dim light towards the woman in the bed. Mrs Leigh-Petty was sitting propped up with pillows and there was no doubt about it but that she was ill. Her face, in the half-light, was a dirty grey, and her narrow hands were clutching convulsively at the bedclothes. She was breathing quickly and she stared at Fanny for a long moment before saying, 'Who was that at the door?'

Seeing she had to deal with a sick woman Fanny checked the retort, 'Why ask the road you know?' Instead, she replied, 'It was me son.'

'Why did he come up here? What did he want?'

Again Fanny checked her natural retort and said, 'Well, surely he's entitled to come up and speak to his mother. Is there any law against that? He came to tell me he'd be late in, and for me not to wait up. Are you satisfied?'

Mrs Leigh-Petty's rapid breathing slowly lessened and her hands, leaving the bedcover, pressed themselves together, and lying back and in an altogether different tone she said, 'Forgive me for speaking like that. Come in, won't you, and sit down.'

'I've got me knitting in the other room,' said Fanny, 'and you'll want to be quiet.'

'No, no . . . it's so rarely I see anyone. Please sit down.'

The request was gracious and Fanny could not do otherwise than take a seat, but she pulled it away from the bed and into a position from where she could view the woman. And the first thing she noticed was that she had a real fine nightie on, a bit old-fashioned with a deep lace collar, but an elegant thing entirely. Furthermore, the bedding was good, but it covered a single bed and this set Fanny to thinking. Where did the lass lie? For besides the child's bed in the kitchen there was only a folding camp bed standing behind the big chair in the corner, and that would be for the lad . . . She must lie on a shake-down somewhere likely.

This room, too, Fanny noted, had a carpet and a fine old-fashioned bedroom suite in it – she remembered admiring it the day they moved in – but it was the number of books in the room that held her attention. There were dozens of them. They lined the mantelpiece and were stacked at each side of the small attic window that came down to the floor, besides filling two small tables on each side of the bed.

'You are looking at my books?' There was a faint smile on Mrs Leigh-Petty's face.

'Aye,' said Fanny, 'you've got enough to start a shop.'

'Oh, I've got very few left, at one time I had hundreds and hundreds.'

'You don't say,' said Fanny. 'And did you read them all?'

'Most of them.' Mrs Leigh-Petty sighed and her head moved slowly on the pillow. And as Fanny looked at her she had the strange idea that the great sockets of her eyes were empty and that the eyes themselves had dropped inwards.

'Things haven't always been as they are now, Mrs McBride.'

Now, thought Fanny, it's coming at last, and so she said, 'No, I guessed that. It doesn't need a great deal of brain to know you've seen different times.'

'Yes,' Mrs Leigh-Petty sighed again. 'Yes, very different times. I've travelled most of the world, Mrs McBride.'

'Have you now?'

'Yes, and seen almost everything in it there is to be seen.'

'Well, you can be happy with your memories.' Fanny gave a little laugh. 'Here is me, never even been to London. But mind, I'll tell you something, in me new job in The Ladies you see as much life as you would on any travels. By! you do that. Would you believe it if I were to tell you I've never been further than Shields for the last fifteen years?'

'Yes, I would.' The tone was flat, and Fanny's lids narrowed. Now what did she mean by that? My God, if she was going to slip double meanings off her tongue she'd get out cos she wouldn't be able to keep her temper.

'Some of us are born to revolve in narrow orbits, but my orbit was large.' The sockets were turned towards Fanny. 'My father was a very distinguished man, Mrs McBride.'

'Was he now?'

'Yes, and we travelled widely together. He was a very cultured man. He retired early and he showed me the world.' Her head moved again, and she concluded, 'There are wicked people in the world, Mrs McBride.'

'I know that,' said Fanny with some stress. 'I've met a few in me time.'

'And women are more wicked than men. Women are very wicked, Mrs McBride.'

'Aye, I've no doubt.' Fanny waited a moment before adding the test question 'Has your husband been dead long?'

'What?' Mrs Leigh-Petty's hands came swiftly from under the counterpane, and she spread her arms across it as if bracing herself.

'I was just enquiring about your husband.'

The weary, pained look lifted from Mrs Leigh-Petty's face and her expression became hard, and for the moment she glared at Fanny as if she hated her, then dropping back on to her pillows, she murmured, 'I've talked too much, my head aches. Where has Margaret got to?' She turned to the table and pulled a small clock towards her. 'She's had plenty of time to get back before now.'

Marian, Fanny considered again, may not be this one's but it was certainly from her that she had acquired her knack of evasiveness.

'The surgery's likely full,' said Fanny, 'and she's got to go all the way to Hebburn. You'll have to pick a doctor in Jarrow.'

'I'll do no such thing. Dr Gruber understands my case.' The tone had changed again. 'But why am I talking, I want to rest. Will you kindly go?'

Begod! Fanny stared at the woman in the bed. If it wasn't that she was indeed a sick woman she'd give her something to think about this minute. Ordering her about as if she was a cross between a child and a lackey. She rose to her feet, and without further ado went into the kitchen and closed the door none too gently after her.

Marian was lying quiet and very wide awake. She had enough sense not to address Fanny, but lay watching her, unblinking, as the needles flew and clicked loudly.

And the lass, thought Fanny, has to put up with this day in and day out. How does she stand it? But perhaps the old woman doesn't take that air with her . . . I wonder if she's back yet? And she wondered how long Philip would be likely to keep her, for she'd be glad when she got down into her own house, away from this strange set-up.

It was almost at this moment that the door opened and Margaret came in, and at the sight of her Fanny pushed an almost finished sock hastily into her bag and, rising quickly, asked, 'Are you bad, lass?'

'Margaret, I want to tell you something.' Marian was sitting up in bed, and Fanny, turning on her, cried below her breath, 'Be quiet you, and lie down, or I'll skelp your backside for you.'

On this unexpected but very definite order Marian lay down, and Fanny, moving closer to

Margaret, whispered, 'You look like death. What is it? Have you had a do with him?'

Margaret shook her head and was about to make some reply when from the bedroom came the imperious command of, 'Margaret! Margaret!'

Margaret did not answer or look towards the door, but she said softly, 'Thanks for staying, Mrs McBride. I'm sorry I've been so long.'

'That's all right, lass.' Fanny was still looking at her, and she added somewhat reluctantly, 'Well, I'll be off now.'

As she moved towards the door the command came again from the bedroom, 'Do you hear, Margaret?' and Fanny turned to watch the girl go into the room. She saw the door close, and she was on the point of leaving when Mrs Leigh-Petty's voice arrested her. It came through the closed door, muted but high and quivering enough to convey its rage. 'Don't tell me you've been all this length of time at the doctor's. You've been seeing that man . . . I'm right, am I not?'

'You're right.' The girl's voice was flat and weary.

'What!' the syllable was like a scream, 'after you promised . . . you promised, do you hear?'

'I promised nothing.'

'You did . . . you did. Do you want to kill me?

Yes, that's what you want. You know what it will drive me to . . . I've tried . . . I've done everything you've said. I've tortured myself to do it, and this is how you keep your part . . . sending that vile, horrible old woman up here, so you could . . .'

'Mrs McBride is a good woman.'

'Good? That great ignorant low creature? Have you thought of her as a mother-in-law?'

'Yes.'

'Margaret' – the voice suddenly dropped and all the vituperation went out of it – 'you can't do it. Oh! you can't do it. You won't do it, will you? What will become of me? Come here . . . oh! come here, Margaret, don't torture me.'

There came the sound now of crying, choked crying, but it aroused no pity in Fanny. All her pity was with the girl. That 'un, as she thought of Mrs Leigh-Petty in her mind, made her blood boil . . . Vile, horrible old woman. By God! it was as well for her that she was a sick creature or she would have gone back in there and wiped the floor with her.

She cast one infuriated glance towards the bedroom door, which included in it the open-mouthed Marian, then went out and down the stairs, telling herself that it would be a long, long while before she came up this far again under any consideration whatsoever.

Philip was sitting by the fire when Fanny entered, and seeing the expression on her face, he rose and asked, 'What's the matter?'

'The matter!' Fanny threw the knitting bag on to the sofa. 'The matter? I'm a vile, horrible old woman.'

'Who said that?'

'That 'un up there. If it hadn't been for the lass, I'd have gone in and given her the length of me tongue and the back of me hand the night, drug-daft as she is an' all.' Fanny paused now; then asked in a more subdued voice, 'How did you get on? Did you see her?'

He turned to the fire again. 'Yes.'

'Well, then, what happened?'

'She was sick.'

'Sick?'

'Yes, just that.' He gave a little laugh. 'I asked her if she would come out with me, and the next thing I knew she had her hand to her mouth and she was making for the kitchen. She was actually sick.' His eyebrows rose in a slightly amused fashion as he added, 'It was a very levelling experience.'

'That lass is ill,' said Fanny, 'and if something isn't done the old 'un will have her as daft as herself . . . Didn't she say anything to you?'

'No, she wouldn't listen. Nor would she let me near her.'

Thinking of what the girl had said, it was on the tip of Fanny's tongue to tell him that he had no need to worry, for she had already accepted herself as her mother-in-law, but to convey this to him as she had heard it would need delicate wording without making him think the lass was two steps ahead of him, so she remained quiet. Instead she asked him a question that had been niggling at her to be voiced. 'If you do take up with the lass,' she said, 'what about the new job? Will you go?'

He turned from her direct look, and picking up a couple of books from the chair he said, 'I don't know, but things'll pan out.'

As Fanny watched him go towards his room she confirmed this. 'Aye,' she said, 'things'll pan out, they generally do.' And as she thumped the kettle into the heart of the fire preparatory to brewing yet another pot of tea her mind, without her sanction or wish, swung to her youngest son, and she thought, Dear God, let it pan out right that way an' all. Make him come, for I, too, am sick, sick for the sight of him.

6

Fanny, opening the front door, was confronted by a solid sheet of rain, and Barry Quigley from behind her said, 'You're goin' to get drenched, Fan.'

'Aye,' she said, 'it looks like it. It's comin' down heavier than ever.'

'Water, water everywhere . . .'

Barry now gurgled in the depths of his skinny neck, and Fanny turned on him a look that caused him to cough and drop his eyes. She would joke as much as the next with a woman, and about The Ladies or anything else, but she knew where the innuendoes of Barry and the like of him led to. She was having none of it . . . she'd had enough of that kind of thing from McBride.

Barry, being sensible enough not to test the temper of his neighbour too far, turned the subject to coal, saying, 'That bloody Johnson hasn't turned up with the coal the day, and we're near froze up there.'

'You should have come down, you could have had a bucket till it comes.'

'Aye, I know, Fan, but Amy said we've done enough borrowing from you from time to time.'

'Oh, if we can't lend, what we here for? Coals are being stored up in hell for them that refuse to lend.'

They both laughed together at this, then Barry, with his voice very low now, said, 'There was some shindy up above in the attic last night.'

'Aye.' Fanny kept her gaze on the steady rain.

'There's something fishy there, Fan.'

'What makes you think that?' Her voice held little interest . . . she knew what tactics to apply to Barry.

'They kept on for hours on end . . . stopping and starting, at least the old one did. It was like switching the wireless on. Amy made me go across to shut 'em up at one time, but I just got as far as the landing . . . You know, Fan, I feel that that lass has done something.'

Now Fanny forgot her tactics and exclaimed sharply, 'What d'you mean, done something?'

'Well' – Barry's head wagged and his thin eyebrows went up into points – 'the old one was threatening her, threatening to give her away.'

'What about?'

'The old one was saying, "I'll tell everybody,

and your gentleman friend, and then what will you do? Will he want you then? Ask yourself." That's what she was sayin'. And more that I couldn't get hold of, Fan, but it didn't need two and two to be put together to know that she'd got something on that lass.'

Fanny turned from Barry and stared out into the rain again. What could she have on her? If the child wasn't hers, what other hold could the old 'un have on her? But there was something here that was twisted . . . she had suspected it all along. Yet the lass didn't look the type to have anything in her past that would give that 'un a hand over her. But then again, you never could tell with the young 'uns today. They were a new kind of creature altogether to the lasses of her own day . . . Well then, if the lass had a past, what kind of a past would it be? A past usually meant a bairn or a man, the man coming first, of course. What other kind of past was there? Not thieving. No, no, the girl wouldn't do that. Well, whatever it was, and say it was a fact, how would her gentleman son react to it?

'There goes Lady Golightly.' Barry was speaking under his breath, and Fanny's eyes were drawn quickly to Mrs Flannagan emerging from her door wearing a white plastic mackintosh and a matching hat.

'I wonder what's driving her out in the rain?' said Barry. 'Perhaps she got a job after all.'

Fanny turned sharp eyes on him. 'Was she after a job for herself?'

'Why, aye.' Barry's small eyes screwed up to pinpoints. 'Didn't you know? She was after yours . . . Mary's.'

'You mean? . . .'

'Aye, the lav . . . The Ladies.'

Fanny's jaw dropped and her mind was jumping back to the morning she had gone to the priest for the reference, when Barry said, 'Lizzie Croft, who does the rough in the priest's house, heard Father Owen telling Miss Honeysett about you and her comin' for references for the same job, but you happened to get in first.'

'Well!' Fanny's bust rose with indignation. The great Mrs Flannagan condescending to go after a job in The Ladies, well, she'd be damned! And she made this statement aloud to Barry, and Barry said, 'Oh, I thought you knew, Fan.' Fanny shook her head. He knew fine well that she didn't know. Oh, she knew Barry's tactics, and now she wanted no more of them. She wanted to get by herself and think, think of that damned, sneaking bitch of an upstart going after her job . . . Mary Prout didn't come in to it now. So plunging into the rain she cried over her shoulder, 'So long, I'll be seeing you,' and hurried as quickly as her swollen legs would carry her up the street to the bus . . .

When she reached The Ladies she was dripping wet, but Maggie's warm welcome as she divested her of her coat made up for all the discomfort.

'By, you're wet through, Fan.'

'It stops when it gets to the skin.'

Maggie laughed. 'Eeh! you've got an answer for everything. Look, I'll hang it over here, near the pipes. And there's a cup of tea ready. There's hardly been anybody in the day. Nobody out . . . who would in this weather? I hope it keeps slack, I want to get me jumper finished. Did you finish those socks?'

'Yes,' said Fanny, 'I finished them and started another pair.'

'Eeh, the socks you knit. By the way, Fan, you know that lass that was outside the night I pushed the funny out, in the Salvation Army bonnet? Well, she came in this mornin' again.'

Fanny remained still, but said, 'Well now, what's that got to do with me, Maggie?'

'Nowt, Fan, just that she was asking after you.'

'And what would anybody in the Salvation Army be wanting with me? I'm a Catholic to the bone, you know that, Maggie.'

'Yes, I know, Fan, but the lass was nice.'

'There's no nice Hallelujahs,' said Fanny.

'Aw, Fan.'

'Never mind "Aw, Fan", what did she say?'

'She just said, politely like, "Is Mrs McBride not at work today?" And I said, "No, she doesn't come in till the afternoon."'

'Well?'

'She asked how you were keeping.'

'How I'm keeping?' Fanny looked down on Maggie, and Maggie looked up at Fanny and nodded, 'Aye, Fan, she was nice and polite.'

'There's no—' Fanny was going to repeat her statement that there was no nice Hallelujah, but instead she said, 'Pour me a cup of tea, Maggie, while I get me shoes off. They're wet.'

'Aye, Fan.'

As Maggie poured the tea out, the door clicked open and she exclaimed, 'Bust!' – then pushing her head out of the cubby-hole she remarked in a relieved tone, 'Oh, it's only Baggy Betty.' Then she shouted, 'D'you want a cup of tea, Betty?' and a croaking voice replied, 'I could do with one, Maggie, I could that.'

Maggie put Fanny's cup at her elbow, then took a mug to the derelict woman standing near the entrance. 'Sit down until you hear anybody comin', then make on you're titivating up.'

At another time the latter part of these directions would have set Fanny's flesh wobbling – to think that the bundle of rags that covered Baggy Betty could be titivated, or that the titivating would delude anyone – but at present Fanny's mind was too taken up with the Hallelujah. So that was the game, was it? She was coming to spy out the land, he hadn't the nerve to come home. He thought he would break the ice through his wife . . . wife! huh! In Fanny's eyes the girl was no wife. Not having had the words of the priest over her, she was to all intents and purposes living with their Jack.

'If Mrs Proctor comes and finds her here I'll get it in the neck,' said Maggie, coming back into the little room, 'but I don't care, I'm not frightened of her. I wouldn't put a dog out, a day like this.'

'Aye, true,' said Fanny absentmindedly.

And that was how Maggie found Fanny all afternoon. She was absentminded, but Maggie didn't mind. She liked the warm comfort of Fanny's presence, whether she made her laugh or was quiet, as she was the day. She didn't care whether Mary Prout ever came back, for she liked this big, fat old woman. She'd never had so many laughs in her life. She had just to look at her bulk of flesh and something about it tickled her.

The door clicked again, and on the sound Fanny left the cubby-hole and her knitting and went into the little glass office. Then, to Maggie's amazement she heard Fanny's voice raised high, like it had been the morning she started the singing, but now it wasn't laughter-making and she was startled by it, for Fanny was yelling her name out as if she was at the bottom of the street. 'Maggie! Maggie! get your bucket and mop ready, you'll need it!'

Maggie rushed out into the corridor, but all she could see was Baggy Betty in the corner and one solitary woman in a white plastic mac, with an expression on her face that would have soured milk, making her way to one of the cubicles.

When the door banged on the woman Maggie turned her perplexed, bird-like face to Fanny, and Fanny, from behind the partition, cried, 'Check up on the rolls! You can never tell with the people you get in here, they'll stick them down their stocking tops or in between their scraggy breasts. Oh, you can put nothin' past 'em.'

Maggie, scurrying into the cubicle, whispered, 'What's up? Who is it?'

'Lady Golightly Flannagan, the one I told you about,' hissed Fanny. 'I just heard the day she was after this job. I just pipped it afore her. She would take the holy water from the dying, that 'un.'

'That sour puss?' said Maggie, nodding back to the cubicles.

Fanny made a deep motion of her head, making her chins ripple. Then with her voice at pitch again she went on. 'This is a very comfortable situation, but they're very particular who they take in it, for there's money concerned. Your character must be of the best afore you get a job like this. You can go to the priest for a reference, but the priest isn't to be taken in. He's not to be deluded by a plausible tongue that covers a black heart. Oh, no, the priests have the insight of God in them.'

As she ended this tirade Fanny nodded down at the pop-eyed Maggie, and they stood waiting.

There came the sound of rushing water, and as the cistern gurgled a door opened and banged shut again. Fanny did not try to compete against the noise, and when Mrs Flannagan stood opposite the glass partition it was she who got the first words in, not Fanny.

'You are quite right, Mrs McBride, I did go for a reference to the priest. But I did not want the position for meself, it was for a poor, witless creature from Gunthorpe Road. She wasn't capable of doing anything that needed either brains or sense, so I thought it would be a Christian action to get her such employment as this.'

Fanny was now on her feet, with her head as far out of the let as she could get it. Her voice was not high now but menacingly low as she said, 'You're a blasted liar, Mrs Flannagan.'

And Mrs Flannagan's was as quiet but weighed with dignity as she replied, 'And you're an uncouth, dirty, fat, big-mouthed galoot, Mrs McBride.'

As Fanny swung away from the partition in an effort to get round into the corridor and at her neighbour, Maggie grabbed her skirt entreating, 'Eeh! no, don't Fan, you'll lose the job. Eeh, no, don't, she's not worth it anyway.'

The small woman's plea deterred Fanny, and she turned again to the glass partition, her breath coming deeply as she cried, 'You're right, Maggie, what's the good of wasting your breath on scum. Jealous, begrudging scum at that, who's never lifted a hand to do a good turn for anybody in their life.'

Mrs Flannagan looked sneeringly down her nose before moving away, then at the door she turned her head and looked back at Fanny's grim face and said, very softly and precisely, 'You are wrong again, Mrs McBride, I do lend helping hands. I lent one last night to the poor girl who stands at the top of the street waiting for your son to marry her and give her child a name.' With this last telling shot Mrs Flannagan inclined her head briefly before making a dignified departure.

Fanny sat back slowly on the stool. The night before last Nellie Flannagan had been extolling the merits of their Philip, but now she was stamping him the father of that lass's bairn, and what she was saying the night you could bet that everybody in the place would be saying the morrow.

Maggie, looking up at Fanny and her curiosity very much alive, asked, 'Eeh! Fan. Is it right what she says, has your lad got some lass into trouble?'

'No!'

Maggie jumped under the bark and blinked as she turned away saying, 'All right, Fan, I was only askin'.'

She could say no, Philip could say no, but would it do any good? What if that madam managed to pin the bairn on him? It would bust up his life, the job, the lass up stairs, the lot. Her flesh flounced on the seat. No, begod! she wasn't going to sit by and see that happen, no, not even to Phil. He could be what he was, a bit above himself and maddening with his fancy ways, but he was her own flesh and blood after all, and no loose piece was goin' to make a monkey out of him. No, begod, and she'd see they didn't.

*   *   *

What with the Hallelujah enquiring after her and the news Nellie Flannagan had made a special journey to The Ladies to throw in her face, Fanny reached home that evening in a very unsettled state of mind; and when she saw the light already on in the kitchen, she thought, 'He's home and what I've got to tell him will put him off his tea all right.' But before she opened the door she knew that it wasn't Philip who was in, but Corny, for Joe's yelping came to her, and as soon as she entered the room the dog was all over her.

'For God's sake get the beast off me. Stop it, will you! Get off me coat, you'll have me on the floor.'

'Stop it! Joe. Quiet! Joe.' Corny admonished his dog and Fanny said, 'What for d'you bring him across the water every time you come? Look at the damage he did last time.'

'But you laughed at it, Gran.' The boy looked up at her, grinning.

'Aye, I might have, but I'm in no mood for laughing the night, so stop it. What's that?' Fanny was pointing to a musical instrument lying on the table.

'It's a cornet, Gran.' Now Corny left the dog to continue its scampering and grabbed up the cornet from the table. 'It's the one me da bought for me.'

Fanny surveyed the cornet; then said, 'Yer da also bought you Holy Joe. What's the matter with your da these days? What did he give for it, three rabbits?'

'No, he got it off a stall in the market, Gran.'

'Why couldn't he get you something sensible off the stalls?'

'I wanted that, Gran. I want to learn it.'

'Learn that thing! Where d'you think you're goner practise?'

There was silence, and Corny turned and put the instrument lovingly down on the table. Then his finger following the round curve of the mouthpiece, he spoke two words very quietly, 'Here, Gran.'

'Oh, no! Oh, no, begod! you won't. A trumpet here? Oh, no! I bet your ma wouldn't have the noise in your own house and that's why you brought it over here. Isn't that it?'

Corny's head dropped a fraction and Fanny cried, 'Aye, I knew it. Well, you're not learnin' the cornet here. Now you take that for final.'

'Aw, Gran.' He raised one pleading eye and eyebrow up to her.

'Never mind, "Aw, Gran", one toot out of that tin whistle and out that door you go.'

'But you haven't heard it, Gran.'

'I've heard cornets afore in me time. I know

what they're like. Banshees aren't in it.'

Corny picked up the cornet, then catching Joe, fixed the lead to his collar and in an attitude that was meant to probe the hard core of his grannie's heart moved disconsolately towards the door.

'Where you off to?'

'To find Tony.'

'Well, when you find him don't start blowin' that thing, not in this neighbourhood. I've got enough trouble . . . d'you hear?'

'Aye, Gran.'

When the door closed on the boy, the dog and the cornet, Fanny stood for a moment looking towards it, and a twisted smile spread over her face. Corny was dear to her heart, very dear . . . but a cornet! Oh, no, begod! Not a cornet.

It wasn't until she went to put the kettle on the fire that she noticed the sheet of paper on the mantelpiece. Taking it down and holding it out at arm's length from her she read, 'Won't be back until seven. Don't make anything for me, I've had a cup of tea.'

So he had been in, and gone. Well! Fanny crumpled the paper up and threw it behind the fire. Then stood for a moment thinking. And the result of this took her swiftly to his bedroom door. If she was going to tackle this madam who was trying to pang a bairn on to him she must know where she stood.

And now she did what, despite her many faults, she had never stooped to before. She began to rummage carefully through his drawers for any letters that might give her an insight into what she thought of as 'his case'. He had received letters from the girl, she knew that, for she had herself stuck them on the mantelpiece. But search as she might she could not find one of them. On a little table below the window stood his books and blotting pad.

There were lots of papers on the pad. And she picked them up at random and looked at them. There was nothing in the nature of a letter. One piece of paper caught her attention, so much so that she read it three times, holding it further away from her eyes each time. But even after the third time she was no nearer to understand what it meant.

'All life is lived within walls
Of flesh, of brick, of wood, of wattle,
Of wattle, or wood, or brick, or flesh;
Only the soul escapes the entangling mesh
And, above clouds of thought where time is the
*   moment*
And nought can be bought or sold or swapped
*   or borrowed or lent,*

Where life is forever and yet already spent,
Draws from the laws of boundless space
Substance to face Life encased within walls
of flesh, or brick, or wood, or wattle.'

In the name of God, what did that mean? Did he waste his time in here writing such stuff as that? Huh! With a disparaging gesture she threw the paper back on to the table. There was nothing in things like that that would get her anywhere. No wonder he got himself into trouble if his head was as mixed up as them lines.

In the kitchen again, she took off her outer things and made herself an extra strong cup of tea, and had just seated herself at a corner of the table to enjoy her first sip when a knock came on the door. And when, after answering it with the usual, 'Come in,' nobody appeared, she got up and lumbered towards it. Pulling open the door and being confronted with a very smart, if heavily made-up, young woman, she had no need to enquire who she was.

'Are you Mrs McBride?'

'Yes, that's me. Will you be wanting me?'

The young woman hesitated, then, giving a little jerk of her head, she said, 'Well, yes, I suppose so. Can I come in?'

Fanny did not add to this, 'Yes, and you're

welcome,' but stepped aside, then closed the door on the stylish piece and said, 'Take a seat over there.' She pointed.

'I'm not staying.'

'Oh, in that case you'll be gone afore you come then.' Fanny walked towards the table and seated herself again near her cup of tea and looked at the young woman. It was evident to her that the room didn't find favour with her visitor, neither with her eyes nor her nose, for that delicate organ was twitching just the slightest.

'Will you be tellin' me then what you're wantin'?'

'I want to see Philip.'

Fanny got up now and went to the hob and ground the kettle once more into the fire. 'In that case I would sit yersel' down for a while, it'll be a good few hours afore he's in.'

Corny, putting his head round the door at this moment, gave her the opportunity to vent a little crudeness which she hoped would all go towards putting this madam off. 'You get yersel' out to play, and don't bring that weak-bladdered animal in these doors again! Wetting all over me chairs. I've had enough.'

Corny, eyeing the . . . smasher, did not want to

go out to play now, and he said, 'But I've never had any tea, Gran.'

'Then you will have a better appetite for it when you arrive home. Go on now, across the water with you.'

There was no fun in his grannie's tone, and Corny turned and went out, saying, 'Can I leave me cornet then?'

'Aye, leave it, and get out.'

When the door closed on her grandson, Fanny, without any preliminary chatter, asked of the young woman, but quite lightly, 'And what d'you want with our Phil?'

The young woman hesitated only for a moment before saying, 'That's my business.'

'I understand you and him are finished.'

'We are not, not by a long way.' The deeply waved head moved from side to side.

'Then somebody's a liar . . . Why couldn't you wait at the corner like you've been doin'?' The girl's eyes widened, and Fanny went on, 'You didn't wait because he's been dodgin' you, and that doesn't indicate to me he's breakin' his neck to see you.'

The girl's face reddened. 'You're insulting.'

'I'm merely speaking the truth, lass. It's far better to face up to it.'

'Face up to it! You're right there, that's what he'll have to do.'

Now it had come, and Fanny waited, her eyes narrowing on the girl.

'Do you know why I've come here?'

'I've a good idea.'

'Oh, have you?'

'Aye, but go on, tell me in your own way.'

This attitude slightly nonplussed the girl, and she hitched up her extremely smart coat on to her shoulders and moved from one spider-thin heel to the other, and when she was just about to speak, Fanny, her head cocked on one side, said, 'Whist! you can hold it a minute, for here he is now.'

She had heard Philip's step in the hall, and now she also heard another step accompanying him and she thought quickly, 'God in heaven! don't let him bring the lass in here the night!'

But that is exactly what Philip did. Margaret came into the room, preceding him, and when he turned from closing the door behind them and saw who was standing facing him, his face darkened and his head lifted.

'Hello.'

'Hello.'

'What do you want, Sylvia?'

His tone was quiet, and Sylvia, glancing from

Margaret to him, waited a moment before answering, 'Well, isn't it evident? I want to see you.'

Philip wetted his lips and moved uneasily, then turning to Margaret he hesitantly made an introduction. 'This is Miss Dawson . . . Miss Leigh-Petty.'

The girls nodded, more wary now, and when a silence fell on the room that shrieked in Fanny's ears, she herself broke into it, saying, 'Aye, well, we won't get very far standin' here like stooks of hay. If you're goin' to stay, sit down.' She addressed the girl, then turning to Margaret she asked, 'Are you going to have a cup of tea, lass?'

Margaret blinked and shook her head, then said, 'No thank you, Mrs McBride.'

Philip and the girl were looking closely at each other now, and the girl's looks were as dark as his own. But as Margaret moved towards the door, Philip's eyes snapped away and he went sharply forward to open it for her; as he did so he made a statement which also sounded like a plea. 'I'll see you later,' he said.

'Perhaps.'

It wasn't Margaret's answer to his statement, but Sylvia's interjection, and it brought both Philip and Margaret round to her.

'It's evident that you don't know about me.'

Sylvia moved forward as she addressed Margaret. 'I suppose he's told you nothing.'

'What is there to tell? She knows all there is to know. We were friendly and it's finished.' In the harshness of his tone there was a faint tremor.

'Friendly! Huh!' Sylvia gave a high laugh. 'Friendly, so friendly I'm going to have a baby.'

Fanny was looking at her son's face as this statement was being made and she saw the anger slide from it and fear take its place as he cried, 'It's a lie, and you know it. You can't trap me like that, and you won't, by God!'

He was scared, he was dead afraid of her, and not without cause either. She knew what she was about, this one. Fanny now watched Margaret as she looked from Philip to Sylvia and back again to Philip. Margaret's face had taken on a blank expression, and for the moment she seemed to grow taller than either the girl or Philip. Then like a waft of wind she was gone, and Philip was standing looking at the closed door. He stood like this for some seconds before rounding on Sylvia, and now the words tumbled out of his mouth, giving proof of his agitation. 'You won't put it over on me. I haven't seen you for weeks . . . weeks and weeks. I told you we couldn't go on. Whatever's happened it wasn't with me, you know that damn well. Anyway, what's come over you, Sylvia?' He peered at her as if trying to see her in this new guise. 'You weren't like this.'

The emotion of pity had never before been aroused in Fanny for this son who, to her mind, could talk the hind leg off a donkey once he got started on some of his high-falutin ideas, which usually centred around the uplifting of somebody or other, usually within the family circle, generally one who was perfectly happy jogging along in his ignorant state. Many was the time when he had sat in the kitchen here pressing home some particular point of improvement, and she had wished him far enough and wished also with vicious intensity that some one of them could cap him with an equally swift flow of words and take him down a peg. Not one peg but half-a-dozen. But now, here he was being brought low indeed, and she was for him with every pore in her body. His fear hurt her, for it was a new element, an emotion she had not hitherto found in any other member of her family. Say the same thing had happened to Don . . . he would have lifted his hand and swiped her one. Or Jack . . . oh, Jack would have thrown back his head and laughed, then said, 'Get goin', Jane.' All such lasses had been Janes to Jack . . . until he met the Hallelujah piece. She switched her mind off the thoughts that bred only pain and to the present situation again and to her son, and saw him rubbing his palms together, making an uneasy, husky-like sound, and she saw his good-looking face draw tight and his lips plying each other for moisture. Then her eyes turned to the girl, smart, sleek and defiant, and she stepped in both mentally and figuratively, for moving between them so that she could face the girl, she said calmly, 'What about the manager at the factory office? Have you met his wife lately?'

If she had struck out at the girl with her fist she could not have startled her more, for her eyes stretched, her mouth fell open and her hands, feeling the need of some support, gripped the top of her bag.

'You feelin' faint?' asked Fanny, then without waiting for confirmation she added, 'Go on, why don't you answer?'

'I don't know what you're talking about.'

'No?' Fanny stared at the girl, and seeing guilty admission in her attitude she made a shot in the dark, saying quietly, 'You didn't get your money for nothing, did you? And wives have a habit of getting nasty when their pay's cut short or they're left alone at nights. Now, me lass, if you'll just take your body and your bairn back to the office I'm sure its father'll be only too glad to see you're both provided for. Of course, that's if his wife doesn't get wind of it.'

The girl was looking at Fanny as if she was seeing a witch, then her eyes lifted to Philip and she said defiantly, 'It isn't his . . . it isn't!'

Philip had been staring in bewilderment at his mother. Now he looked at his late girl-friend, and after hesitating a moment, he said, 'I don't care whose it is, the only thing I know is I'm not responsible. And you know that, too.'

He seemed to have regained some of his coolness, for he added, 'You really must take me for a fool.'

'It is yours. You said you loved me and you'd do anything for me.'

'Except father your bairn.' It was Fanny speaking. And she added, and not so unkindly now, 'Get goin' lass, and my advice to you is to go and see your old boss and threaten to go to his wife if he won't do anything for you. That'll fix him.'

Undoubtedly Fanny's knowledge had upset the girl's plans, for she looked deflated as she turned her eyes from one to the other. Then making one last stand, she confronted Fanny, saying desperately, 'It is his.'

'Get goin', lass.' Fanny spoke quietly and went to put her hand on the girl's arm, but it was struck away. 'Don't touch me!' The mascaraed eyes flicked around the room, then came to rest with derision now on Philip. 'No wonder you would never bring me to your home. No wonder you forbade me to come near the house . . . you, with all your high and mighty ideas and supposed education. My! you had a nerve, and there's no doubt about it.'

Philip's face was suffused with colour, but he spoke quietly and there was neither fear nor anger in his voice as he said, 'Get out!'

'Yes, I'll get out, Mr Lord Almighty, but don't think you've seen the last of me, cos you haven't. And' – her head bobbed defiantly as she exclaimed – 'and I'll take you to court. I'll prove it in a court of law, you'll see. You won't get off with this.'

She went towards the door, but before going out she turned and looked on Fanny and threw at her one dart. 'Not that it would be to my advantage to enter this family and be connected with you!'

Before Fanny could come back with a retort the door had banged closed, and there they were left standing in the middle of the room in a strange, uneasy quiet, looking at each other.

Philip's head moved slowly and he wetted his lips, then brought out a single word below his breath. 'Thanks,' he said.

Fanny turned towards the fire, giving a great haul to her bust but saying nothing.

'How did you know . . . about her boss? Is it true?'

'I should say that it was more than likely, for didn't she bring the evidence of it?' Fanny spoke casually. 'It was a bit gossip Mary brought over some weeks ago, and I put two and two together and seemingly made four. But, God help her' – Fanny now laughed and flicked her gaze over her shoulder towards her son as she added – 'I hope it doesn't turn out that number, that would be too much of a good thing.'

Philip did not smile, he only tugged at his collar, and Fanny, turning and facing him now, asked with indelicate pointedness, 'Could she have been right about you?'

'No. No, she couldn't. I've told you.' His voice was loud. 'There was never anything like that. She was always so damn proper – at least with me. My God!' He turned from her and rubbed his hands across his eyes. 'I can't believe it. What if she should . . . ? Anyway, it's nearly four months since we broke it off. She didn't seem to mind much then. I never saw her until she turned up one night at the corner and asked if we couldn't just be friends. I went out with her twice after that but had to tell her it was no good. But she wouldn't let it go at that, she started waylaying me.' Now he paused and stared at Fanny before finishing. 'And Margaret . . . you saw her face?'

'Aye,' said Fanny; 'you'll have a little explaining to do in that quarter.'

'Blast it all!'

Fanny's eyebrows raised themselves just the slightest. He was almost human this lad of hers, that's what trouble did for you. 'Aye, blast it all,' she said. 'But come and have your tea, you need it to fortify yourself. And if you were to ask my advice, the easiest way out for you would be to take that job and skedaddle, make a clean break of it, for although the lass up above is all right you're goin' to be saddled with something up them stairs if you go on.'

It had taken some unselfish strength of mind for Fanny to offer this piece of advice, and she could not but recognise the surge of relief when he said, 'It's too late for that, I've turned it down.'

'You've turned it down?' She paused in the act of pouring out some tea. 'Why?' She was asking the road she knew, and he knew it, too, and didn't answer, except to shake his head. And Fanny, as she cut the bread, was set to wondering if the entire loss of this last son wouldn't have been preferable to a closer association with the drug-taking lady up above, and she realised that in one part of her heart she was hoping that the latest development with Sylvia had put paid to his chances with Margaret, yet knowing the tenacity of man she thought it best just to wait and see.

But some minutes later, as she sat alone at the table, she could not resist talking at him as he changed his coat in the bedroom. 'The only one of the lot of them to get into this fix, and whichever way you jump you're goin' feet first into a ready-made nursery. Begod! the first McBride to be let in for anything like this.' Then some part of her make-up which did not allow of her to kick anyone when they were flat out led her to take a gulp of tea to drown her ending, as she said, 'That's what comes of trying your hand at being different. Education!'

7

Fanny came from the market square laden. She had been to the shops to draw her Christmas clubs – it was a bit early to do so but she wanted the stuff off. It had taken her two hours to choose the Christmas boxes for her family. That she chose seven of the same kind made no difference, for they would be despatched to different parts of the country. She felt pleased with herself, she always felt like this when buying presents. The four and elevenpenny ties, the four and elevenpenny socks, the aprons and the tea towels that went to make up the presents for the adults, and the games and clockwork figures for the children, each brought, if not joy, a definite satisfaction, and gave her a feeling of affluence that a more up-to-date grandmother might have experienced in presenting her sons and her daughters with electric razors and expensive cosmetics.

Mary Prout usually came with her on such occasions and gave her a hand, but Mary's leg after four weeks was still troubling her. Fanny had chided herself earlier for a 'Thank God', and she was now missing Mary's help, for her arms were breaking and her feet were burning. But still it had been an exciting day buying all the stuff, and the weather, too, had helped, for it was bright, with a steely brightness, and the air cut at your throat as it went down. There would be snow. She liked snow at Christmas, she had always liked snow at Christmas, but like everybody else, the weather, too, could be perverse, and would bring snow before its appointed time, and what would they have on Christmas Eve but slush as always?

Before she was half-way home her hat had slipped to one side, her breath was coming in short gasps, and she told herself that her tongue was hanging out for a drink of tea. If only she was home and had the tea-pot on the hob.

She crossed over Ormond Road, sniffed at the new council flats, and came into the labyrinth of small streets and breathed a long sigh as she turned into Burton Street. Thank God, it wouldn't be long now afore she had her hand on the tea-pot and her feet up.

She was half-way down the street when the noise came to her, but she did not pay it the least attention – there was always some old fellow blowing his trumpet in the back lane, but of course, not half as many as afore the war. Then you could have music of a sort for breakfast, dinner, and tea. But a little further on she was suddenly made to pay attention to the ear-splitting strains being emitted by the trumpet, for these were accompanied by the distressing sound of yelping, a weird yelping. And she took in swiftly, even through the thickening twilight, that she wasn't the only one who was aware of the odd combination, for on the pavement outside Mulhattan's Hall she could make out Sam and Clara Lavey, and Amy Quigley from upstairs, and on the opposite pavement, talking across to them, was Lady Golightly herself. And various doors, too, she now noticed, were open, showing protesting faces.

She had proceeded but another few yards when the shuddering truth sprang at her . . . that noise was coming from Mulhattan's Hall, from her house to be exact. It was Corny on that trumpet, accompanied by Holy Joe . . . my God! The sounds put her teeth on edge, and she wanted to screw up her face in protest. It was like the wailing of lost souls. Wait till she got her hands on him . . . only wait . . . And the street out! She'd swing that dog by the tail to hell, you see if she didn't. As for the trumpet player, she'd make him swallow the infernal instrument, she would begod!

As she neared her door the gesticulating died away and the talking ceased, but the accompanying strains of the cornet and the dog increased, if anything.

Believing firmly in the method of attack in any battle, Fanny, addressing her near neighbours, shouted, 'And what may I ask is the gathering for? Is somebody dead?'

'No . . . not de . . . dead, Fan,' stuttered Sam Lavey, 'b . . . b . . . but . . . but nearly d . . . d . . . deaf. Li . . . listen to that.'

'It's your Corny, Fan,' said Amy Quigley; 'and it's been goin' on now since three o'clock.'

'Couldn't you have knocked on the door and told him to be quiet?'

'I did, Fan, and rapped on Miss Harper's floor from above. And there was nowt but cheek out of him. He said he was practisin'. Miss Harper went out, she couldn't stand it.'

Fanny, having her own work cut out to stand it, cried, 'The child's right, he's got to practise some place, he's takin' lessons.' Then raising her voice even further so that it would be carried above the wailing and across the road, she yelled, 'Some folks' bairns can be tied to their tinny pianos and made to practise until the neighbours are ready for Sedgefield, and nothing is said about that, eh?'

As Mrs Flannagan drew herself up in

preparation to sending back a shattering retort, Fanny turned sharply away, mounted the stone steps and went into the hall, to be covered and torn with sound the like of which she had never heard before, not even when the lot of them were young and galloping mad about the house.

Bumping the door open with her hip and quickly closing it again with a thrust from her bust, she was about to cry out in protest and demand silence when Corny stopped.

'Hallo, Gran.'

Corny wiped the spittle from his chin with the back of his hand and grinned at his grannie, and Fanny, pitching her parcels on to the table, cried, 'Shut up that dog,' for Joe had not ceased his accompaniment.

'He won't stop, Gran. He only stops when you give him somethin' to eat. What'll I give him, Gran?'

Joe was sitting comfortably on his haunches, his head well up, his mouth wide open, and contrary to all opinions on wailing dogs, enjoying himself. And when he released from his straining throat a crescendo wail, Fanny screamed, 'Give him! I'll give him poison or a hammer on the head. Go and get him some bits out of the pantry, anything, meat off the dish, anything. Shut up, will you!'

With arm raised she made for Joe, and whether out of fright or compassion Joe's wailing ceased abruptly and he suddenly flopped to the floor and rested his head on his outstretched paws.

There settled on the room a blessed silence, and Fanny, breathing heavily, stood stock-still until Corny entered the kitchen again when she turned her attention to him. 'For two pins I'd tan your backside until it was red raw, me lad.'

Corny stopped, swallowed to get rid of the piece of meat he had confiscated, held out a hand with some scraps towards Joe, and enquired innocently, 'What for, Gran? Me? . . . I've done nowt.'

'You've had the neighbourhood raised, since three o'clock they say. Why didn't you stop when they asked you?'

'Who?'

'Don't you who me.'

'But Gran, I've got to practise some place. I've got to learn it.'

'Then learn in your own house, that's the place. I told you you couldn't learn here.'

Corny's head now drooped as he muttered in genuine dismay, 'I can't, Gran, me ma won't let me have it inside the door. I've got to leave it in the hen cree. I hid it in the coal hoose and our Harry stuffed it full of coal-dust. And in the hen cree I've got to stick it under the straw in a nest box, and I can only do that for this week cos it's our Bob's turn to clean it out next week and if he found it he'd swop it for a spare tyre, he said he would.'

Fan, looking at the doleful musician, had difficulty in curbing a rising chuckle, but willing herself to keep a straight countenance she said, 'Get your da to put his foot down then; he bought you it, didn't he?'

'He won't do nowt. It was him who stopped me playing it inside . . . it was when Joe started to howl.'

Slowly now into Corny's eyes there crept a twinkle and he looked up at Fanny. 'He howled for two hours, Gran. Nowt we did could stop him until we give him something to eat.' There was pride in Corny's voice for Joe's accomplishment, and Fanny, well imagining the pandemonium that must have reigned, said, 'Well, me lad, I don't care where he howls but there's one thing I'm certain sure of . . . it's not goin' to be here. You've had your first and last practice under this roof.'

'Aw, Gran!'

'Never mind "Aw, Gran", that's final.'

'But Gran, couldn't I just leave it here? I'll practise outside, away over on the salt grass, or in the park, or by the quay corner.'

'I've told you I don't care where you practise, but if you as much as put your lips to that infernal instrument in this house once again that'll be the end of it . . . and very likely you if you're not quick on your pins. But enough now of you and your instrument, get the cups out and the tea-pot, I'm parched and me legs are droppin' off.'

'Will I mash the tea for you, Gran?'

'Aye, and put five teaspoonfuls in, I want something to stiffen me . . . And by the way, when I've time to think of it, why are you here at this time of the day and you not broke up yet?'

'Wor Ann's got the measles.'

'My God! the measles now, she gets everything that child. Go on, do the tea, but mind that kettle.'

As Corny struggled to up-end the huge kettle over the tea-pot, he remarked conversationally, 'You know what, Gran, Tony's mother asked me to go a message the day and I couldn't say the thing she wanted.'

'Tony's mother?' said Fanny, dropping her eyes to Corny while relieving herself of her hat. 'Where did you see her?'

'As I was comin' along, she was near Baker's, the chemist, and she said to me would I go in and get her sixpennyworth of' – he paused, then made a dash back to the fire with the kettle and when it was resting once more on the hob, he said – 'para-gumic. I had a job to remember the name,

I couldn't say it, and she kept saying it over and over.'

'Paregoric, was that it?'

'Aye, that's it, Gran. You know it?'

'Did they give it to you?'

'Aye, and when I came out and give it to her she never even said ta or owt.'

'Has she ever asked you to go a message afore?'

'No, Gran.'

'Well, if she does again, say that you haven't got time.'

Corny looked at Fanny understandingly. 'OK, Gran.' Then he added, 'I saw her over our way last week, Gran. She was walkin' up and down the High Street.'

'Well, she's got a right to, hasn't she?' Fanny dismissed Mrs Leigh-Petty with this sharp retort, but she thought to herself that the woman would walk from here to hell if the craze was on her. Tilly Concert used to tramp all the way to Sunderland for methylated spirits or laudanum, or whatever she could manage to get from the chemist and she would come back as full as a lord, not able to stand on her feet. Apparently this one wasn't affected like that, the stuff seemed to go to her head rather than her legs.

'Are those Christmas boxes, Gran?' Corny eyed the table.

And Fanny said, 'Aye, and that's your share of 'em, me lad.'

Her tea drunk and wanting to sort her packages away from Corny's curious eyes, she said, 'Give me me purse there,' and when Corny handed her the worn leather bag, she opened her purse and picked out threepence, saying, 'Go on, get yersel' some bullets, and take that one for his run and see he does something afore he comes back.'

'Aye, Gran. Come on, Joe.'

When they had gone Fanny did not immediately start sorting her parcels but she sat thinking about the woman upstairs, and Philip. God in heaven! but he was goin' to have a job if he married that lass, for as like as not she would fall for a bairn straightaway, and there he would be with a wife and child and three others to support. It would have been bad enough if the old 'un had in her the makings of a normal mother-in-law, but to be responsible for a drug-besotted creature like her was going to be a burden that no man but a blasted fool would take on.

The thought agitated her, and she rose up and began sorting her parcels, pulling pieces of paper off the edges here and there to make them recognisable. But one package, a slim box of about a foot long, she did not untie, but held it in her hands looking at it. And the question came to her, Would he come for it? This was no ordinary present of a pair of socks, they were nylon at nine and eleven. What if he didn't turn up at Christmas either? Oh, away! The small parcel seemed to leap from her fingers and dropped on top of the others on the table. It was still a fortnight until Christmas, and if he didn't turn up before he would turn up then, he would never let Christmas go by without coming to see her, never. Of that at least she was sure. But it would mean something different altogether if he came before, for then it would be herself who was drawing him and not the sentimentality of the season.

She picked the package up again and, taking it to the dresser, stuffed it in the back of the top drawer.

The table cleared of her Christmas shoping, she was in the act of shaking the cloth over it preparatory to laying the tea, when her hands became still and she turned her face towards the window, for from just below it there came the raised, angry voice of Nellie Flannagan.

With an agility that gave no evidence of her legs dropping off her now, she made for the door and pulled it open just as Corny with a head-long plunge was attempting to enter. Her voice stopped his rush, and with her hand on his collar she demanded, 'What's all this? Why the tearing hurry?'

'I couldn't help it, Gran.'

'Couldn't help what?'

'You might well ask.'

Fanny's head jerked towards the hall door and to a really infuriated Mrs Flannagan. The sight of her enemy's wrath already aroused gave Fanny a feeling of advantage, and she asked with a pained, insolent calmness, 'What is it now?'

'What is it now!' cried Mrs Flannagan. 'Just this, Mrs McBride. This is the end, I've stood enough from you and those connected with you. Mad . . . clean mad he is, running wild. And that dog should be locked up . . . put down . . . done away with. I'll stand so much and no more.'

Clearly Mrs Flannagan was beside herself.

'Go on . . . Go on, I'm listening,' said Fanny, aggravating the situation further.

'Yes, I'll go on,' cried Nellie, now pointing at Corny. 'That foul-mouthed ragamuffin should be in Borstal.'

Mrs Flannagan was now almost foaming at the mouth, which sight caused Fanny to ignore the insult to her offspring once removed and to enquire with rage-evoking calmness, 'What's he done?'

'What's he done? What's he done? All my

beautiful clean washing trod in the back lane, my sheets and towels in the gutter!'

Fanny saw it all now and she laughed. She threw back her great head and she laughed.

'It'll be the first time they've touched dirt in their existence then. Was it your new-drawer wash you had out? Your best sheets and towels that you hang out every week that God sends to show off to the neighbours?'

'Oh! you wicked creature.' Mrs Flannagan's head was now flapping from side to side. 'I'll have you up for . . . for . . .'

The poor woman could not go on, and Fanny asked, still quietly, 'And what do you intend to have me up for? Go on, tell me. For isn't it every soul from here to Shields Pier knows about your drawer-wash and Flannagan's two shirts that you dip in the water and won't let him wear but hang out for the eyes of the world to behold, while you dry his old rags on the oven door?'

It now appeared that Mrs Flannagan's thin body might snap, so far back did she endeavour to bend it as she cried, 'I'll have you up, I will! I've stood enough, I can't stand any more. Years and years I've had of you.' And presumably for sanity's sake, she turned her attention from Fanny and addressed the face of Sam Lavey peering out of his door. 'There I was, Mr Lavey, after a hard day's wash, about to take me clothes in when that foul-mouthed ruffian and that wild animal dashed down the back lane, knocked me prop off, snapped me line and let me clothes trail in the dirt.'

Fanny now turned to Corny, a subdued-looking Corny; then her eyes fell to Joe whom the boy was holding with unnecessary firmness. Joe, for once, was standing perfectly still, being weighed down it would seem by his wrong-doing. His tail tucked between his legs, his head drooping, he cast a mournful eye which pleaded for understanding up at Fanny.

'What have you got to say?' asked Fanny sternly of her grandson.

'I couldn't help it, Gran, we was only playin' and runnin'.'

'Playin' and runnin' – like hooligans!' cried Mrs Flannagan. 'And why should you run in my back lane? There's your own, or the street.'

'Listen to her,' cut in Fanny, all calmness gone now. 'Her back lane! Note, forty-two houses on her side and it's her back lane . . . not our back lane.' She poked her head enquiringly towards her enemy. 'Have you bought the lot up?'

Mrs Flannagan, drawing herself to her full height, explained haughtily, 'I want no cross-talk with you whatever, Fanny McBride, and it's just like you not to stick to the point. I'm not going to demise myself by silliquising with you.'

'Oh, begod! here we go with the big words, I thought they were a long time in comin'. You just stay long enough, Sam,' Fanny cried, 'and it's educated you'll be, for as you know, there's not a finer flinger of words than Nellie Flannagan. Like kerbstones they are, big enough to knock you out. Now . . . go on, Mrs Flannagan, I'm listening.'

'Oh, you can sneer, Mrs McBride' – Mrs Flannagan's first rage was dying, she was now falling back on her dignity – 'but I was privileged to be brought up properly, not dragged up. None of my family were brought up on vile language.'

'And who of my family, may I ask you, Mrs Flannagan, has been using bad language in your refeened hearing?'

'Your grandson there.' Mrs Flannagan's disdainful gaze fell on Corny, and Corny staring back at her unblinking, pulled with a grimy hand at his earlobe, endeavouring, it would seem, to banish it into his outsize earhole.

'What have you been saying?' Fanny turned on him. 'Come on, out with it.'

'Nowt, Gran.'

'Now come on.' Fanny's voice brooked no shillyshallying, but Corny persisted, 'Nowt, Gran.'

'Oh! God forgive you, boy.' Mrs Flannagan's eyes caressed the ceiling.

'All right, all right,' cried Fanny at this point. 'If I want any intercession for me family I'll do it meself.' Then turning to Corny again, she said, 'Is it so bad you can't repeat it?'

Corny squinted up at her, the suspicion of a grin now on his face. 'No, Gran, it was only what you say.'

'What!'

Now a pink hue spread over Fanny's face. She couldn't remember one quarter of the names she had called her neighbour over the years she had lived opposite her, but she could remember enough to pray that her grandson had picked on only one of her minor sayings. She did not press him further but waited, and as Corny looked back into his grandmother's face his grin spread and he said, 'When her line snapped and the things fell in the mud I said' – he paused and looked from one to the other; then his eyes settling on his grannie, he ended lamely – 'I said, "That's put paid to old Nelly-jelly-belly's odds and sods."'

With great difficulty Fanny checked the sound that rose in her throat, and a number of conflicting expressions passed quickly over her face, and with her eyes now riveted on her grandson, she said, 'You say I said that? Now shut up!' She snapped her finger and thumb at him like the bill of a duck. 'Not another word out of you. Bejapers, she's right for once, you do need someone to intercede for you. Away inside you get this minute afore I strike the hunger off you.' She pointed to her door, and Corny, with a half-concealed laugh on his face, did as he was bidden. Then Fanny, hitching up her breasts, turned once more to Mrs Flannagan. And now her voice was airy. 'You can't hold me responsible for the sayings of twelve-year-old bairns, can you?'

'Twelve-year-old bairns,' said Mrs Flannagan, 'must hear things to repeat them.' What further remarks Mrs Flannagan would have added were cut short, for at this point she was pushed violently in the back by the door opening, and she turned angrily towards it to be confronted by Mrs Leigh-Petty, a fortified Mrs Leigh-Petty very much on her high horse.

Mrs Leigh-Petty's heightened perceptibility must have informed her that there was a row going on, and recognising Mrs Flannagan as an intruder she turned on her immediately and in her most highfalutin tone demanded, 'And what, may I ask, are you doing in my house?'

This attitude took Mrs Flannagan completely

by surprise, and before she had time to retort in like manner Mrs Leigh-Petty lifted an admonishing hand towards her and said, 'I want to hear nothing further from you. Kindly get away to your own quarter . . . Go now, without further ado.'

Fanny wanted to explode, she wanted to let out a roar at the sight of these combating birds of a feather.

'You're drunk!' Mrs Flannagan, being a staunch tee-totaller, was aghast.

'How dare you! Get out!' It looked as if Mrs Leigh-Petty was going to spring on Mrs Flannagan. And Mrs Flannagan, too, thought this, for she retreated swiftly.

Fanny watched the strange creature from up above bang the door shut, then turn to the Laveys' door which was being discreetly closed, then lastly direct her gaze on herself. And now it took all Fanny's willpower not to take her mighty arm and knock the woman on to her back, for when passing her on her way towards the stairs Mrs Leigh-Petty exclaimed with cool hauteur, 'She's not so much to blame as you are, you're the instigator of all the trouble in this house. You should be evicted.'

In dead silence that dripped with her amazement, Fanny watched Mrs Leigh-Petty mount the stairs. Then she turned slowly into her own room, and to Corny's surprise as she made her approach towards him she said not a word about the odds and sods, but puzzled him by looking right through him and muttering, 'Our Phil can't be let take on that, he can't.'

8

It was Fanny's week-end off from The Ladies. Part-timers got one week-end in four, and although she missed the chatter of Maggie and the busy busyness of her job, she was thankful for these two days, for on Friday night she had felt a bit off colour and had fainted.

She had felt as bad many times before, she told herself, and no oration made about it. Perhaps she had passed out, she couldn't remember, but there had been no need to run round like a scalded cat for the doctor as Phil had done. And she hadn't thanked him for his thoughtfulness, for now she could no longer boast that she'd never had a doctor in her life except for the bairns; and there had been times when they had turned up too late for them, when the last big push had been achieved by the help of God and Mary Prout.

All the doctor had said after examining her was that she must rest. Dear God! there'd be plenty of time to rest when she was dead. Then last night

Philip had brought her in a drop. She hadn't known where to put her face for she couldn't thank him. It was the second time lately he had done the same thing, and it put her all on edge to have to accept anything from him that wasn't her due.

Today she had struggled out to First Mass, and on her return had busied herself with the dinner. Following dinner Phil had insisted on washing up before he went out, and even then only by pushing him with her tongue had she made him go. But once he had left the house she sat down thankfully and remained sitting on and on until the evening. And not a soul had called in, and the hours had seemed to stretch into days in endless time. It was her thinking, she knew, that made them so long.

In the fading light she looked around the room. The old couch with the colourless cushion stuffed neatly into the hole where the springs had come out; the dresser, as usual, cluttered with objects. She saw that the kitchen chairs needed a good scrub and the grate an equally good black-leading. Everything wanted a clean up. Her eyes went to the mantelpiece and travelled over the six brass shoes alternating with flower vases of varying sizes and shapes and full of oddments and rubbish. She looked around at her pictures. There were thirty-five in the room, and they ranged from a

Persil advert to a huge picture of all the Popes from Peter. There the Popes stood right opposite to her, in a number of half circles, each with his name at the bottom of the picture. Fanny believed that picture to be of great value and she had been known to tell people that it was priceless; moreover, even if she should be in want of bread she wouldn't part with it. But she never enlightened her hearers that the value she was referring to was spiritual. She was wise in people and knew that anything of spiritual value that she could show them would not impress them.

The upholstery on the armchairs was lost under a layer of dirt and grease made by countless impressions of dirty hands and feet. The pair of them, meaning the chairs, she decided as she looked at them now were very nearly like herself . . . past it. She eased her seat off a familiar spring and leant her elbow on the arm of the chair and rested her head on her hand. She would be glad when the morrow came and she could get back to work. She prayed her legs would carry her that far. Yet what, she asked herself, would happen when Mary got better? Would the days be all like this one? They had been long enough and lonely enough before she got the job, but the loneliness would be of a deeper intensity once the job was finished. What you've never had you never missed was the phrase, but she'd had it, it being company, and liked it these past few weeks, and it had taken her mind off herself and her worries. When she lost her job, and should Phil go, there'd be nothing to do. No need to go out, no meals to get ready, no shirts to wash, no-one to grumble at or listen to, nobody to do anything for, except herself, and she'd just sit here waiting for Corny coming and the occasional visit of the others. She shook her tousled grey head slowly, and asked again, 'Would the days be like this one until the end?' Quiet like the grave. Even the noises in the house today and the bairns yelling from the street were different noises, muted by the dread on her . . . they were not intimate enough. She wanted the noise and bustle about her, tiring her, making her wish that she was rid of it for five minutes so that she could sit down in peace. How often over the years had she longed for just five minutes alone, the house all to herself, to be quiet in. Now she had all the quiet she wanted; perhaps years of it ahead. Dear God, no! She rose hastily from her chair. She was low the day, it was that faint she'd had. She'd make herself some tea. Yet with her hand on the kettle handle she stopped. Should she wait to see if Corny came? He might show up. He hadn't been for some days, not since the day of the odds and sods. The suspicion of a smile touched her wrinkles. She hoped the measles hadn't caught him. She should have gone across the water last week to see how things were but the truth of it was she was scared to leave the house in the evenings now. Aye, it had got as bad as that. She was scared to move away from the door after six in case Jack should show up, for she knew his heart would soften one night and he wouldn't be able to wait another minute; he'd come tearing round, and she knew exactly what would happen. There'd come a rap on the door – oh aye, he'd knock this time – and she would go all unsuspecting like and there he'd be, and the pain in her side would increase until she'd think she was going to die.

'Hallo,' he'd say; 'can I come in?'

She'd make her face blank of all expression and she'd turn from the door saying, 'It's open.'

Slowly he'd follow her into the room, taking off his trilby. Oh, aye, he'd have his trilby on just to show her how far he'd advanced since he'd got out of her clutches.

There'd be one thing certain, she'd have to sit down. But first she'd pick up the tea-pot from the hob and pour herself out a cup of tea, and all the while he'd be standing there in the middle of the room looking at her, uncertain just which way she was going to jump. Then, 'How you keeping?' he'd say.

She'd take a long drink of tea before answering, 'As you see.'

She'd watch his hands uneasily moving round his hat, pulling its good brim all out of shape, and she'd chide herself, 'Let up. Let up, or else you'll be sorry.' Then she'd say, as off-hand as she could, 'If you want a cup of tea you know where the cups are . . . you don't want me to run after you, do you?'

On this she'd see the tenseness would go out of his face, his eyes would crinkle at the corners and almost like an obedient child he'd go into the scullery and return with his own special pint mug in his hand. And that would mean he was coming back. No! no! She shook her head at this thought. Somehow she didn't want that, for that would mean everything had gone wrong for him. Oh – her head actually wobbled on her shoulders. Dear God, please understand her, for she couldn't understand herself. She had done all in her power to stop him marrying the lass and now here she was afraid of a split between them. Anyway, she'd say to him, 'Can't you sit down?' And he'd sit down with the mug of tea in his hand and a silence would fall between them, a silence that screamed to fling itself into words.

And at last he'd bring out, 'I'm sorry, Ma,' and she would be unable to answer.

Then he'd say, 'I meant to come sooner.'

Still she wouldn't be able to answer.

'It was all my fault, Ma,' he'd say. 'You always played square with me; I should have told you how things were going and it wouldn't have come so hard on you.'

Then she'd draw herself up from her chair, and going to the fire and taking the poker she'd rake vigorously, while lifting her apron to wipe away the sweat from her face. And then, perhaps, she'd turn to him and say kindly, 'What's done is done, it's no good raking over the past. Will you have something to eat?' And they'd eat together. And likely as not, they'd laugh. Oh, aye, they'd laugh.

She almost leapt from her chair when the knock came on the door, and with her hand pressed tightly against her ribs under her left breast she went slowly towards it. And when she opened it and saw Margaret standing there, she felt physically sick for a moment.

'Aren't you well, Mrs McBride?' Margaret was in the room now, leading her back to her seat.

'I'm all right, lass. I get the wind now and again. Sit down.'

'Sit down yourself. Perhaps it's cold you've got, it's such a raw day.'

'Yes. Yes, it is cold. Will you have a cup of tea?'

'Yes. No, don't get up, I'll pour it out.'

When she had poured out the tea, Margaret sat down on the other side of the hearth, and sipped at the tea slowly, not speaking. As she looked at the girl the pain in Fanny's side ebbed away and with it the shock she had felt when she had imagined her wishful thinking to have taken concrete form.

'Is there anything wrong, lass?'

'No, nothing.' Margaret's eyes dropped as she went on, 'Mother's in bed and the children are out . . . at Sunday school.'

'Philip's out an' all.'

'Yes, I know.' Margaret's eyes were still cast down.

Which meant, thought Fanny, that she wouldn't have come down if she had known he was in, for she had been evading him. He hadn't said a word about it, but his manner had spoken clearly enough. Nor had he heard from the other one, she had asked him point blank about this. The next news she would glean about Madam Sylvia would come through Mary Prout, no doubt.

Margaret caught her interest sharply by saying, 'I've got to go away for a couple of days shortly, Mrs McBride. I wondered would it be too much to ask' – she hesitated – 'would you give an eye to them?'

'I'll – I'll do what I can, lass, but you know I'm out half the day.'

'Yes, I know, but if you could just–'

'Have you got to go away?'

Not only Margaret's gaze, but her head dropped now until her chin was touching her chest, and she looked almost as young as Marian. But when she said, 'Yes, I've got to go,' she made the statement definitely, and it did not encourage further enquiries, for she rose to her feet. But Fanny, not to be put off so easily, looked up at her and asked, 'Are you goin' to see a friend or someone?'

'Yes. Yes, I'm going to see a friend.' It was a parrot-like repetition.

Fanny's gaze did not waver from Margaret's averted face as she persisted, 'Would it be a man you're goin' to see?'

Now she was looking at the girl's back, and as Margaret once again almost repeated her words, saying, 'Yes, it is a man I'm going to see, Mrs McBride,' Fanny felt a quick surge of anger against her. She liked the lass well enough, she liked her more than a good many she had seen, but there was something fishy about her, and she said so bluntly in her own fashion. 'Then if that's the case you should tell my lad, because as you well know he's got notions about you. But I may as well tell you here and now, although I've got nothing against you, lass, I'm not for him saddling himself with your family.'

Fanny's tone brought Margaret round, and although her voice was low there was a sharp note in it as she replied to the first part of Fanny's statement. 'And he had notions about that other girl, hadn't he?'

Fanny spoke kindly, as she said, 'Well, you need take no heed of what that one said. That was over and done with long afore you came on the scene. That one's a scheming piece, tryin' to palm something on to him. I know my lad, no-one better.'

But even as she said this Fanny was asking herself if she did know people, especially when they were men. Weren't men made for the precise purpose of bringing trouble to women? Legally or otherwise, it was all the same.

'Well, it makes no difference really, Mrs McBride, for there's nothing can come of it.'

There was a listlessness apparent in both Margaret's voice and body now, and Fanny, easing herself to her feet, said, 'You don't know with things like that. I happened to hear what you said to your mother the other night, lass, and what she said to you. You were quick enough in his defence that time.' She watched the colour creep over Margaret's face, then added, 'I wasn't at the door when you started, I had no intention of listenin'. It was thrown at me as it were. But you see, I'm a bit puzzled when I hear you say one thing one minute and the opposite the next, so to speak.'

Margaret walked slowly to the door, and when her hand was on the knob, Fanny said, 'Can't you tell me who it is you're goin' to see?'

Margaret did not turn around as she muttered, 'I'm sorry, Mrs McBride, but I can't.'

The door closed and Fanny was alone again and as she sat down once more she asked herself was the girl lying about her age. She might be nineteen, but she could be twenty-three or four. Marian could be hers after all and she was going to see the father. Yet in that case why should she have spoken up that night as if she wanted their Phil? As she'd said earlier on, there was something here that would need a lot of digging down to.

But the interest in the girl's affairs could not really hold her, and within a moment of being alone again she was thinking, 'My God, what a shock I got with that knock on the door. Another dose like that and it will finish me.'

After another half-hour, she asked herself should she go to Benediction, to make a break in the monotony. But she dismissed the idea almost as it was born. You never knew, he might turn up, Sunday night or no Sunday night. This was the main night for the Salvation Army, the night it banged its brains out on the drums. This might be the one night he'd had enough and come home.

9

As Fanny punched the tickets behind the glass partition and eyed each customer, she thought to herself, 'Begod! the town's out.' Four times this morning there had been a queue as far as the door. And the morrow, without a doubt, they'd be longer, it being Christmas Eve and everybody running around like scalded cats getting in their last-minute shopping.

Fanny had been put on mornings this week and she didn't like mornings. They were always much busier in the mornings, not that that mattered, but it was the getting here. And then again, this wasn't the whole of it, it was a long time from half-past one until she went to bed at night. True she had her work to do and a bit shopping, but the afternoons at home didn't seem to pass as quickly as the mornings. And her legs seemed to have got into their swing and ready for taking a walk by mid-day, whereas first thing she could hardly get her shoes on. Even so, if it hadn't been for the gnawing ache in her heart she would have said she was enjoying herself, for there was Maggie, running up and down the corridor, quipping with the regulars, exclaiming loudly at some untoward happening such as a toilet roll missing or a wet floor; there were the people passing, ever passing before her window, short ones, skinny ones, ones as big as herself, all carrying the exciting aura of Christmas around them. And, believe it or not, she'd had eight tips this morning, amounting to four shillings altogether. Now who would believe anybody would tip you in this place. It had both tickled her and pleased her.

At home, too, everything was set for Christmas. Everything, including her heart, was full of expectations. The house was all cleaned up in a very special way that the event of Christmas alone warranted. Last week she had done her top. Defying all Philip's entreaties to leave it till he got home when he would do it, she had covered what furniture couldn't be shoved into the bedroom and with the help of Sam Lavey, who held the bucket, she had stood on the table and slashed at the ceiling with whitewash. It had been almost an easy matter while the table and herself had the support of the walls, but the centre patch left by the uneven square was another matter. A nerve-racking matter, that called for such ejaculations

from Sam as 'Oh, m . . . my G . . . God, Fan, you'll
be . . . be over . . . Oh! m . . . my G . . . God, Fan,
you'll break yo . . . your neck! W . . . watch your
pins, Fan, f . . . for if you fall on them, that'll be
. . . be the f . . . finish, they'll never c . . . carry
you again.' And finally he had cried, 'F . . . for
God's s . . . sake! Fan, l . . . look w . . . what
you're up to or you'll f . . . fall on me and the
bl . . . bloody bucket!'

With her ceiling finished, Fanny knew one thing
– that was the last ceiling she'd ever do, for it had
set her all a-tremble and brought on the wind in
her side. But tomorrow was Christmas Eve and
she was all done. The cupboards were turned out,
the furniture had been scrubbed – there was no
polish left on any of it – and the range was showing
a depth of shining blackness that gladdened her
eye when she opened her door. Her cake was
made and she had two puddings in the pantry. She had a chicken ordered for Christmas
Day and a piece of sirloin; she had a pretty full
cupboard of odds and ends, which alone, in the
past, would have been enough to gladden her
heart. But now the terrifying feeling, and it was
a terrifying feeling, that perhaps, just perhaps, her
youngest son, being made of the tough stuff of
herself, might carry his stubbornness too far and
not show up was casting a dark shadow over

everything. During the past days she had said he'll come the morrow, it would be the morrow he'd walk in. Every day it was the morrow, and now the morrow was Christmas Eve.

There came a cry from Maggie declaiming another toilet roll gone. 'It's always the same at Christmas and the summer holidays, they've got their families comin' or visitors and they want to swank. They forget that the name's on every piece. The things people do . . . it's a good job the pans are screwed down.'

'Merry Christmas. Merry Christmas.'

'Merry Christmas,' said Fanny, as she picked up another sixpence, 'and thank you.' People were kind. If she went on like this, who knew, she'd likely gather a pound or more by the morrow, and together with what Maggie picked up the split wouldn't be too bad at all.

'Merry Christmas.'

When the old lady pushed the threepenny-piece at her, she replied, 'Merry Christmas,' and was about to push the coin back towards her, for, God help her, the poor soul looked as if she needed all her threepenny-bits herself, but the face was so kindly that Fanny could not hurt her, and so she said, 'Have a good time, lass.'

The smile broadened and the donor said, 'By! . . . aye, I'm gonna enjoy meself, life's short.'

Aye – Fanny nodded to herself – there was no truer saying. It was short and it slipped away unknowing, and you found yourself one day . . . old, old inside and not able to stand up to things, not able to say, 'Oh, to hell!'

She was punching the next ticket when a voice said, 'May I wish you a Merry Christmas?'

Before she looked up Fanny knew who was speaking, and her eyes were hard as she stared at this girl who had taken her son and brought anxiety on her and the constant pain under her ribs. Her common sense told her that her best policy would be to say, 'Aye, you can wish me a Merry Christmas and the same to you,' for the lass would go back and tell him, and if nothing else would bring him that would, that she had been civil to his wife. But at the moment her common sense was at a low ebb, and she retorted bitterly, 'You can wish me nothin', you have done me all the harm you can. I'll thank you not to speak to me, and you can tell me son that if he thinks I'm sitting waitin' for him he's sadly mistaken. We can all be done without . . . there's better fish in the sea than's ever been caught, tell him that. And I didn't know it until he left the house.'

Dear, dear God, what was she saying! Why didn't she shut her mouth? But the words seemed to be spurting from another individual altogether and she couldn't stop them. 'I want nothin' from him or you. He's forgotten his duty as a son besides his duty to God, and no good will come of it. Mark that.'

'What's the matter, Fan? You havin' trouble?' It was Maggie at her elbow. Then looking at the girl moving towards the cubicles, she said, 'Oh!' then bending towards Fanny, she whispered, 'Why, that's the lass that keeps asking after yer. What's up, Fan?'

With a resounding clang Fanny punched another ticket for an invisible customer and exclaimed bitterly, 'I want no-one to ask after me, Maggie. No mealy-mouthed, sanctimonious, come-and-be-saved hypocrite . . . for that's how she got him, with her mealy-mouthed . . .'

'Got who?' said Maggie enquiringly.

'Oh, it makes no odds. Listen, there's somebody callin' you.'

'Aye,' said Maggie, moving away reluctantly. 'Aye, they've never been done callin' this mornin'.'

As she punched the tickets Fanny kept her eyes on the departing clients, and when she saw the girl going slowly out, her head cast down, some part of her wanted to cry out, 'Hold your hand a minute. Come here.' The locked room in her heart wanted to burst its door and the disused voice of tenderness cry out, 'Tell him to come, and you come with him.' But she couldn't bring herself to assist the rusty hinges to swing back, so she went on punching, punching, and punching, answering, 'Merry Christmas.' Punching and punching, and all the while punching at the pain and the desire in her heart for her youngest son.

With her hat still on Fanny went quickly through her Christmas cards. There was a pile of them, but there wasn't anything to show that their Jack had remembered she was still alive. She was tired both inside and out, and added to it was a soreness now as she looked up at the mantelpiece. She had got a lot of fine cards. That's about all she ever got from her family, a lot of fine cards. What had they sent her this Christmas? Bert and Jane had sent a special 'Dearest Mother' card with a letter enclosed to say how tight things were; Frank had sent her ten shillings and Molly five shillings, and Peggy a half-crown postal order, and she with her man working in the London docks, who never had less than fourteen pounds a week to pick up; Davie's wife had sent her a pair of lisle stockings, and Owen and his wife their love. Well, they knew what they could do with that. From Don and his wife she expected nothing at all, and that she knew would be what she would get.

Don had come in yesterday and remarked on her looking tired. He had said that she should give up the job in The Ladies and she had laughed in his face, for she could hear his wife speaking. What were they coming to, with his mother working in the lavs now! He had gone on to say she should get herself out and join the Old People's Club and go for trips and suchlike. Once upon a time, he had reminded her, she had complained about never being able to get across the door, so now she should take the opportunity and go places.

Go places! She sighed . . . she had never been further than Hartlepool in her life, and that was in a brake trip before she was married. She'd never had the chance after. Years ago she had imagined herself going to London to visit Peggy but that dream had faded long ago, and now she didn't want to go anywhere apart from The Ladies. And when The Ladies job was finished, and it wouldn't be long as Mary's leg was getting better, there would be nothing to take its place. She was too old to go jaunting now, and she had no desire to join old people's clubs – she saw enough of old people. You could live too long . . . aye, you could that. God, she thought, should so arrange things that when the work He had given you was done He should take you. Aye, and give you a big bonus for having put up with some of the jobs He'd dished out. Oh, she was weary these days, she couldn't pull herself up at all.

She sighed again and looked about the room. What did she want anyway? Oh, she knew what she wanted, let her face it, she wanted just one of her bairns to need her . . . Well, didn't Phil need her?

This reply seemed to come out of the air, and she nodded her head to it. Aye, it was strange, but she had come these past few weeks to know that he needed her, and it was God's way of working, she supposed, to make the one she liked least of all her brood treat her the best. In some ways it was a slightly humiliating experience. As if the Lord wanted to humble her by showing her she had loved the specked and not the good fruit of her body.

Phil was worried over the lass upstairs and was going round like a bewildered hare. Of late he seemed to have lost his lordly air. When she had told him that Sunday night that Margaret was going away he had asked, 'Do you know where?' and she had said bluntly, 'No, but I do know she's goin' to see some man or other. I think it only right you should know it, for you don't want to be led up the garden a second time.'

He had looked pretty sick on this, and although she had felt sorry for him, she was ashamed inside herself that the whole business, vital as it might be to him, was really of little concern to her. At times it would seem that she had borne only one child, for if every one of her brood had turned up in the kitchen this very minute, and Jack not among them, the loneliness in her heart would not have eased. She shivered, took off her outdoor things, then made herself some tea, and after drinking it she drew a chair up near to the fire and sat staring into it.

It was a long while later when the knockers banging in the street aroused her. It was the extra post. She didn't tell herself what she hoped the post would bring, but she rose and pushed in the latest cards here and there on the mantelpiece, then straightening her apron she went to her door and waited. There was the sound of a motor van drawing up outside, and a moment later a lanky youth came into the hall. He smiled broadly at her, saying, 'McBride, Quigley and Lavey.'

'I'm McBride,' said Fanny. 'The Laveys are over there and the Quigleys upstairs.'

'Well, there's a parcel for the Laveys.' He looked at the parcel. 'That's all for them. And there's four cards for the Quigleys.'

'And mine?' asked Fanny quietly.

'Oh, there's none for you.'

'But I thought you said . . .'

'Aye, the other fellow's bringing it off the van.'

As the boy dived up the stairs the door was pushed open again and another plain-clothes postman came in carrying a hamper.

'McBride?'

Fanny could only nod.

'Well, here you are, mother. I'll take it in for you.'

'Is it mine? You're sure?'

'Yes' – he looked at the label – 'if you're Mrs Fanny McBride and this is Mulhattan's Hall . . . Is it?'

'Aye, it is.'

'Well, then, this is yours, and I'll just dump it inside.'

He stood the hamper on the table, saying, 'That should see you over.' Then added, 'A happy Christmas to you.'

Fanny dragged her eyes from the hamper to the man going out the door. 'A happy Christmas . . . just a minute!' She scurried to the mantelpiece for her purse and opening it she hesitated between sixpence and a shilling, then extracting the shilling from it, she said, 'Here.'

'Ta . . . oh, thanks, mother.' The man stood looking at her for a second, during which he seemed to take her and the whole room in. Then he went out, banging the door so hard that the building shook.

She went slowly to the table, her eyes fixed on the hamper, but she didn't open it; instead she stood surveying it. It was about two feet high and eighteen inches across. There were two labels on it, and she searched for the postmark. Aye, there it was, Jarrow. Yet why, she asked herself was she troubling to see where it was from . . . she knew where it was from and who had sent it, didn't she?

Her heart was bounding and thumping, and her breathing became so difficult that she had to press her hand to her side. He hadn't forgotten her after all, but if he had only brought it himself, or just come himself . . . oh, if he had only come himself. Oh, that pride. Well, this was to break the ice, she knew his way . . . What a Christmas! A hamper, a real Christmas hamper.

Years ago when they were all young she had often said, 'You know what I would like, I'd like the postie to stumble in that door carrying the biggest Christmas hamper in the world.'

None of them had thought to buy her a hamper, even a little one, until now. Oh, Jack. Only Jack would have thought of something she had said years ago. Her eyes were hot and burning and her body was trembling. She sat down and as her hand caressed the wicker-work the door burst open and Corny came in.

'Hallo, Gran.'

'Hallo, lad.' She turned a beaming face to him. 'Look at what's just come. Come and see what the postie's brought.'

'Coo! Gran. A hamper!' He put his arms about it and tried to lift it from the table. 'Coo! it's heavy. Who's it from?'

'Guess.'

'Me Uncle Frank?'

'No.' Her brows drew down. 'Not your Uncle Frank.'

'Go on, open it, Gran.'

'Aye, I will. Bring me the gully so's I can cut the seal an' the cord.'

After she had cut the seal Fanny began to roll the cord neatly into a ball, her eyes on the hamper the while, until Corny's patience giving out, he cried, 'Aw! never mind the string, Gran, let's see what's in it. Open it. Aw! go on, Gran, let's see in it.'

As if she expected the hamper to hold china, Fanny removed the top and then the packing, and there, revealed to her own and Corny's eyes, was the first layer made up of a small ham, two decorated boxes and a fancy tin.

'God in Heaven!' Even as she voiced her wonder her hand went to the envelope pushed between the boxes, and with trembling fingers she opened it. After a moment she looked down at Corny, and her face was such a mixture of expressions as to be comical. But Corny did not laugh at her for he saw that his grannie was upset.

'It's a grand hamper,' he said in a small voice. 'Who sent it to you, Gran?'

He watched her draw in her breath; then slowly dragging her eyes back to the hamper again, she said, 'Phil.'

'Uncle Phil?'

'Aye, Uncle Phil,' she repeated, looking at the paper again. She hadn't read what was written on the paper, she had looked first at the bottom just to see Jack's name there, which would mean that everything was all right between them in spite of the Hallelujah. But it was Phil who had thought of her and her longing for a hamper, not Jack . . . Phil, with his desire to be different, with his flair for words, with his mania for clean changes, with his pet hobby that had gone on, seemingly to her, since he was born, the reforming of herself. Yet it was he who had thought of her and bought her what she liked most – food. He was as miserable as sin because of the lass upstairs but he could think of her like this. He had never bought her anything to equal this before. It was as if he knew just how badly she was feeling about Jack and was trying in some measure to make up for his brother's neglect. Yet he never guessed the extent of her feelings for his brother, she was sure of that – she had, she felt, treated them all alike, on top.

'Fancy me Uncle Phil sending you that. Eeh! it must have cost a lot. And I've brought you a Christmas box an' all, Gran.'

'Have you now?' She forced a smile to her face.

'Aye, but you haven't got to open it till Christmas mornin'.'

'No. No, I won't. Of course I won't.'

'Guess what it is?'

'A five-pound note.'

'Why no, Gran!' He turned his head to the side, but did not take his eyes from her.

Fanny looked at the small parcel, about six inches in length, and gave another impossible guess. 'A pair of slippers?'

'Coo!' he laughed, 'look at the size of your feet, Gran . . . There are two things in it . . . three of one,' was how he described the handkerchiefs, 'and . . . oh' – he considered the number of hairpins there would be in a packet – 'about thirty of the other.'

'What! all that? By! I'll never guess in a month of Sundays.'

'I've bought them with me own money, mind, Gran. Nobody helped me.'

'Did you, lad?' Fanny looked at him tenderly. 'That was kind of you. And now,' she added, 'I suppose you're broke and you've come on the cadge?'

'I haven't, Gran . . . no, I haven't, I've one and ten left, look.'

Fanny nodded as she looked down at the palm full of coppers; then picking up the ham she turned away and made for the scullery. The flat look had returned to her face, and Corny, after staring at her back for a moment, furtively slid the note from the table and with one eye on the scullery door he hastily read it:

Dear Mother,

How often have I heard you say you wanted a hamper! It gives me great pleasure to be able to grant your desire. I hope you find it to your liking.

PHILIP.

His Uncle Phil always talked like that . . . proper. He had always been a bit scared of his Uncle Phil, but his da said his Uncle Phil was better'n any of 'em. That was after his Uncle Phil had come over the water to their house the other day and asked his ma to go and see his Uncle Jack and ask him to go and see his grannie. His Uncle Phil said he wouldn't go hissel' cos they had never hit it off and Jack would be more likely to stay away if he went and asked him. His ma said she couldn't go cos she was bad. She wasn't bad properly, Corny knew, but she was goin' to have triplets. That's what his da said. But she was goin' to have a baby anyway, so she couldn't come across the water. But she had written a letter to his Uncle Jack, and his Uncle Jack would have got the letter this morning, so he might be here at any minute now.

He looked towards the door as if it would open under his desire and show his uncle standing there. He knew his grannie had thought the hamper was from his Uncle Jack, and she was upset because it wasn't. But anyway, his Uncle Jack would come, he was bound to come, for his ma said she had given it to him hot and heavy in the letter. He had liked his Uncle Jack; he was always good for a lark and a bit carry on. His Uncle Jack used to tease his gran and call her names and laugh at her, and she used to go for him, like she did for himself in fun. Perhaps when his Uncle Jack came in he'd have a bit lark. He wished he would come in cos he was getting that funny feeling in his chest.

When his grannie was upset it disturbed him in a way he did not like and could not understand. He was made to feel sorry inside, and his mischievous and laughter-loving nature jibbed at this lowering feeling. And so he was but presenting a prelude to what he hoped would take place when he said off-handedly to Fanny as she returned from the kitchen, 'I saw me Uncle Jack the day, Gran.'

Fanny's hands, raised to dip into the hamper, became still.

'Where?' she asked.

'Ormond Street.' You were bound, sometime or other, to see everybody in Ormond Street.

'Did he speak?'

'Aye.'

'What did he say?'

'He said, "Where you goin'?" an' I said, "To me grannie's."'

'Aye, go on.'

'Well, he said, "I'll be seein' you soon."' Corny paused.

'Which end of the street was he at?'

'The top end.'

'He wasn't goin' to the ferry?'

'No, Gran.' Corny was studying intently a large jar of lump ginger in syrup.

'Was he alone?'

'Aye, Gran.'

'What was he doing? . . . Pay attention . . . look at me.'

He had started something. Why had he said he'd seen his uncle? Didn't he know what his gran was like when she once got asking questions?

'He was looking in a shop, Gran.'

'Whose shop? . . . Which shop?'

Corny's face was averted again and his eyes strayed to Fanny's feet, which gave him a clue and he muttered, 'A shoe shop, Gran.'

A shoe shop. He was on his own . . . he was in the town and was looking in a shoe shop. What would he be looking in a shoe shop for when he never bought a stitch of his own, and wouldn't go into a shop if you paid him? There was only one explanation, he couldn't come to her without some present; he was likely looking for some slippers for her. Hadn't he said to Corny he'd be seeing him soon? That meant he was coming. It couldn't mean anything else could it? There was nothing else it could add up to. He was on his way, likely at this very minute.

'Here,' she cried, her voice crisp and her face alight, 'lets get this thing emptied and the stuff put away . . . come on now.' And she drew one thing after another out of the hamper; a small cheese, a box of chocolates, a bottle of port.

'Coo! Gran, what's in this glass thing?'

'Walnuts,' said Fanny, 'pickled. Push them in the cupboard.'

'Why not stick them all on the sideboard, Gran, then everybody can see them?'

'Put them in the cupboard.'

When Jack came into the room, she did not want him to be confronted by a galaxy of stuff that Phil had bought for her. That would put them off on the wrong foot for a start, for he'd never had any time for Phil. Phil, he had considered, had always been a bit of an upstart. Yet of the two who had acted the upstart lately? . . . Here! here! she wasn't going to think like that and him likely to be in any second.

'There,' she said, 'now put that hamper in the scullery, it'll do for stickin' wood in.'

Corny took the hamper to the scullery and set it soberly on top of the wash-boiler, after which he stood contemplating the sink while he gnawed at his thumb as if he intended to relieve his hand of the member. His Uncle Jack would come. His mother had written to him, hadn't she, and told him what he must do, so he would come.

But as he stood gnawing, an uneasiness rose in him which made him reluctant to re-enter the kitchen until drawn there by Fanny's voice bellowing, 'What you up to in there? Come out of that pantry.'

'I wasn't in the pantry, Gran.' Corny came into the kitchen. 'Gran, I'm goin' to see if Tony's comin' out.'

'You can save yourself a trail, he's out. You can help me get the tea and get things ready. And after your Uncle Jack's been in a minute or so, you can go out to play, you understand?'

'Aye, Gran.'

'By the way,' said Fanny, 'I'd forgotten to ask you, where's Holy Joe the night? Your Uncle Jack'd laugh at Holy Joe.'

'Me ma wouldn't let me bring him; he's tied up. He got in the hen cree and scared the life out of them. A hen dropped its egg and broke its leg, and me ma carried on. We're having it for Christmas.'

A great surge of happiness and humour was flooding up in Fanny, and she cried, 'Havin' Holy Joe for Christmas?'

'No, Gran, the hen,' said Corny solemnly. 'Me ma says she'll have him put down if I don't get a proper lead and collar . . . Joe, I mean.'

Corny was trying hard not to give his grannie any further material for laughter, for he was depressed beyond understanding by her gaiety.

'Well, are you goin' to get one?'

At the sight of her grandson hanging his head, she added, 'You've only got one and tenpence, haven't you?' She let out a laugh as she went to the mantelpiece, and taking a whole half-crown from her purse she handed it to him, saying, 'There, stick that to your one and tenpence and go and get him a proper lead.'

Corny's face slid into a smile. 'Oh, thanks, Gran.' Then dashing to the door in relief, he called, 'I'll be back, Gran.'

Fanny looked at the gaping door, and as the wind whistled round her ankles she did not cry out in protest, but went towards it laughing a laugh such as she hadn't laughed for many a day.

It was now four o'clock, the light was on, the table was set, and the fire was blazing merrily, and Fanny sat in one armchair, her knitting on her knee and her back to the door. This was a defensive position which would allow her time to control her feelings when he walked in. Corny now sat on the edge of the other chair, and so restless were his movements that Fanny said, 'For God's sake! sit still. It's as if you were on a griddle.'

'It's the springs, Gran, they're sticking in me.' This was only part of the truth.

When the clock had ticked slowly on to half-past four and there had been no knock on the door, of one kind or another, Fanny put down her knitting and looking straight at her grandson, demanded, 'You sure you saw him?'

Not even the fear of eternal damnation could have made Corny speak the truth in this moment . . . a more adult and braver soul than Corny wouldn't have dared to crush the hope in Fanny's eyes.

'Aye, Gran.'

'Which shop?'

'I told you, a shoe shop.'

'But which one?'

Corny said swiftly, 'Smedleys.'

Smedleys, that was near this end. He had never been so near since he had left this house, she was sure of that, and he couldn't come so near to her and not come all the way.

'What time was it when you saw him?'

'I told you, Gran, just afore I came in . . . Gran' – into Corny's mind had sprung an idea that would effect his escape and perhaps temporarily placate his grannie – 'will I go and look in Smedleys and the other shops around and see if I can see him? He's . . . he's likely got stuck somewhere cos the shops are packed.'

Fanny hesitated. She couldn't see what good it would do, for he could be anywhere by now, yet if only the lad could confirm that he was still shopping it would take away the fear that was creeping through her veins again. 'All right,' she said, 'get yersel' away and don't dawdle. Go on now.'

Corny went. Like an arrow he shot out of the door, and Fanny, taking a stern pull at herself, took up her knitting again. The minutes passed sounding loud and clear as the clock ticked them off. When she had counted fifteen Fanny's heart missed a beat as she heard the front door open and close, but it settled painfully back again as she recognised the footsteps as those of Margaret. So the lass had got back then? She heard her mount the steps rather slowly for her, then within another minute her footsteps came racing down again, and she had her call of 'Come in' ready as the knock came on the door, but it was an impatient invitation for she didn't want to be bothered with anybody at all at this minute. Yet on the sight of the girl she was forced to be concerned. 'What's the matter now, lass?' she asked.

'Where are they, Mrs McBride? Has anything happened?'

'No, lass, not to my knowledge. What's the matter with you? Sit down.'

'No, no thanks, I've just got back. There's nobody in. But there's . . .' She stopped and rubbed her hand across her eyes, then went on, 'Do you know where they are?'

'Your mother and Marian went out just as I was coming in. She seemed all right . . . quite all right, normal like, and Tony I saw in the town as I was getting off the bus.' Fanny pulled herself to her feet as Margaret leant against the table. 'What is it, lass? What you frightened of?'

Margaret was clutching the front of her suit, holding it as if she wanted to tear it from her body. 'Oh, Mrs McBride, I think I am going mad.'

'Now calm down, we want none of that talk.' For the moment Fanny's mind was lifted from her waiting. 'Look, sit down. Have you had a cup of tea, or anything to eat the day?'

'I – I don't want anything. I'll have to go out and find her. She promised me she wouldn't leave the house, she swore she wouldn't . . . Mrs McBride.' Margaret put her hand across her eyes.

'What is it, lass? Come, sit yersel' down, you're as white as a ghost. Look . . . have a little drop of something . . .'

'No, no, I don't want anything.' Suddenly Margaret leant forward and clutched at Fanny, and with her eyes staring out of her head, she whimpered, 'I know I'm going mad, I know I am. There's something going round in my head all the time.'

'Now, now,' said Fanny sternly, 'that's enough of that. Look, I'm goin' to give you a wee drop of something, it'll still your nerves for you.' Fanny went to the cupboard, and taking out a half-bottle of whisky she poured a generous measure into a cup, then taking it to Margaret she ordered, 'Drink that up, and don't leave a drop.'

With a number of gulps and coughs Margaret finished the whisky and Fanny, as she took the cup from the girl's trembling hand, exclaimed, 'There now, and don't let me hear any more of that talk.'

'But, Mrs McBride, you don't know, you don't know where I've been.'

'No, I don't unless you choose to tell me, lass.'

'I've been to a prison to visit my father.'

Fanny stopped with her hand on the table and slowly turned to the girl, and Margaret went on, 'He's in for life, he murdered a man.'

Coming back to the girl, Fanny lowered herself into her chair and she opened and closed her mouth twice before she brought out in awe-stricken tones, 'In the name of God, lass!' Then after she had stared at Margaret in amazement for some moments more she added, 'Now I can understand . . . it's driven your mother . . .'

'She's not my mother!' The denial was emphatic.

'She's not . . . not your mother?'

'No, my mother's dead.'

Fanny blinked and wetted her lips. 'Well . . . well, who is she then?'

Margaret's eyes dropped to her twisting hands. 'It's a long story, but if I don't tell you now I know I'll go off my head, I know I will.'

Fanny did not contradict her this time, but she said softly, 'Clear your mind, lass, and tell me what you want to, and you'll feel better.'

Margaret's head began to wobble on her shoulders as if she wanted to throw it off, and then she muttered, 'I should be out looking for her instead of sitting here.'

'You're not going out of this room,' said Fanny, 'until you feel better, and you won't feel better until you've got someone to share what's on your mind, so go on. The quicker you get it off, the quicker you're eased.'

But even as she said this a section of her mind was in revolt, for if he walked in now she wouldn't be able to give him her attention, at least not as she had planned. Wasn't it just like the thing? Damn it all!

Margaret was now pressing her hands between her knees and rocking herself, and Fanny said again, 'Go on, lass.'

'Well, you see, my father was sea-going, and my uncle, his younger brother, lived with us . . . my . . . my mother and him.' She stopped and swallowed and Fanny waited silently.

Margaret lifted her eyes now, and staring unblinking at Fanny she spoke rapidly. 'My father didn't know – it had been going on for years – and when he found out he didn't do anything . . .

not right away. If – if he had it would have made things easier for him later, but he pretended to go back to sea. And then he' – she closed her eyes as she said – 'did it, and he got away and someone else nearly got the blame.'

Her son for the moment entirely forgotten, Fanny, pulling herself to the edge of the chair, put out her hands and gripped those of Margaret. 'Oh, lass, why didn't you unburden yersel' afore this? God help you. Yet it's no fault of yours, you've got nothing to be ashamed of. But tell me. If that one's' – she lifted her head to the ceiling – 'if she's not your mother, who is she?'

The fingers moved within Fanny's hands, clutching at them. 'She's no relation at all. She had a room in a house opposite where we lived. She was at the trial and . . . and when nearly everybody was down on my mother she was kind to her. My mother was about . . . about to have Marian, and we had to move away from the neighbourhood. She came with us. My mother died when Marian was born and there was no-one who wanted us, and if she hadn't looked after us we would have been separated and put in homes. I was terrified of being separated from Tony, he had always seemed to belong to me more than to my mother, for I'd had to see to him from a baby. I left school and went straight to work. I didn't earn much and sometimes things were awful. There were times when there wasn't enough to eat; then there'd be times when the house would be packed with food. This was when she got, what she told us, was her quarterly allowance. She never had any allowance, she used to . . . to shoplift. I was seventeen when I found out the truth. Since then life has been a series of nightmares. You see, Mrs McBride, we had grown fond of her and she adored Marian. She has an obsession about Marian, she thinks that she's her own child. We were forever moving. We left the Midlands and came back to Newcastle where she had once lived, and then we moved to Hebburn. It was there that I met Doctor Gruber, who had known her when she was young and he told me all about her.'

There came a rattling, as of a door out in the hall, and she paused and listened. And Fanny, too, listened, her mind jumping to her own concerns again. Then she said, somewhat dully, 'It's nobody, lass, it's only the wind. And anyway, they don't know you're here. If they come in they'll go straight upstairs. Go on.'

'The doctor told me her father had been a wealthy man and had spoilt her. Then he married his housekeeper who had been in his service only a short time and she never forgave him. They had a dreadful quarrel and she attempted to kill herself.

Then she left home. She was then in her late forties and had never been trained to anything, but she had travelled and could speak several languages, so she went as governess to families, but never stayed more than a few months at each, for she couldn't stand being under anyone. Then she took to drugs and shoplifting and she's been in prison for it. It is that – that awful fear that she'll be caught that haunts me. She's been good to us, keeping us together. She liked playing mother, for she insisted we call her mother. For a time she gave up the drugs and the stealing, then at the beginning of this year she started again and has got steadily worse. I never know a moment's rest if she goes out. She promises me she won't, but if she can get money she can't stay in. You know . . . Oh, Mrs·McBride, the thought of her being in prison makes me ill. When I see my father . . .'

She stopped and covered her eyes with her hand and Fanny said softly, 'Lass, you should have told me all this afore now. It's too much to carry alone. No wonder your head's in a whirl. But look now' – she patted the hand still clutching at hers – 'you're not alone any more, for there's my lad. Aye, now don't draw away, he thinks the world of you, and there's nothin' against him, that lass was only trying to trap him. You can take my word for that. I happened to find out weeks ago that she was carrying on with her boss, so don't hold anything against him. And mind, although I say it meself, you'd go further and fare worse for he's a good fellow.'

Margaret looked past Fanny to the far corner of the room. 'Who am I to pick and choose? Anyway, he wouldn't want anything to do with me if he knew.'

'Nonsense!' said Fanny brusquely. 'There's one thing I can do, I can speak for me own flesh and blood and I know, if anything, it would draw him even more to you.'

Margaret shook her head violently. 'That only makes it worse.' She now looked up into Fanny's eyes. 'You see . . . you see it's the fact that . . . that I might marry that has set her back this last year. There was a man at the factory. He – he called and asked to see me, and that was the beginning of her starting again. You see I can't part her from Marian, and I can't leave Marian with her. Tony and Marian are my responsibility and if someone . . . well, would have the heart to take us all, what would become of her? That's what the trouble is, that's what's worried her and set her off again.'

'Lass, she should be in a home.'

'Oh, I know that, Mrs McBride, and she knows it, but to mention it drives her mad. Doctor

285

Gruber has tried to persuade her, but she won't hear of it. What am I to do?'

Fanny considered for a moment, then looking at Margaret with tenderness, said, 'Well, lass, I admit it's a problem, but take heart, there's a solution to everything. And you know what mine would be in your case?'

What Fanny's solution was she had no time to voice, but the sound of the outer door opening and a well-recognised cough gave a clue to it and she exclaimed, 'Here's Phil now.'

Her words brought Margaret swiftly to her feet.

'Now, lass, hold your hand a minute.'

'I must go, I can't see him now. I'll go out the back way.'

'Wait just a minute.'

'No! no!' She was already at the scullery door. 'I can't, not now. I'll come back.'

As the back door closed on her Philip came in, and Fanny saw his glance sweep the room and a look of disappointment come over his face. Then pulling off his coat he asked offhandedly, 'Post been yet?'

She made herself face him as she said, softly, 'Aye, lad, it's come. And – thanks. It was the biggest surprise of me life.' She did not add 'and disappointment', and as she watched his colour mount she felt forced to speak the truth. 'You're the only one, lad, who's ever done a thing like that.'

The pleasure in his eyes hurt her somehow, and she felt strangely humbled when he said, 'I started too late. I should have done it years ago . . . I always wanted to.'

Aye, she thought, and you would have an' all, there's no doubt, but your nose was put out by the other one. She sighed again, then said with forced airiness, 'Well, I've got a Christmas box for you, I think it's the one you would want most.'

His eyebrows went up, and he said, 'Yes?'

'Sit down,' she said, 'although it won't take long in the tellin'.'

In a bewildered fashion he sat in the chair that Margaret had just vacated, and without taking his eyes off his mother he waited and watched while she poured out a cup of tea and handed it to him before seating herself.

'It's about the lass.'

'You know where she's been?'

'Aye, I told you she was goin' to see a man, didn't I?'

He did not speak or make any indication, and she went on. 'It's her father, he's doin' time for murder.'

Philip was on his feet looking down at her in much the same way as she herself had looked at the girl a few minutes earlier. 'You can't mean it!'

'I can and do. And that one isn't her mother, she's no relation. She's a thief and a drug-taker, and she's been along the line an' all. But she was kind to them when the father was in trouble and now, to cut a long story short, she's terrified Margaret'll find some man and that'll put paid to her hold on the lot of them. And there you have it in a nutshell . . . What you going to do?'

She watched him pace the mat for a moment, then walk to the window and stand with his back to her, and as she looked at him a dread came on her that equalled any pain she had felt over Jack, and she thought, 'God in Heaven! don't let this make him back out, one of me own blood.'

He turned round. 'It's a wonder she hasn't gone stark, staring mad.'

A long, steady breath escaped Fanny as she said, 'She's on the point of it, and if she doesn't have some help she'll at least have a breakdown that'll be equal to any madness.'

'Where is she?'

'Well, she slipped out of the back door when she heard you come in. She may be upstairs, or she may be gone to look for her, for she's out on the rampage again.'

She offered no further word of advice, and he turned abruptly and went out of the room, and when she heard his feet taking the stairs two at a time her flesh fell into heavy folds that, but for the pain in her side, would have spelt contentment. He'd make the lass see sense, he had a way with him when he wanted anything, and he liked the bairns. But what would happen to the other one? Ah, well, that remained to be seen.

After a few moments when she did not hear Philip's step coming down the stairs again she sighed and thought, 'Well, that should settle that,' and like a wash that had been finished or a floor that had been scrubbed she put it out of her mind as something that needed no more thought, and her whole attention returned to her own business, and to the pain-filled channels of expectation. Corny had not found him, he had been gone long enough to search the town.

She stood with her thick forearm on the edge of the mantelpiece and stared down into the fire until the red leaping flames brought a red leaping anger into her heart, and its intensity promised to consume her. And as her head came up preparatory to her hand striking out blindly to swipe the mantelpiece clear of cards her eye was caught by a tinsel-bespangled picture of the Nativity, and her anger melted as, joining her hands together before it, she began to pray, 'Holy Mary, Mother of God, mother of a son . . .'

10

It was about one o'clock on Christmas Eve and there was a lull in The Ladies when Maggie, supping noisily at a cup of cocoa into which she had slyly poured a drop of rum, said to Fanny, 'You know somethin', this is the happiest Christmas I've ever known.'

'Well, I'm glad of that,' said Fanny, looking down on the little woman.

'Oh, I wish you were stayin', Fan . . . for good, I mean. Mary Prout's all right, but she's not like you.' Maggie dug Fanny in the hip, and Fanny said, 'Give over now or I'll have you up for assault and battery.'

This set Maggie off into a gurgle of laughter, and she was in the act of taking another gulp of her cocoa when she nearly choked herself on the sight of Mrs Proctor coming through the door. Pushing the mug on to a shelf and under cover of an old apron, she hurried out of the little cubicle to meet her boss, but Mrs Proctor apparently had not come to see her, for there she was, standing opposite Fanny at the glass partition, her head lowered to the aperture.

'You're not wantin' a ticket?' Fanny was laughing at the solemn face of Mrs Proctor, and Mrs Proctor, taking her seriously, said hastily, 'No. No, thank you.'

'I thought you wouldn't be. If you can't go free I wonder who can.'

'I'm in a bit of a fix, Mrs McBride.'

'Oh, aye?' Fanny's eyes widened.

'I've just had a note from Mrs Craig saying that she won't be able to come, and I've no-one to fill her place, and I can't leave Maggie here on her own.' She cast a swift glance towards where Maggie was standing, her ears wide. 'Do you think you could stay on, Mrs McBride?'

Fanny's chin dropped and her eyes lowered to the counter. It was Christmas Eve and she had a lot to do, but something more than that, she wanted to get home, the reason being the ever-present one. What if he came and she wasn't in?

'I'll see that you get time and a half.'

'Oh, I'm not worrying about that.'

'And I'll have some dinner sent to you from the central kitchen.'

'You're very kind,' said Fanny. What could she do but stay? 'I'll have to send a note to me son,' she said. 'He'll be wondering what's happened to me if I don't turn up.'

'Yes, yes, of course,' said Mrs Proctor. 'I'll see that he gets it. I'm going that way, I'll drop it in myself. It's very good of you, and I won't forget you.'

Fanny took a scrap of paper and wrote a note to Philip, telling him briefly why she would not be home; then she handed it to Mrs Proctor, who said, 'Thank you very much, Mrs McBride,' in a tone which made Fanny comment to herself that certain folks could be very civil when they were getting what they wanted.

When the door had closed on Mrs Proctor, Maggie said, 'Aye, thank you very much, and I won't forget you. And that's all you'll ever get out of her. Not even a tanner.' Then going and joining Fanny in the cubicle and uncovering her now cold cocoa, she added, 'What did I tell you, Fan? I told you I saw that madam coming out of the station last night sozzled. I knew it was her, although she dodged me. She's got a hangover, that's what's the matter with her. Wait till I see her, she won't put on any airs with me again . . . But Fan – ' She dug Fanny again in her fleshy hip, then ended, 'Eeh! but I'm glad you're stayin' on, 'specially the day, it makes it more Christmasy somehow.'

'Oh, aye,' said Fanny briefly, while forcing a smile to her face. Wouldn't it be just like fate if he landed in this afternoon, probably straight after work, and she not in.

The door opened, admitting a customer, and she banged on the puncher thinking, 'Why the devil didn't I tell her to punch the blasted tickets herself? Convenience, that's all she's makin' of me . . . convenience.'

The afternoon was a long one, even with business pretty brisk and Maggie's chatter and laughter at its height. The door opened and banged with incessant regularity, for it was a biting day and people seemed to be glad to get out of the snow-filled wind for a few minutes. Fanny had seen so many faces that by now they were all beginning to run into one, until, the door bursting open yet once again, Mrs Leigh-Petty came in.

Slowly Fanny slipped from her seat to her feet and stared at the woman, for she looked as if she had seen a ghost, and not one but a company of them. She came and stood with her face close to the glass and attempted to say something. Then after glancing furtively back towards the door she turned away into the corridor, and when a few seconds later she came stumbling into the office Fanny exclaimed, 'What's up with you, woman?'

'Look after them for me, will you?' The shivering creature thrust into Fanny's hands a hold-all and a leather bag. 'I'm very tired . . . I'm not well. Will you – will you take them home for me?'

'Take them home?' Fanny dropped the bags on the floor as if they were red-hot, and said, 'Now look here, woman, what you up to? What's in these bags?'

'Nothing, nothing. I've just been doing some shopping. Keep them there for me, will you, please? Oh, please.' She leant towards Fanny, touching her as she made this entreaty. Then before Fanny could make any retort whatsoever she had dived out of the office and into one of the cubicles.

Fanny stood staring down at the bags until the sound of the door opening again drew her attention, and when she saw the blue uniform of a policewoman she suppressed a muttered, 'My God!' and looked her straight in the face over the distance, while dribbling the bags under the counter with her feet. Then casually gathering up a newspaper from a shelf she shook it out and threw it down beside the bags before going to the window.

'Good afternoon.'

'Good afternoon.' Fanny hawked in her throat,

then blew her nose loudly. 'You come to pick me up?' She forced a smile to her face.

'Now I shouldn't be surprised at that,' laughed the policewoman. 'I'm sure it isn't all flesh you've got under that apron.'

Fanny had come to know this lass over the weeks she had been in The Ladies, and she replied jocosely now, 'I have a witness, I'll have you up on that. What do you say, Maggie?'

Maggie came out of the corridor asking, 'What's that you say, Fan?' then seeing the young woman she exclaimed, 'Oh, hallo, who you after?'

'Oh, just a light-fingered lady. Had anybody in here with too much to carry?'

Maggie shook her head and looked at Fanny, and Fanny said, 'Drunk, you mean?'

'No, not drunk, light-fingered I said.'

'Are you on somebody's trail?' said Fanny.

'Yes, close enough, she came this way.'

'Do you know her?'

'Yes, we know her. She's tried to clear most of the shops in the main street today.'

Fanny gulped and forced a laugh as she said, 'Good luck to her. I wish she had taken me along with her.'

'You would have had a free Christmas dinner then at any rate.'

'Aye,' laughed Maggie, 'and free beer and a

party on Christmas Day, that's what they give prisoners, Fan.' Then looking up at the police-woman, she added, 'There's been nobody in here, only . . .'

'Only herself,' put in Fanny, hastily, 'and she's the biggest lifter from here to the Swing Bridge, she's even tried to lift me.'

This remark sent Maggie into a fit of laughter.

Then as Fanny watched the policewoman move away to take in the complete view of the cubicles she went hastily out to join her. There were only three doors closed now and when after a few moments and the thundering clang of the cisterns there remained only one door still shut, Fanny, in spite of her knowledge of . . . the creature, felt a surge of pity for her. God in heaven, it was awful! Christmas Eve and all. But surprise brought her head back and her eyes stretching when, the door opening, a fat middle-aged woman emerged, who certainly wasn't Mrs Leigh-Petty.

The policewoman nodded decisively at Fanny, then to Maggie, and turning on her heels she went out, and Fanny as quickly made her way to the yard.

The yard in which there was no exit was small and the light from the corridor flooded it, but peer as she would, Fanny could see neither hilt nor hair of Mrs Leigh-Petty. Then her astonished gaze took in a stack of boxes in the corner. In the name of God, the woman had climbed the wall! But how had she managed to get down the other side? It was a good eight feet drop if an inch. The wall formed part of an alley-way, separating The Ladies from a builder's yard. The alley was unlit, and it was unlikely that anyone would have seen her drop into it. She could be lying on the other side with broken bones for all anyone knew.

Fanny returned to the corridor, where Maggie demanded, 'What's up, Fan? Somebody in the yard?'

'No, who could be there? I just wanted a breath of air.'

'Well, if you breathe much of the air the night it'll cut your throat, and then you won't be able to breathe at all, or worst still, all your drops of tiddly'll run out.' Once more Maggie went into a gale of riotous laughter, proving that the hot rum was still carrying on its exhilarating work in her stomach. But she cut off her merriment abruptly as a knock came on one of the opaque windows high up in the wall at the top of the corridor, and she exclaimed angrily now, 'There's them at it again, they'll break the glass. I bet it's them lads trying to see in, the dirty beggars.'

Taking no heed of the knocking Fanny returned to the cubicle where her eyes were drawn to the bags beneath the newspaper. What in the name of God was she going to do with them?

Before any kind of an answer came to her, her eyes were lifted upwards. The lads had evidently come round to this other side of the building, for now just above her there came another sharp rapping on the window, and the next moment she thought she was either going daft or the drop she'd had earlier on was having a delayed action for she distinctly heard a voice come hissing through the pane calling, 'Mother! Mother!'

'It is them lads again,' said Maggie coming in. 'I wish I'd told the polis on 'em.'

'The lads?' repeated Fanny bemusingly. 'Aye, yes, it's the lads.' For a moment she had imagined she heard their Philip's voice. There must be something wrong with her, it was that damned woman and her capers, it couldn't be the rum.

When the rapping came on the window again, both Fanny and Maggie turned and looked upwards in a sober fashion. The knocking was a too-ordered knocking to be the pranks of lads, and Fanny was thinking, It can't be her, she wouldn't have the nerve to come in here again, when she almost rose from the floor as she heard a voice crying angrily, 'Take your hands off me, will you, I only want . . .'

'I know what you want, and I know what

you're goin' to get!' It was the policewoman's voice, and it made the situation so clear to Fanny that she was out of the cubicle, along the corridor and in the street almost, she felt, before she had drawn another breath. And when in the lamplight she saw the blazing, but startled face of Philip glaring at the policewoman, and she with her strong hands on him, some part of her wondered why she didn't laugh, why with this wonderful and unique situation she didn't let out a great roar. A few weeks ago this would have been her instant reaction. That Phil had been pinched for trying to peep into The Ladies would have tickled her to death. Anything would have tickled her that would have taken down her gentlemanly son. But now she found herself saying anxiously, 'What is it, Phil?'

'You know this man, Mrs McBride?'

She looked at the policewoman and saw that the best way to tackle the situation was to take a funny line because a thing like this could easily be taken seriously, too seriously, and his good name would be gone forever. She had known things like this happen afore, so she said, 'Well, if I don't somebody played a dirty trick on me when he was born, he's me youngest but one.'

The policewoman looked back at Philip and asked, 'Why were you at that window?'

'I've told you, I was trying to attract my mother's attention.'

'Why couldn't you go to the door and knock?'

'What!' Philip pointed to where a number of women were now entering The Ladies. 'Knock on that door!'

The policewoman saw his point, but she still stuck to her own, saying, 'You could have asked someone to tell your mother.'

Philip's face was red and Fanny saw that he was angry, for his words were of the crisp, polite kind that always showed his anger. 'I wished to speak to my mother, the matter was important and I was in a hurry.'

'How did you know she would be likely to hear you through that particular window?'

'Because I heard her voice near it.'

At this moment on to the scene came a policeman, and his appearance didn't evoke Fanny to any quip about the police force turning out, just the contrary, for she turned towards him with a rush of relief as she said, 'Aw! Ned, thank God to see you. Will you straighten this out? This conscientious young lady here won't believe that Phil was wantin' to speak to me. You mightn't believe it, but she imagined he was . . . picture-hunting . . . him, Phil, picture-hunting!'

The policeman looked at Philip, then said in a light fashion, 'You've got yourself in a jam this time, Phil.' Then to Fanny's dismay she saw that Philip was in no mood to take anything lightly, not even his reprieve, for he turned on Constable Bolton and with his meaning directed towards the policewoman he said, 'Instead of the police trying to concoct cases they should be out after shoplifters and such. It may be news to you that there's one been rampaging round the town all day today.'

Proof of Fanny's gasp came when her escaping breath floated in a misty cloud in the lamplight. She never thought he would give the old 'un away like this, no matter what the circumstances. It was another thing if you were caught out by the polis but to let on on anyone in a jam! She felt a wave of shame warming her against the raw wind.

'What do you mean, Phil?' asked Constable Bolton quietly.

'Just what I say,' said Philip.

'Keep your tongue quiet!' Fanny's tone was her old, loud, arbitrary one.

'It's no use,' said Philip, turning on her, 'it's got to come out. You should see what she's done. There's things in all our cupboards . . . even under your mattress.'

'Under me mattress!' Fanny's voice was high in

her head. 'What'd you mean?'

'Just what I say.' He was talking now as if they were alone. 'The woman's gone stark, staring mad since Margaret told her about us. She's bound to be caught, and she knows it and is trying to incriminate you and me, especially me. You should see the things she's put in my room and the places she found to hide them. You wouldn't believe it.'

'You mean to say all this has happened since I left the house this morning?'

'It must have. It was Corny who put me wise. He came to see you and couldn't get in, but he heard somebody in the room and looked through the window, and there she was. The boy even tackled her, and you know what she said, she told him that if he opened his mouth his grannie would go to prison for receiving stolen goods, for you and her worked hand in hand. And the stuff's so cleverly mixed up with our things that we wouldn't have spotted them for some time, not until it was too late, if it hadn't been for Corny.'

'I think we'd better go and investigate.' Constable Bolton's voice was quiet as he addressed himself to Philip. But it was Fanny who answered in a long cry, 'Aye, and the sooner the better. Hold your hand a minute till I get me coat.'

Fanny disappeared into The Ladies again, and grabbing her coat and hat from the hook, she gabbled at Maggie, 'I'm sorry, lass, but I've got to go. Anyway, we're not far off closing time. There's trouble at home.'

'Trouble, Fanny? What trouble?'

'Well, it isn't ours, not rightly, but we're in it. Oh—' she shook her head – 'I can't explain now, but I'll see you after the holidays and tell you everything.' As she pushed a hatpin through her hat, her downcast eyes were brought to the crumpled newspapers and she thought, 'My God, what am I gonna do with them?'

'Look, Maggie –' she pulled her into the office – 'you see these two bags?' She lifted the papers. 'Don't touch them on your life. Don't give them to anybody except meself or a polis.'

'Polis!' The word was an awe-stricken whisper.

'Aye, a polis. Now mind what I've told you, and if I don't see you, a Merry Christmas, lass.' She patted Maggie's head, and Maggie, hurrying out after her, said, 'But, Fan, what's it all about?'

'I'll tell you later,' called Fanny. 'A Merry Christmas, and I'm sorry to go like this.'

It hadn't taken her more than a few minutes to get her things, but when she reached the street again she saw a police car standing at the kerb, and when Philip, taking her arm, said, 'Come, get in,' she pulled back saying, 'I'll do no such thing. How did this get here anyway? I've never been in one in me life and I'm not goin' to start now.'

'Jungle telegraph,' explained Constable Bolton laughing. 'And it's all right, Fanny, it isn't the Black Maria.'

'Get in, Mother,' urged Philip under his breath. 'I don't know what's happening back there, but I'm scared, I'm scared for Margaret and all of them. That woman's insane.'

Seated at the back of the car, Fanny told herself ironically that the first car she had ever sat in would have to be a police car.

When almost in a matter of seconds she saw that they were whirling down Burton Street, she commented privately that anyway they had their uses for they couldn't have got here quicker if they'd all had wings. But before the car had actually come to a stop, Fanny knew that there was something up in the house, for the light was streaming from the doorway down the steps, and she could make out the Laveys, both of them, and other figures standing silhouetted against the light.

As Philip was easing her from the car a scream ripped out of the house and its impact brought Fanny to her feet with startling suddenness. She paused for a second and looked upwards, then made for the steps up which Philip was already bounding, with two policemen and the police-woman following him.

In the hall Sam Lavey greeted Fanny with, 'S . . . somethin's g . . . goin' on here, Fan. S . . . sounds as if one of them's b . . . being mur . . . murdered.'

Fanny did not stop to hear any more from Sam, but as another scream rang through the house she mounted the stairs, pulling herself up by violent tugs on the banisters.

On the first landing Miss Harper, with her hands to her thin bosom, was exclaiming aloud, 'It's awful, awful! The way they've been goin' on. On and off all day. Oh, Mrs McBride!'

'Out of me way!' With a thrust of her arm, Fanny pushed Miss Harper back and reached the attic stairs, and as with a final puff she pulled herself on to the crowded landing Ted Neilson was saying, 'They've been at it tooth and nail, the old wife goin' for the young one, and the bairns yellin'.'

Philip was now shaking the door and calling, 'Open the door! open the door! Do you hear? Margaret, open the door!'

They all remained quiet, waiting for an answer, but none came except the sound of muffled scuffling.

'Get back there.' Just as one of the policemen made a wide motion with his arm for clearing a space in which to ram himself against the door, Tony's voice came to them, full of chilling fear, crying pleadingly, 'Don't! oh, don't! Leave go of her, Mother! leave go of her! Margaret . . . Margaret.'

Philip's voice now filled the house as he shouted, 'Open the door, Tony. It's the police here.'

Fanny pushing Ted Neilson aside and also elbowing the policewoman out of position, cried, 'Look through the keyhole, can't you, and see what's up.'

Before anyone could follow this suggestion Constable Bolton hurled himself against the door. Nothing happened. When the constable hurled himself at the door a second time Philip's shoulder was with his. Yet except for a shudder the door remained firm. Again they hurled themselves against it and again they made no impression. On the fourth attempt the lock gave suddenly and the door swung open as if it had been pulled violently from inside and the two men catapulted into the room and measured their lengths on the floor.

For a second Fanny's eyes remained on them before taking in the room. There, almost within reach of Philip's outflung hand, she saw the lass lying, and if blood was anything to go by, looking as though she might well be dead. As an expression of horror, taking the form of 'Name of God!' left her lips, there came a scream from the bedroom and when following it there was an echo from the street below the hairs on her head seemed to rise up.

Almost as quick as the policewoman she was in the bedroom. The attic window which reached to the floor was open, and by it lay Tony clutching Marian to him, as if he were trying to press her into his thin body.

Getting to her knees with difficulty, Fanny, side by side with the policewoman, peered down into the street and on to the dark form lying in the shadow outside the light cast by the street lamp. When she turned from the window the policewoman was gone, and putting her arms about the huddled pair of children, she said soothingly, 'It's all right, me bairns, it's all right, me bairns. Come on now . . . quiet now, quiet, it's all right.'

When Tony tried to speak no sound came, and she pulled him to his feet, while his arms still held on to Marian, whose body was shaking with deep, shuddering sobs.

'There, there, now.' She engineered them towards the door. But there Tony stopped and whispered, 'Margaret.'

'She's all right,' said Fanny, shielding his sister from his gaze with her bulk. 'Go on downstairs, straight into my house.'

In a moment she passed them over to Amy Quigley, saying, 'Take them downstairs, Amy, I'll be there directly.' Then she went to where Philip was kneeling with Margaret's head in his lap.

'How bad is she?'

He shook his head and nipped on his bloodless lips before answering, 'I don't know, there's a gash in her head. I think she must have hit the fender.' He did not look up as he went on, 'What's happened in there?'

'The bairns are all right. She's . . . she's jumped from the window,' said Fanny quietly, as she stared down on the death-like face of Margaret, commenting to herself that she didn't like the looks of her and the quicker she was in a hospital the better.

Voices from the stairs penetrated the room and she straightened her aching back, saying, 'I'll get the house cleared, otherwise they'll never get up the stairs with a stretcher and that crowd about.'

When Fanny reached the landing a babble of comments reached her.

'She's done it, and I'm not surprised.'

'Why did she have to pick this night of all nights? Christmas Eve!'

'She was a queer card, I could tell that from the first.'

309

'Aye, she was, and I could see this coming off.'

'Aye, you can always prophesy things after they've happened,' commented Fanny dryly. 'Now get downstairs with you out of the way.'

'How many of you live here?' The policeman's voice came from the lower landing, and Fanny cried to him in muted tones, 'I'll tell you that.' Then stabbing her finger down at three women and a man lining the stairs she exclaimed, 'You, you . . . and you and you, get going to where you belong. My God! you couldn't all have been quicker on the scene if it was a free-gift day. Get out will you, and back to your own houses, and your own business. Anyway, I'd have thought you'd have found more interest in the street than up here.'

'Has she murdered the lass, Fan?'

'She has done no such thing. Now get going.'

Fanny pushed the non-residents of Mulhattan's Hall before her, making cryptic remarks with each push. Nor was Miss Harper spared. 'And if you were to get indoors you'd be one less an' all, for you're obstructing the traffic standing there.'

When at last the stairs and the hall were cleared, except for policemen who, Fanny commented, must be coming up through the drains, there were so many of them, four in all, she did not go into the street to see what was taking place there – she did not wish to see Mrs Leigh-Petty again, dead or alive – but she went into her own house and closed the door. She lifted Marian up into her arms and sat down heavily on her chair and rocked the sobbing child to and fro, exclaiming tenderly, 'There, there, me bairn. There, there.'

As she looked towards Tony, standing with his back to her and his hands pressed to his mouth, she said, 'Don't worry, lad, everything is going to be all right from now on.' And when she saw his shoulders heaving, she added quickly, 'Go on into the scullery and get it up.'

A few seconds later as the sound of his retching came to her she nodded to herself; that would ease some part of him.

Now she looked about the room, but could see nothing that she could not recognise. She hadn't a doubt though that she wouldn't have far to search. But there was time enough for that.

A matter of seconds later, there came the sound of the ambulance in the street. They'd pick the old 'un up first. She wondered if she might be still alive. Very likely, and that was why they hadn't attempted to bring her into the house. She had no desire to go and see what had really happened to the woman, for there was little pity in her for the creature now. It seemed only by the grace of God that she hadn't done in at least two of the three; there was no doubt she had tried to finish off the girl, and by the looks of things had tried to take the young one with her when she jumped. It would be a long time before these bairns would forget this night.

She heard the ambulance men go up the stairs, and after a very short while come down. And Philip's step was with theirs.

When the front door had closed on them there was a deathly stillness left on the house, for even Marian had stopped her sobbing. Then into the stillness came a sound that brought Fanny upright in her chair. So quickly did she jerk that Marian almost slipped from her knee. The sound was that of a carol . . . Come All Ye Faithful. As yet it was in the distance, which told her that the band had just entered the top end of the street. And which band would it be but the Salvation Army's? God in heaven! After a day like she'd had and after what had just taken place in the house, and now this. Had God, like her son, forgotten her altogether that He could allow her to be inflicted with this last torment and shame? They would parade the street and likely stop outside this very door.

> *'Come all ye faithful,*
> *Joyful and triumphant.'*

What if he had come with the band? No, God above, he wouldn't do that! But she had insulted his wife and, like herself, he was capable of anything when in a temper. And yet she wouldn't be able to find out if he was with them or not, not for herself she wouldn't, for she wasn't brave enough to go and see. But if he was there the neighbours would soon tell her. Aye, begod! Before Christ was eight hours old she would know.

> *'O come ye, O co . . . ome ye to Be . . .*
> *ethlehem.'*

The music came nearer, louder, more clashing, more joyous. And then it was on her. It actually stopped outside the house.

In small aggressive jerks she began to rock Marian. Begod! if she had a machine-gun she'd stand behind the curtains and pick them off one by one, she would begod! this night, this Christmas Eve.

Good will to men!

God asked too much of human beings.

11

It had been the strangest Christmas Fanny had experienced, as she said to herself, like something you'd read of in the paper. Newspaper men, police, hospital, questioning . . . oh! the questioning. The same things, over and over again. Had the one upstairs ever tried to sell her anything? 'No,' she had lied stoutly. Had she ever found in her flat before any articles that did not belong to her? How had the woman gained entry into her flat on the afternoon of Christmas Eve if she hadn't a key? To which Fanny had replied, 'Your guess is as good as mine.' Why hadn't she handed over the two bags in The Ladies to the policewoman? Why should she? she had asked . . . to her they were ordinary shopping bags. Had she expected Mrs Leigh-Petty to jump over the wall? Why hadn't she informed the policewoman that Mrs Leigh-Petty had jumped over the wall? 'Name of God!' she had cried, hadn't they tried to run in her son for peeping into The Ladies at that very moment. Oh, the questions, the questions. You would think that she was the culprit instead of the old wife.

Mrs Leigh-Petty's past had been made public, everything, that is except that she had been in prison before. This would not come out until after her trial, so Phil said. Again that is, if there was one. She was still a very ill woman, with a broken hip-bone and ribs and other things and if she were to recover and, after being tried for stealing, attempted murder of the child, and suicide, be presented with the alternative of prison or going into a home as her doctor had already suggested, there was little doubt now but that she would do as she was told. One thing was final, she had severed herself from the family she had adopted.

Margaret's head injury had proved nothing more than a nasty scalp cut, caused by the end of the steel fender, and after some days in hospital she had returned to the house, white and drained-looking and much depleted. Yet the strained look had gone from her eyes, and when Philip had brought her into the kitchen she had cried in Fanny's arms tears of weakness and relief.

As for the repercussions of this whole affair on Philip, Fanny saw her son in a new guise, for he was already acting like the father of a family. This attitude of his had dated from Christmas Eve when the two single beds for the children had been brought downstairs and the boy's placed in his bedroom and Marian's in the kitchen at the foot of her own. During all this week when he wasn't at the hospital, he had been busily burrowing into the affections of Tony and the child, who were from now on to be his responsibility.

Aye, it had been a week and a half during which she had been kept very busy. Nearly too busy to think, but not quite, for the pain ever present in her heart was a sharp reminder that her lad had let her down. But only on Boxing Day had she indulged herself in reviling this son who must know that she would be waiting for his coming. For on that day Sam and Clara Lavey's two sons, who with their families were visiting them for the Christmas, had looked in on her. Then there was the Quigleys' lad, come all the way from South Wales; and there was Miss Harper's niece and her family who had come to visit her on Boxing Day. They all had someone come from outside, while there was herself who had reared eleven out of twelve of them, and had only one with her. As she had sat alone by the fire, Philip having taken the children out, she had asked herself angrily, why, why were things like this for her? Hadn't she given the lot of them her life? Hadn't she always seen they had full bellies? True, she must admit it, her house had never been much cop.

And who was to blame for that? Had she ever had a chance to have a fine house? Did any of them ever offer to stump up and buy her new furniture? No. When they started earning big, they started courting big. They had kept her nose to the grindstone. Her nose had always been on the grindstone. First with McBride, then with one after another of them, working, slaving for them. She had been a fool. This was nineteen fifty-eight, near fifty-nine. There were women going about today of her age and looking young, dressed up to the nines and painted . . . aye, painted. Off to the over-sixty clubs, pictures, whist-drives, aye, and even old-time dancing. Why hadn't she started earlier and said, 'To hell with the lot of you, I'm goin' to enjoy meself.' Why? And all the remainder of the week she had asked of the pantry shelf and the fire, and the puncher in The Ladies, Why? And only last night when she went to bed tired and weary did she give herself the answer. She wasn't made that way. Her life was in this kitchen, and the strength of her life had drained through this bed, on which she had brought her family into the world. Her very heart's core was in this untidy, shabby room. And she had really wanted nothing else as long as it held the one part of her body that had given her joy . . . Jack. And Jack was here no longer, Jack would not even come to see her, not even the glory and forgiveness of Christmas had softened his heart.

Last night she had brushed her black coat and hat and squeezed her swelling feet back into her decent shoes and gone to confession. She'd had to wait a long time to get in to Father Owen, but she preferred that to going to Father Bailey. Father Owen always soothed her, and instead of making her feel guilty as Father Bailey did over her numerous sins, rather he left her the impression that she was a good woman. And last night he had brought a sting to her eyes as he talked to her after the absolution, talked to her as nobody else had done or could do, talked about their souls, not only her soul, but as if he was as bad as herself, and that he, too, had said things against God.

'Fanny,' he had said, 'worry no more about such things, for if we didn't get our back up at God He would think that we were dead perhaps and He hadn't noticed.' He'd made a small noise that could have been a laugh. 'You've got to look on Him as a real father, and which one of us hasn't thought at one time or other that they knew better than their father. If He has put burdens on you, Fanny, and you have resented them and not put a tooth in it about letting Him know, don't worry, we all do it. I've done it meself. And when I've gone back to Him to say I was sorry and made Him a promise never to sin again, I've even heard Him chuckle and say "Until the next time".'

Aye, Father Owen had a way of putting the Almighty over that didn't stick in your gullet. He had touched her so much that she had even started her confession again, and against her better sense, she had said, 'Nellie Flannagan, Father, she always makes me want to go hell for leather for her.' And he had said, 'It's understandable, it's understandable. But I would like to see you two friends, for she's a good woman, a respectable woman, and she tries hard like all of us, God help her.'

Before he had finished extolling Nellie Flannagan, Fanny wished sincerely that her conscience hadn't gone mad and made her say that. Father Owen might speak well of Nellie Flannagan, but he never stayed long in her home when he came visiting, and she had seen him scurry past the door more than once. She'd always had a strong suspicion that when he talked well of Nellie it was just to tease her, to get her own goat. But just as she was leaving he had lain a balm on her soul as he said, 'God bless you, Fanny. And for the next three nights I'll say a special prayer that the desire of your heart may be granted.'

When this morning she had dragged herself out of bed in the bleak, shivering dawn and made her way to church to receive communion, she prayed in her own inimitable way as she went along through the dark streets, 'I'm offerin' me communion, Holy Mother, so that he might come, and I promise you I won't go for him when he turns up, or say a word against his wife, I won't so help me, God.' And as the Host was placed on her tongue she did not breathe, 'Oh, God be merciful to me, a sinner,' but 'Bring him. Won't you bring him?'

The anger and resentment had now gone and the longing was back, and with it hope. What was Christmas anyway to a northerner, it was only for the bairns. New Year was the time. Of course it was, New Year's Eve, this was the time for forgiving and forgetting . . . Should auld acquaintance be forgot . . . Should your own flesh and blood be forgot? No, this was the time for forgiving and forgetting, during the long, long day of New Year's Eve.

The children's beds had been moved back upstairs, and once again Fanny had the house to herself. She was not sorry the children had gone. They had been no trouble, the boy was quiet and Marian had been subdued, unnaturally so, for the terror was still with her, yet they weren't her own, not like Corny, or her other grand-bairns, although she seldom saw these except on escorted visits. But bairns, she found now, tired her, and what was more she couldn't think with folks in the house. She wanted the place to herself to think and wait in.

Now on this New Year's Eve she had all the day to wait in, for she was finished at The Ladies. It had been touching how upset Maggie had been at her going, but she had promised to come round and see her.

She knew she wouldn't be bothered much with Philip in the house for the next few days, for he'd be up the stairs most of the time if she knew anything. Then there was the time coming very soon now when he'd be gone altogether, and she'd be left alone. It was odd but she was finding that when she tried to think of this now something eluded her. Was it that the fear of loneliness was leaving her? She didn't know, but somehow she couldn't see further than the New Year and Jack coming. His coming would decide many things.

There came a tap on the door, and Mary Prout put her head round, saying, 'All by yourself, Fan?'

'Aye, come away in.'

Mary came to the hearth, a strange jauntiness about her that brought Fanny's eyes to her as she said, 'Sit yourself down, off your leg.'

'Oh, me leg's fine now, Fan. By, the doctor was right. Rest, he said, and rest I did, and thank God

I'm better again. But as I said, Fan' – Mary bent over Fanny – 'thank God for you an' all, cos I could never have had that rest but for you.'

Fanny peered hard at Mary, and a twist of a smile came to her lips as she said again, 'Sit down.'

Mary sat down, and looked across at Fanny with an oily beam splitting her face as she said, 'Well, another New Year's Eve, Fan. By, we've seen some together, haven't we?'

'Yes, we have that,' said Fanny flatly.

'It's been a week, Fan, hasn't it? I've never known such a week, not all the years I've lived in Burton Street. And you know what I heard Nellie Flannagan say the day?'

'It would be nothing new,' said Fanny.

'It is, Fan, for I heard her meself tellin' Mrs Peters that she saw it all from her window. The whole struggle and her throwing herself out . . . what d'you think of that?'

'I think she's keeping to pattern,' said Fanny, with unusual calmness. 'She's got to say something to keep her name up for being the biggest liar on God's earth.'

'You're right there, Fan, you're right there. And you know what's more, Fan? She said she offered to have the bairns, but . . .' Mary paused and Fanny said, 'Well, go on.'

Mary did a little wriggle on the chair, then bending nearer to Fanny she whispered, 'She said, Fan, you pushed your nose in. That's what she said, Fan. And you know what . . . you know what I said, Fan? I ups and told her she was a liar. I did. I did, honest to God, Fan, I did!'

Fanny looked at Mary stretching her meagre height with the glory of her integrity, and she said, 'Well, that's something to your credit. Her have the children! I can see her, when she won't allow her own child to bring a bairn into the house in case it disturbs the mats. Her have the bairns!' Fanny lifted up her bulk. 'I wish I'd heard her.'

'And there's something else, Fan. You mind me telling you about our Monica working with the lass your Phil used to go with?' Mary was emphatic in her use of the past tense. 'Well, Monica came in last night, and she said Phil had had a lucky escape because Sylvia had come to the office, and when the boss sent word to say he was engaged she had rushed in on him and caused a shindy . . . At first that was. And then what d'you think?'

Fanny waited, making no comment.

'He left the office with her, her walkin' with her head up, as brazen as brass, Monica said, and the bairn showing in spite of all her efforts to lace up.

323

Monica said the boss looked green, and when his missus had finished with him he'd likely be black and blue. Monica said she'd never seen anybody look more cowed or guilty. What d'you think of that, Fan?'

Mary had never paused for breath, and Fanny said, 'I think she's had a hard job to father it, but I think her memory's serving her well, she's hit on the right one. As for the man, I wish him luck, and the same to all of his kidney.'

'Yes, yes, you're right, Fan. Is Phil goin' to marry the lass upstairs?'

'Aye, he is.'

'Well, now . . . well, now.' Mary's tongue set off again. 'And takin' on the bairns? He's a good lad, Phil, but you're goin' to feel a draught, Fan, on your own with just your pension. And then being lonely.' Mary's eyes took on a sadness and a moisture. 'It's no cop being on your own, Fan. Fifteen years I've had on me own, Fan. But there, you're different; you have your family, and your grand-bairns. It makes a difference . . . Has Jack been along yet, Fan?'

Fanny prised herself to her feet, then took up a bucket of coal standing by the side of the fender and with one swing deposited it on to the back shelf of the grate. Then taking the raker she pulled some lumps down on to the already blazing fire before she answered, 'I'm expecting him any minute. I've heard tell he's poppin' in.'

Not even to her lifelong friend could she say what was in her heart.

'Oh, Fan, I'm glad for you, I am.' Mary, now becoming recklessly brave, went on. 'He's like you, you know, Fan . . . Now you can say what you like, he is.' Mary wagged her finger up at Fanny, and she spoke as though there had been a denial to her statement, whereas in fact Fanny had said nothing, nor had her face given her away even as she thought, 'Aye, don't I know it, and aren't I suffering for it. For if he wasn't such a big chip of meself he'd have been along afore now.'

When there was still no comment forthcoming from Fanny, Mary said, 'No offence meant, Fan, no offence meant.'

Now Fanny stood and looked down on this woman whose nature was fundamentally timid, and suddenly she laughed. She put her head back and she laughed, the first good laugh she'd had for some time, in fact, since Joe had caused the shindy, and she laughed the more when Mary's laugh joined hers.

'I didn't think I'd laugh the day,' said Fanny, wiping her eyes. Then looking down on Mary again she said, 'You've had a drop, haven't you?

You're so full of Dutch courage at this minute you'd have a job to decide on your nationality.'

'Now, now, Fan. No! no! I haven't,' protested Mary.

'Aw, away with you,' said Fanny. 'How else would you have stood up to Nellie Flannagan?'

'Now, Fan!'

'And me.'

'Oh, Fan . . .'

'Aw, be quiet, I won't give you away for breaking the pledge.'

'Fan, but I—'

'Be quiet, I tell you, and don't try to hoodwink me.'

'But it was only a drop, Fan, a small port and—'

'I don't care what it was. Come on and have another sup to wash it down; you've given me a laugh that I never expected to have.' She went to the cupboard and brought out the half-bottle of whisky which was now getting low. 'We'll have a drop together for old times' sake, eh, Mary?'

And Mary, the beam splitting her face again, nodded a gleeful nod.

So they drank together and they laughed together and they talked of life as they had seen it, and Mary told Fanny she was the best friend she'd ever had, and her tongue becoming really loosened she told her what she would like to say to Nellie Flannagan, to Father Bailey, and not least to Mrs Funnell, who kept the outdoor beer shop, and lastly to Mrs Proctor of The Ladies. Oh, the things she would like to say to Mrs Proctor! And when at last she took her leave and Fanny sat alone again, she thought, 'Aye, it's good to laugh on the last day of the year; it's good to see it going out on a laugh.'

She felt that her laughter would bring luck. She had laughed in the morning of New Year's Eve, then she would laugh in the evening, and she would see the old year out on a laugh. Yes, something good would happen the day, and what better than . . . She let it go at that and took another drop of whisky.

Fanny laughed at Philip when he came in with Margaret. She laughed at their obvious happiness, and when she had succeeded in making them laugh, she laughed the louder.

To Corny's delight when he dashed in to see her she let him play his trumpet, with Joe accompanying him, and as she sat with her fingers in her ears, she rocked with her laughter, and the louder she laughed the louder Joe sang. And so the day wore on, and when Corny left she embraced him closely, and he returned her embrace, and she patted Joe, who in turn licked her furiously in saying his own particular goodbye.

And so the evening came.

She set her table quite early with all her good things, which was the customary way to greet the New Year. She packed Philip off to where his heart lay, upstairs, with orders not to come down till just on twelve to bring in the New Year. The order had a double motive for she wanted the house clear. She had steadfastly refused the offers of the Quigleys and the Laveys, and various neighbours to come and see the New Year in with them. She had never been out of her house on New Year's Eve, and nothing short of an explosion would have driven her out this night of all nights.

The warming influence of the whisky kept the bubble of laughter on the surface of her mind, but beneath she was waiting. She knew, in spite of the veneer of merriment, that she was waiting, and that the waiting had an apprehensiveness about it. She knew that she had taken more liquor today than ever before. She was no whisky addict, she liked a drop now and again when she was feeling low, but she had suffered too much from its effects on McBride to want to indulge in it. But today was an exception, today it had, as she put it to herself, saved her face, for if she hadn't laughed she would have cried, and she was afraid of crying. She had never allowed herself this indulgence, except in the secret hours of the night when there was no-one to see or hear her. But the hours of waiting would, she knew, have worn her down this day, and she would have bubbled at the first kind word and she would never have been able to live it down. No, the whisky had saved her the day. But she knew when to stop, and she was having no more, only a nip to toast in the New Year with the lass and Philip.

Then to bring her laughter bursting forth again Maggie came in saying she could only stay a minute but she felt she just had to look in. She held Fanny's hands as she said, 'Oh, Fan. Eeh! but I am sorry you're not comin' back.'

'Me, too,' said Fanny.

'There's been nobody like you in The Ladies afore, Fan.'

'And won't be again,' cried Fanny, her laughter filling the room.

'What a pity you hadn't come years ago,' was Maggie's last comment, as Fanny thankfully saw her to the top of the frozen steps.

As she returned to the warmth of her room again, she thought aye, it was a pity she wasn't goin' back, for The Ladies had taken her out of the world, so to speak. When she was younger she had washed and scrubbed for the wives at the top end of Jarrow and at times she had thought, 'Who are they, anyway? They're no better than meself, the only difference is their bit money. And they've only got that through the steady jobs of their men.' But in The Ladies it had been different. There, there had been no class feeling, if anything she had felt superior. Was she not taking the money and seeing them all at a disadvantage, as it were? Aye, begod! for, after all, nature's indignity had been put upon rich and poor alike.

This last thought pleased her and sent her chuckling to her chair to wait and to hope that nobody else would drop in.

But Don did, not ten minutes after Maggie had gone. He walked up and down the mat and filled the room with his awkwardness. She was aware that he was finding her unusually quiet the night and she enjoyed the sensation and kept it up. She even puzzled him further by sending good wishes to his wife. But unfortunately this had the wrong effect and delayed his departure by several minutes, during which he said he would look in again the morrow and bring Jeanette with him. She didn't want to see this particular granddaughter, for the child was too much like her mother, but she could say nothing . . . This is what happened when you weren't yourself.

* * *

Between ten and eleven o'clock the streets were abustle with life, banging doors and hurrying feet, any pair of which might turn up the steps of Mulhattan's Hall and into the kitchen.

Between eleven and a quarter to twelve there came a stillness on the street, as if it, too, was waiting. Then came the sound of voices again, calling now to each other, mostly thick, foggy voices, telling that the loads were already heavy, even before the real drinking in of the New Year had begun.

As the few first-footers joked in the street below, the ships' hooters started and the whistles blew, and the church bells rang out and Philip banged twice on the door, and Fanny, opening it to him, said, 'A Happy New Year, lad.' And then she did a strange thing; she not only kissed him, but she put her arms about him and held him to her for a brief moment before pushing him with high laughter towards Margaret.

As they all drank to the New Year just born and Fanny plied them with plates of ham and pickles, mince pies, and cakes, she did not glance towards the door. There was a pause in her waiting now for she knew he would not come at this particular time. As like as not he was being his own first-foot for the first time. But in a little while, when people started to move from one house to another . . . then.

At half-past one Philip took Margaret upstairs, and when he came down again Fanny was sitting in the chair by the fire, and he stopped by her side and said quietly, 'Are you going to bed now?'

She looked up at him with a kindly smile. 'Not for a moment, lad, but get yourself away.'

'No, I'll stay . . . Listen to the Laveys, they're going it, aren't they?' He laughed.

'You'll do no such thing. Now get yourself away to your bed, I'm goin' to turn in in a minute, I'm just goin' to warm me feet.' She held her feet nearer the fire. She didn't want him sitting with her when . . . She rose. 'Go on, you've had a long day . . . a long week for that matter.'

He stood before her, tall, good-looking, still making her wonder how he ever came to be of her flesh. Then as she looked up at him, he said, very softly, 'Thanks, Mother.'

'And what would you be thanking me for?'

'Everything.'

She turned her face to the fire saying, 'It's soft you're goin', lad.'

There was a long pause during which she wished him gone, and then he said swiftly, 'I want you to know now, you won't be alone. I'm not leaving the town. And Margaret's with

332

me whole-heartedly in this, we want you to come and live with us when we're married . . .'

'Oh, away with you, man.' She turned sharply on him, laughing. 'Now would anyone get me out of these four walls? Go on with you, away to your bed.' She pushed out her hand but did not touch him, and as he turned slowly from her to go into the bedroom, she said, 'But thanks, lad, I won't forget that you've asked me. No, I won't forget that. Good night, and a Happy New Year to you . . . and her.'

He paused and looked back at her. 'Goodnight, and the same to you.'

The door closed. The kitchen now all her own, she pulled her chair closer to the fire in a series of jerks and settled herself to further waiting.

She was still waiting at three o'clock when Philip's door opened again and he asked gently, 'Are you going to stay up all night?' Then coming slowly towards her he added, 'It's no use, you know.'

When he stood looking down on her, she pulled herself to her feet saying nothing, then angrily pushed the chair to one side and shambled to the light which she switched off before saying shortly, 'Get yourself to sleep!'

Without a word now he went into his room, and in the firelight she groped her way to the bed and, sitting on its edge, she began to rock herself back and forward, back and forward. And after a while her rocking ceased and she was about to slide to her knees on the floor and implore God of His mercy to take this lonely longing from her heart when her whole body was consumed by a furious anger. It rushed through her like a torrent sweeping a gorge. The anger cried out against God, against her entire family, against this son that she loved more than anything on earth. What had she done to deserve such treatment? Hadn't she given him everything? With every ounce of her flesh and every fibre of her heart she had given to him, depriving the others of love to give to him, and what thanks had she ever got from him? But she had never wanted his thanks, only for him to laugh with her, joke with her, tease her, as if she was a bairn or lass, and for that small return she had given him everything, her life, the whole of her life. Damn and blast him! he was an ungrateful swine . . . an unforgiving swine. Blast him to hell! . . . She hoped . . . she hoped . . . There was a great lump in her chest like a weight of iron. It rose, pressing itself upwards in her throat. She gripped her neck to suffocate the sound that was endeavouring to escape, then as the tears spilled from her eyes she turned and pressed her face into the pillow. So intense was her emotion that it seemed to her that she was crying through every pore of her body, for the whole of her huge bulk was aching with a queer ache like a cramp, and as a cramp will converge to one spot all the aching gathered itself into a knot in her side where the wind usually was, and so intense did the pain become that it even stilled her crying, and she slowly straightened herself up, her hand gripping at the flesh under her breast. She tried to call out to Philip, but there was no sound in her throat.

She knew she was in her chair by the fire again, but she couldn't remember moving from the bed. The pain had stopped. It had been shoved away by a blackness that for a brief moment terrified her and checked her breathing. She was now lying in the blackness. It was as if a mighty hand had been placed over her mouth and eyes and even over her inward sight for she could see nothing, not even in her mind.

Slowly the fear of the darkness left her and she lay in it, almost calmly, waiting as she had been doing all night, and for days and weeks past, waiting, waiting. And when at last the darkness slowly lifted and she was able to glance once more about the firelit room, she noticed a very odd thing, so odd that, to put it still in her own words, her heart nearly shot out of her mouth, for sitting in the other armchair right opposite to her, literally dead to the world, was herself.

With a strange lightness upon her now she rose from her chair and moved nearer to the great, slumped figure and stood staring at it in a kind of awe for a moment. Begod! she wasn't a pleasant sight, not a bit like she thought she was. She stroked down her apron, as if in an attempt to put a semblance of tidiness on herself, and the thought struck her that it was . . . queer . . . it was, that she could do this, make herself tidy . . . yet that other one of her was not affected by it. As she raised her eyes and looked slowly around the familiar room, with every detail clear and distinct before her eyes, although there was nothing but the dim light of the fire to show them up, it came to her with a sort of great pity, overwhelming pity, that she had died, died in that spasm of pain and anger and doubt, and all her waiting was over, all the recriminations, all the worries of being left alone. Everything she had tired herself out with these past months had been a useless waste of good time.

Then she stood straight up and stretched herself, and moved her hands down her body as if to get the feel of the strange lightness that was on it, and as she did so she was overwhelmed by an urge to go quickly away from this room that had held her life, to go now, at this very moment. The urge promised happiness and peace . . . even, strange thought, adventure, and the thought of adventure was in no way incongruous to her now. In the very act of moving towards the door she stopped. She could not go yet, she would have to wait a little longer. But the waiting didn't matter any more, for it was without pain. She sat down again, quite calmly, and looked at herself sitting slumped in the chair opposite, looked at herself down the years to when she was a child and felt light and springy as she did at this moment.

It was dawn now. Soon the house would be astir. With no sense of time at all she waited, and when the bedroom door opened and Philip came out and she watched him spring across the room and lift up her drooping head, she cried, 'Don't look like that, lad . . . aw, don't man!' She watched him fall on his knees and bury his head in her lap, and as his sobbing twisted his body she went to him and put her arms about him. Why was he taking it like this? 'Look, man,' she said, 'give over, I was never worth all that. Aw, come on now.'

It was strange but he did not knock her flying when he sprang up and placed his head near her breast as if listening. Then she watched him rise and stumble to the door, and she listened as the house awoke from its first sleep of the New Year.

When Margaret came in she, too, knelt before her and she took her hand and held it to her face. Margaret was a nice lass . . . aw, she was, none better. And she was for Phil, the very one. Then came Amy and Barry Quigley and Ted Neilson, and between them all they lifted her on to the bed. And, begod, she had to admit they had their work cut out. She knew she was a size, but not all that weight!

She moved aside out of the hubbub, and as she watched them the urge to leave the house increased. Yet she didn't go. Then the doctor came, and as he walked through her she said, 'You're late again . . . too late this time.' She watched him fiddling about with her, and it didn't look decent somehow. Then without warning the blackness descended upon her again.

When it cleared the doctor was no longer there, but Mary Prout was standing over her. There was a muzzy feeling in her head and she thought vaguely, I'll be launched afloat if she cries any more. And now the light, airy feeling came on her again and the urge to get away was almost overpowering, and she said to herself sharply, 'Go on.' But still she didn't go.

And then he came in.

His face was grey and he was thinner, and he looked much older than on the day they parted.

He came and stood looking down on her, all the muscles of his face working and his teeth biting into his lip. He did not cry as Phil had done, his crying was slow and painful and hurt her. She patted his arm and said, 'It's all right, lad, it's all right. I knew you'd come. Come on now, come on, stop that. I'm not mad at you for not showing up, I was just impatient . . . as ever. Give over. Give over now. I tell you I understand.'

And she did understand. She made several valiant efforts to tell him so. But his teeth still ground into his lip, and she knew as she looked at him that for the remainder of his life the pain of coming too late would be with him.

Then Phil started on him. He was standing at the other side of the bed and the look on his face was one that she hadn't seen there before, for it was a reflection of her own when in anger as he ground out, 'You've done this! You've finished her years before her time.'

She watched Jack drag his eyes from her and say with surprising meekness, 'What could I do? She'd have gone for me like a tiger if I'd put me nose in the door.'

'Gone for you!' Philip's voice was full of scorn. 'Did she ever go for you? She gave you everything and the rest of us nothing . . . nothing, do you hear? And these past weeks it's been hell just watching her waiting for you, but you, big-head as usual, wouldn't come unless she sent for you. Well, now it's too late, and you'll remember it's too late for the rest of your life.'

So Philip had known how she felt. Well, well. She put her hand on his arm, saying, 'Hush now, hush now. Enough of that.' And she laughed as she added, 'You mustn't quarrel over the dead, it's a useless game.'

Then she looked from one to the other, but the affection in her gaze was still not equal, and being aware of this she felt a slight return of pain. But she could do no more, she could not alter herself, it was too late. She was finished with this life anyway, and this room. The urge within her told her this and, obeying its pressure and with only a faint sense of regret, she left it and the people in it and went into the hall and towards the main door. But when she opened the door she was brought to a halt, for there, coming across the ice-covered road towards the house was none other than Nellie Flannagan.

Begod if she isn't coming to make sure I'm dead, thought Fanny, and if she goes in there and moans over me I'll rise up and spit in her eye, so help me God, I will!

Mrs Flannagan reached the pavement. She reached the steps. And when she had mounted to the third one Fanny went to meet her and with a great sweep of her hand she was aiming at her unsuspecting enemy to bring her, she hoped, chin first on to the steps when a voice saying sharply, 'Now! now! none of that,' checked her.

The voice, a strangely familiar one, stayed her hand, and she turned to see, in the far distance, in fact right at the top of the street, a figure she recognised instantly, and the recognition gave wings to her feet and a great lift to her heart. So light did she feel that her bulk wafted it-self like a feather up the street.

She knew that she was smiling all over her body, and her mind was more joyous than it had been in the whole of her life. It was true then, all that they had promised . . . they had sent the blessed Michael himself to fetch her. And within a jiffy now she'd be in one of the mansions of Heaven.

So great was her haste to take up her new abode that she almost floated past him, but a hand, not as soft as down but as hard and as gnarled as any navvy's stopped her progress.

'Where you off to?'

She looked at him, surprise stilling her tongue for the moment. He had a voice like a number of people she could put a name to . . . Father Owen, Father Bailey, Phil and, most surprising of all, Corny.

'You ask me that?'

'I do.'

His tone annoyed her, so much so that she forgot his mighty power and nearness to the Throne and found herself answering him in a manner similar to that she would have used on a lesser celestial being.

'What you asking the road you know for? I'm off to get me just deserts, for God Himself knows I've earned them.'

'Then you're going the wrong way.'

His voice boomed the words as his mighty hand lifted and pointed down the street, and she turned her startled eyes to behold, standing outside Mulhattan's Hall, no other than McBride himself. The same yet different, for above his great thick ears where the tufts of hair used to stick out were now horns, not big ones like those associated with the Devil himself, but big enough to show clearly which side he was on. And even after all these years of enforced abstention she saw with her widening eyes that his nose was still bulbous, knobbly and red.

At this juncture she found that the pain had returned to her side, brought on no doubt by fear. She flung herself round to Saint Michael, crying, 'I'm not goin' along of him, I've had enough.

As God's my witness, I'm not havin' another existence with McBride.'

'You're a hypocrite, Fanny McBride.'

As he said this she was set to wondering how anyone could dislike an archangel, but she did at this moment. She knew why he had called her a hypocrite. He was getting at her for the Masses she'd had said for McBride, supposedly to get his soul out of purgatory. But the proof of her duplicity was before her, for he was still there; in fact, by the sight of him, a bit lower down.

The pain in her side was getting worse and she pressed her hand to it as she answered his accusation with, 'Then I'm not alone.'

On this she expected his wrath to come down on her and kizzen her up, but instead he laughed, just like Father Owen would have done. And just like him, he asked, 'And how do you make that out?'

Ignoring entirely now his great majesty, she replied. 'Because I've prayed to you for years, not knowing what you were really like.'

Again his laughter filled the street. But she did not laugh with him, nor did her heart become light as it had done when she had first rushed to meet him, the only feeling that remained now was the urge to go . . . to go on . . . on, on, and up. And she voiced this in saying wearily, 'If we're goin', let's away now.'

'You're not going anywhere, Fanny.'

His voice was kinder but held a note of finality.

'Well, what's goin' to happen to me?' There rose a feeling of panic in her.

'You're going back.'

'No! No!' Her voice sounded like a moan and it filled the street. 'No, don't send me back, I've had enough, I've suffered enough, I can't bear the heartache over again.'

'The heartache was of your own making; you're stubborn and pig-headed. You've been the same all your life.'

'You rear eleven and try and be anything else. It's the likes of you who could never tackle such a job who are the first to tell others how they should go on.' She was angry now and quite fearless of this great being.

'True. True in all you say.' He nodded solemnly down on her. 'But apart from McBride you've made your own heartache with your children.'

'How d'you make that out?' She was aggressive now.

'You've brought them up to the best of your ability, but you didn't love them, did you, except one? Not that they were a gang you could love very much, I admit, being self-seeking, the whole bunch of them . . . But again I say, except one, and he wasn't the one that you loved . . . you understand me?'

She moved her body as she said, 'I understand you well enough. But I'm as God made me.'

'Oh, no you're not.' Saint Michael's voice was sharp now. 'Don't you lay the blame on Him. He simply gave you a pattern, the making up lay with you. And you liked the look of what you made so much that when you saw it reproduced in your son, Jack, you fell in love with it. That's it, isn't it?'

She was hot, very hot, and she flung her arms wide as she cried, 'You can't help where you love.'

'Then you should realise that your son Philip cannot help loving you, and he is the one who deserves your affection, not the other one. And what is more, I'm telling you now that your beloved Jack doesn't need your love, for he has inherited all your weak and bad points, he can do without you very well. But Philip's different. He needs you, always has done, and you're going to be given the chance to fill that need, you're going back.'

'You don't know what you're talking about. He's goin' to be married, what need will he have of me then?'

'You're a stupid woman, Fanny McBride, a stupid and stubborn woman.' His voice was rising and the anger was showing on his face. 'For two pins I'd countermand the orders I've got and send you packing down to McBride, so if you're wise you'll be on your way before I do just that . . . And mind, I'm warning you. You stint your affections towards Philip and I'll have you back here and in the arms of McBride before you know you have come and gone . . . Now away you go.'

'But . . .'

'No buts. No buts . . . NO BUTS.'

The boom of his voice sent her body tumbling down the street, and it was only at the foot of Mulhattan's steps that she managed to right herself. Then, strange . . . strange thing, she found she was standing on the steps above Nellie Flannagan with her arm thrust out in the same position as it had been when it was checked by his voice. He had said nothing about Nellie Flannagan, not a word, although he had made his mouth go about other things. Well begod! she'd have some satisfaction of some kind out of this episode. So, with a mighty downward swing of her arm, she whipped Mrs Flannagan's feet from beneath her.

The street was filled with a cry as from a scalded cat and she watched the thorn of her flesh rise some way in the air, before landing flat on her face at the bottom of the steps.

With her body wobbling with laughter and dusting her hands she marched up the steps and into the hall again. But here, the stuffiness of the house after the clean air outside caught at her throat and almost choked her. She began to cough. And the coughing racked her body and dragged at her, pulling her down. Down she went, and she clutched at the black air about her. And when out of it came a hand she hung on to it with all her might.

'Thank God!'

She opened her eyes slowly to the voice and at the same time to a loud cry. From the street.

'Oh, Mother!' She looked at Philip, whose hand she was gripping; then with eyes that had weights dragging at them she turned them on Jack. So he had come. Why didn't it matter so much now? She didn't know, she was so tired.

'Go to sleep, dear.'

It was Phil's hand that was taking her wet hair back from her brow. Aye, she would go to sleep. She felt at peace somehow. She would talk later.

The voices were whispering all about her; the room was full of them. There were 'Thank God!'s and 'She'll pull through now' and 'It's a miracle, if there ever was one.' Then a whisper, distinct from the rest, said, 'That cry in the street, that was Mrs Flannagan. She's fallen down the steps and twisted her ankle badly. They've had to carry her across home.'

With a quirk to her lips Fanny went to sleep.

THE END

THE RAG NYMPH
by Catherine Cookson

In the heat of a late June afternoon in 1854, abandoned by a panic-stricken mother in an all-too-obvious flight from the law, Millie Forester burst into Aggie Winkowski's life like a bolt from the blue. Aggie, who was known hereabouts as 'Raggie Aggie', for trading in rags and old clothes was her long-established business, knew well enough the dangers waiting for such a strikingly pretty girl left alone in this rough and vice-ridden quarter and could see nothing for it, other than to take her in.

But what began as a compassionate expediency led to the establishment of a new relationship that would grow and deepen, moulding Millie's destiny and giving new meaning to the life of Aggie Winkowski.

Millie Forester's advance through the coming years to the threshold of womanhood is the core of *The Rag Nymph*, as gripping and socially concerned an historical novel as Catherine Cookson has ever written. Her superb skills of narrative and characterization provide a spectrum of the good and evil of the Victorian era, frankly confronting the terrible menace of child corruption, which remains a constant issue in our own time.

0 552 13683 2

MY BELOVED SON
by Catherine Cookson

Ellen Jebeau married a man who did little but dream, and who then died with debt his only legacy. Whatever else her marriage had lacked, however, she had her son Joseph. She resolved he should have all in life she had missed and to achieve that end, she would stop at nothing.

It was Sir Arthur Jebeau, her late husband's brother, who came to her aid, and soon Ellen and Joseph were living at the old family seat at Screehaugh. It was a convenient arrangement, one which Ellen was not slow to recognize could work to her advantage, for Sir Arthur was a widower and Screehaugh had no mistress . . .

That was in 1926, but the working out of so many increasingly intertwined destinies would continue for twenty more years and only come to final resolution with Joseph Jebeau's escape from the traumatic heritage of his mother's ruthless ambition and his emergence as his own true self.

My Beloved Son will rank among Catherine Cookson's most compelling and deeply moving novels and her portrayal of Joseph Jebeau is as sensitive and percipient as any this well-loved author has achieved.

0 552 13302 7

THE HOUSE OF WOMEN
by Catherine Cookson

Emma Funnell is the matriarch of Bramble House, built for her as a wedding gift. Now, in 1968, she is in her seventies, with the avowed intent of living to be a hundred. And, as she has always done, she continues to rule the roost, for apart from herself three generations of the Funnell family live in the house – all of them women.

There is widowed daughter Victoria, increasingly a hypochondriac, granddaughter Lizzie, who bears the brunt of running the house, as well as enduring a loveless marriage to Len Hammond; and Peggy, her sixteen-year-old daughter, now trying to find the courage to drop the bombshell of her pregnancy into their midst.

This explosive situation provides the springboard for a powerful and absorbing novel that explores, over a period of fifteen years, all that fate holds in store for the dwellers in *The House of Women,* reaching its climax with a frank confrontation of a major social issue of today.

'The author's grip on the novel never flags . . . her crown rests assured'
Sunday Times

0 552 13303 5

A SELECTION OF OTHER CATHERINE COOKSON TITLES AVAILABLE FROM CORGI BOOKS

THE PRICES SHOWN BELOW WERE CORRECT AT THE TIME OF GOING TO PRESS. HOWEVER TRANSWORLD PUBLISHERS RESERVE THE RIGHT TO SHOW NEW RETAIL PRICES ON COVERS WHICH MAY DIFFER FROM THOSE PREVIOUSLY ADVERTISED IN THE TEXT OR ELSEWHERE.

□	13576 3	THE BLACK CANDLE	£4.99
□	12473 7	THE BLACK VELVET GOWN	£4.99
□	14064 3	THE BLIND MILLER	£3.99
□	11160 0	THE CINDER PATH	£4.99
□	14063 5	COLOUR BLIND	£3.99
□	12476 1	THE CULTURED HANDMAIDEN	£3.50
□	12551 2	A DINNER OF HERBS	£4.99
□	14068 6	FEATHERS IN THE FIRE	£4.99
□	14069 4	FENWICK HOUSES	£4.99
□	10450 7	THE GAMBLING MAN	£3.99
□	13716 2	THE GARMENT	£3.99
□	10916 9	THE GIRL	£4.99
□	13621 2	THE GILLYVORS	£4.99
□	14071 6	THE GLASS VIRGIN	£4.99
□	12789 2	HAROLD	£3.99
□	12608 X	GOODBYE HAMILTON	£3.99
□	12451 6	HAMILTON	£3.99
□	13300 0	THE HARROGATE SECRET	£3.99
□	13303 5	THE HOUSE OF WOMEN	£4.99
□	10267 9	THE INVISIBLE CORD	£3.99
□	10780 8	THE IRON FACADE	£3.99
□	14091 0	KATE HANNIGAN	£3.99
□	14092 9	KATIE MULHOLLAND	£4.99
□	14078 3	THE LONG CORRIDOR	£3.99
□	14102 X	THE MAN WHO CRIED	£3.99
□	14085 6	THE MENAGERIE	£3.99
□	12524 5	THE MOTH	£4.99
□	13302 7	MY BELOVED SON	£4.99
□	13088 5	THE PARSON'S DAUGHTER	£4.99
□	14073 2	PURE AS THE LILY	£4.99
□	13683 2	THE RAG NYMPH	£4.99
□	14075 9	THE ROUND TOWER	£3.99
□	10630 5	THE TIDE OF LIFE	£4.99
□	14076 7	THE UNBAITED TRAP	£3.99
□	12368 4	THE WHIP	£4.99
□	13577 1	THE WINGLESS BIRD	£4.99
□	10541 4	THE SLOW AWAKENING	£3.99
		(Catherine Marchant)	
□	13407 4	LET ME MAKE MYSELF PLAIN	£3.99

All Corgi/Bantam Books are available at your bookshop or newsagent, or can be ordered from the following address:
Corgi/Bantam Books
Cash Sales Department
P.O. Box 11, Falmouth, Cornwall TR10 9EN

UK and B.F.P.O. customers please send a cheque or postal order (no currency) and allow £1.00 for postage and packing for the first book plus 50p for the second book and 30p for each additional book to a maximum charge of £3.00 (7 books plus).

Overseas customers, including Eire, please allow £2.00 for postage and packing for the first book plus £1.00 for the second book and 50p for each subsequent title ordered.

NAME (Block letters) ....

ADDRESS ......